Editkének szeretettel,

THE ANGIE CHRONICLES:
Angie's Story

Also available from Eva Fischer-Dixon:

The Third Cloud

One Last Time (Previously titled "For One Last Time)

A Song for Hannah (Previously titled "Hannah's Song)

A Journey to Destiny (Previously titled "A Journey to Passion)

The Discovery

The Forbidden

Fata Morgana

"Eighteen"

The Chava Diamond Chronicles: The Shades of Love and Hate

The Bestseller

A Town by the River

Five 'til Midnight

Thy Neighbor's Wife

The Roma Chavi (The Gypsy Girl)

My First Son

By the Book

The Angie Chronicles: Six Summers & One Winter

THE ANGIE CHRONICLES:

Angie's Story

A Novel by

Eva Fischer-Dixon

Copyright © 2015 by Eva Fischer-Dixon.

ISBN:	Softcover	978-1-5035-6108-3
	eBook	978-1-5035-6107-6

All rights reserved. No part of this book may be reproduced or transmitted in any form or by any means, electronic or mechanical, including photocopying, recording, or by any information storage and retrieval system, without permission in writing from the copyright owner.

This is a work of fiction. Names, characters, places and incidents either are the product of the author's imagination or are used fictitiously, and any resemblance to any actual persons, living or dead, events, or locales is entirely coincidental.

Any people depicted in stock imagery provided by Thinkstock are models, and such images are being used for illustrative purposes only.
Certain stock imagery © Thinkstock.

Print information available on the last page.

Rev. date: 04/22/2015

To order additional copies of this book, contact:
Xlibris
1-888-795-4274
www.Xlibris.com
Orders@Xlibris.com
711830

*For those who never gave up
on finding true and everlasting love*

Contents

New And Old 1
Captain Mark Hegyes 7
Christmas And New Year's Eve, 1967 14
A Birthday And A Surprise 18
Happy 18Th Birthday To Me (Sort Of) 30
. . . And There Was None 35
The Happy Couple 42
What Comes Around, Goes Around (Maybe) 51
It's Christmas Time Again 56
A New Life 62
Work, Work And More Work 72
Attila, The Hunter And Joe, The Returnee 84
The Visitor And Mrs. Toldai 98
Love And Marriage 122
My Life As I Knew It 133
The Aftermath 140
Someone From The Past 149
The Birthday Surprise 158
Good Things Comes To Those Who Wait 163

Epilog 165

NEW AND OLD

LIFE WAS MOVING on slowly and without any apparent dramas. Another year went by and Andy and I were still engaged with no prospect of an apartment anywhere, rental or otherwise. It was a very sore subject as it became even more questionable if we could get married the following year. Andy promised me over and over, and again that our plan would become a reality just as he envisioned from day one. The problem was that I had become more and more unsure that it was a realistic plan, but my love for him never wavered and he was still every girl's dream.

At my place of work everything was going fine. After my year of probation was over, I became more involved with other projects in the office complex, until one day Colonel Toldai informed me that he was getting promoted to Lieutenant General (LTG). Needless to say that with the big promotion came a change of scenery for him, he was going to work in the Defense Ministry, which meant that a new Commanding Officer was scheduled to take over Colonel Toldai's position at the garrison. The news was incredibly bad and sad news for me, because I got to know him so well that I even knew when he was taking a breath, so to speak. Seeing my sad face he burst out laughing. "You should be happy for me, Angie," he said as I stood in front of his desk with tears in my eyes. I shook my head. "Promoting me means promotion for you."

"I don't understand," I whimpered.

"You thought that I would leave you behind? Not in a million years," he said and made a face at me when he saw my first teardrops rolling down my face.

"Excuse me, sir, you mean that I will be working there too?" I asked almost unable to believe what he was saying. He nodded.

"I am more than pleased with the job you are doing for me, and your work ethics are commendable," he said while he was getting up from his desk. He stretched his hand for a handshake. "Congratulations Angelina Aranyi, you are going to be the youngest executive office manager in the entire building."

I was so happy that I even forgot to ask him about how much I was going to earn, but I gathered that with a promotion, no matter how much, there would be a salary increase. My parents hugged me and congratulated me and I could hardly wait until Andy came over so I could tell him the good news. He also kissed me and wished me well, but something about the way he acted hurt my feelings, so I asked him if he was not happy about my promotion.

"Oh, I am and if anybody deserves it, it got to be you," he replied. "My concern is that you will be in contact with some powerful senior ranked people who surely realize what I noticed about you right away, how special you are. What if somebody wants more than just your assistance? What if they realize that technically you are this sweet innocent girl who is not familiar with the way of life?" I couldn't believe my ears.

"Are you jealous of me?" I asked. He shrugged. "You don't trust me that is what you are saying?"

"I trust you, but you are a desirable woman, that is all I am saying." He said and it was not to my liking.

"Why don't you marry me then?" I inquired with growing anger.

"I would if I could," he answered and looked at my mother who acted as if she didn't hear us. *Fine,* I thought. *I have nothing else to say about the subject either.*

Two weeks later I said goodbye to my colleagues and to some of the soldiers who also worked in the administration building. My new office was incredibly large, almost an equal to LTG Toldai's, minus the conference table. Technically speaking it was not entirely my office; I had to share it with the General's aid. For almost a month I enjoyed the office all to myself as the aid; a Captain in ranks was in the process of transferring. Within a short period of time I met a lot of great and interesting people, and Andy's concern that I was going to be noticed was not without merit. There were a lot of young people; naturally nobody was as young as I, just passed seventeen years of age. Because I always looked older than I really was, nobody suspected and I would not give away my real age.

As always, the cafeteria was a good place to meet people and there is where a lot of senior ranked officials also got their nourishment, unless they had a working lunch or meeting someplace else. I must admit, and not to my surprise, the cost of the food was just the same, yet it was much tastier than what was cooked and served at the Army Garrison.

I picked up a somewhat different workload, instead of having garrison level assignments and projects; I was in the BIG league due to my promotion. Almost half way through my second month there, I was busy transcribing a dictation by LTG Toldai into a typed speech he was scheduled to present on the following day, when I heard a knock on the door. "Enter," I yelled without looking up.

"I am Captain Hegyes, I am here to report to LTG Toldai," he said and I finally looked up. I dropped the sheet of paper from my hand as momentarily I thought that Joe was standing in front of my desk. The Captain (CPT) was tall, very well fit in his spotless and wrinkle free uniform. He had short military cut blonde hair and his blue eyes were focused on my somewhat surprised face.

I had to clear my throat before I was able to speak. "Welcome CPT Hegyes, the General will be pleased that you have finally arrived." I said trying to be nice.

"Would be too much trouble for you to get up and tell the LTG Toldai that I am here?" He asked sarcastically. *So,* I thought. *That is how things are going to be. I am ready for you.* I forced a smile on my face and picked up the phone.

"Sir, CPT Hegyes managed to make it here and he is anxious to finally meet you. Would you like me escort him into your office or should I issue him a map to the building?" I asked and I looked up at Captain's face that had an *"I will get you for this"* look on his face. What I heard on the phone as a response, I couldn't help myself, I laughed out loud. So, okay, the General and I got along very well and he *"got"* my snotty introduction. He immediately knew that we might have a "problem child" in our little family.

"Do you think that he will need potty training?" LTG Toldai said, that is why I laughed. Yes, I know that it was way out of being professional, but one had to know the General who was a true patriot and who hated stuck up officers who looked down on civilians, or on soldiers under their command. LTG Toldai also learned and knew a lot about me, and he knew that he didn't have to worry about me handling the Captain, this was a subject that later came up during a conversation while I brought in his morning coffee. He asked me if I thought that I would have a problem working with Captain Hegyes, to which I replied that I was looking for that challenge. He sipped from the black coffee that he liked with one cube sugar and put the cup down. "I feel sorry for the Captain," he said and winked at me. I didn't reply, I nodded and went back to work.

One of my major assignments was to organize appointments, garrison visits, to which I accompanied him on occasions when dictations had to be taken from certain meetings, setting up meetings, basically organizing and controlling his entire day and weekly schedule. During an official function, I met LTG Toldai's wife and daughter and they were seemingly nice people.

There was a lot of typing involved as well as transcribing from dictations, basically running an office smoothly. The Captain's job was to be a liaison between LTG Toldai and other senior ranked military and civilian personnel; he escorted LTG Toldai on all of his meetings, even the ones to different garrisons where I was present too. He also picked up LTG Toldai at his home to bring him to work and took him home. Normally there was a driver assigned to senior ranked officers and higher post civilians, but LTG Toldai refused to pay somebody for driving when he had an aid who was perfectly capable to do so, and whose apartment was near the General's residence.

The Captain's desk was on the opposite side of the office so we faced each other. I tried to ignore him as much as possible because every time I looked at him, I thought about that certain night when Joe attacked me. At home, I didn't even dare to tell Andy about the Captain's appearance, until one day Andy had some time on his hands and stopped by for a visit. When he walked into the office he smiled and came directly to my desk where he kissed me. When he turned around, he saw that the Captain was looking at us.

"Good Lord," Andy exclaimed. "How could you stand seeing him all day?" He asked.

"I ignore him," I whispered to Andy. "Why don't you be nice and introduce yourself to him." I suggested. I had to give him a *"look"* to do it. He walked over to the Captain's desk and introduced himself.

"I am Andrew Horváth, Angie's fiancée," he said and reached out his hand for a shake. It must have been an excruciating task for the Captain, but he finally got up and accepted Andy's hand.

"Captain Hegyes," he said dryly.

"How should I call you?" Andy asked him jokingly as he didn't give Andy his first name.

"You may call me Captain, or sir," he said in a most unfriendly voice.

"May be I just won't address you at all," Andy replied and returned to my desk. "Honey, you have my deepest sympathy working with this jerk." He whispered.

"It's not bad at all, we just don't talk about anything else but business," I told him. He had his back to the Captain and faced me.

"I miss you," Andy said and smiled that certain smile that I only saw on rare occasions. The door to LTG Toldai's office opened and he stepped into our office. He saw Andy and right away stretched out his hand for a handshake.

"It's good to see you Andy," he told him with friendliness. "So when is the big day, she won't tell me anything." He complained jokingly.

"It's coming," Andy replied curtly. It was a very touchy subject with me and the smile disappeared from my face. I glanced towards the Captain's desk and our eyes met. I swallowed hard because in his eyes I saw Joe's reaction when he talked about our wedding day. *What was that about?* I wondered.

LTG Toldai chatted with Andy about his military service, and then Andy excused himself that he had to go because he was on a supply run not far from our building, he explained his reason for stopping by. He gave me a quick kiss and then headed for the door where he turned around. "Honey, I'll see you later." I nodded and watched him leave. LTG Toldai who had business to attend in another office two doors down the hall followed Andy out. Normally, when my boss left his office and ours, he would tell us where he went, unless he went to use the bathroom.

I looked at the Captain before I returned to typing and noticed that he was still watching me. "How long you have been engaged?" He asked me. I took a second look at him.

"Why do you want to know?" I asked. He shrugged.

"Just curious," he commented.

"As the saying goes, curiosity killed the cat," I replied and went back to typing.

"I was just wondering because you didn't seem to be happy about having no wedding date yet," he said not without sarcasm. I took a deep breath and turned back toward him from my typing. This was only the end of 1967 and there were no computers in those days in my native country yet. I liked my typewriter; it was a Remington, which was placed on a side table to my right.

"Look, CPT Hegyes," I tried to reply in a civilized tone of voice. "We have worked together almost half a year now and not once did you express the slightest interest in anything that involves me, or my personal life. Since you don't know anything about me, and you do not truthfully care about me, let's just leave it that way."

"Don't be such a spoiled brat," he hissed at me.

"You are a bonafied jerk," I yelled at him. There was only a problem, the door was not closed all the way to our office and LTG Toldai heard the whole discussion by standing near the open door. He stepped into our office and I had never seen him so angry. *The question was, whom he was angry at?* I wondered.

"In my office, both of you," he ordered us.

Captain Hegyes being a jerk, just as I called him, walked in right front of me, which was not a gentlemanly gesture. LTG Toldai looked at the Captain and then at me as we stood in front of his desk, I leisurely, the Captain at attention.

"My simple question is; is this a government institution or kindergarten?" He asked and he did not expect or want a response. "Captain Hegyes, let's start with that you walked into this office before letting a woman in ahead of you. While it is not in any government or military regulations, it was not polite. Ms. Aranyi, I am disappointed in you because I thought that you were smarter. Why did you even bother to respond to his question when you knew that he was just trying to give you a hard time?" I did not reply I began to scan his desk in front of him for anything out of the ordinary.

"Sir, if may say something," Captain Hegyes began to try and explain whatever was on his mind.

"No, you may not," LTG Toldai said firmly. "I want the two of you to get along, and that is an order. Understood?" He asked.

"Yes, sir," we both replied.

"Dismissed," he said and ignored us.

"Excuse me, sir," I turned around from the door. "Would you please tie your shoe laces so you would not trip over them," I said somewhat boldly and with a grin, well knowing that he was wearing military issue boots most of the time. "I am just saying." I added.

"Smart ass," he said with a smile and motioned with his hand for me to get out there.

The Captain and I tried to avoid each other as much as possible. We barely talked, and when we did, it was all business. In the cafeteria, we would sit at different tables, sometimes at tables that stood next to each other. Usually someone would ask me if they could sit with me, mostly young men, military or civilian, and even other female employees too, just to chitchat.

There was most definitely a tension between us and I just could not get over how much he reminded me of Joe. I was desperately trying to forget about him, both in my heart and in my brain. I even tried to forget his appearance, but seeing the Captain every day, it was simply impossible.

CAPTAIN MARK HEGYES

A COUPLE OF WEEKS after the incident in the office, LTG Toldai informed us that we were required to go on a two day trip to a garrison that was located near at the southern border of the country. Andy hated those trips that took me away for more than one day, but it was part of the job and I could not get away from it. Usually we had a car from the carpool, and sometimes we even got a driver, but not on that particular occasion. LTG Toldai said that perhaps the Captain and I could switch driving half way. I reminded the LTG that I was underage and I didn't know how to drive. The Captain assured LTG Toldai that he had no problem driving all the way, and then he gave me a puzzled look.

It took us almost six hours to get to our destination and because it was late in the evening, we were shown to our quarters at the garrison. We faced two major dilemmas right from the beginning; one was that at that particular garrison there were no female employees, therefore there were no restrooms for women at all. Secondly, I would have to share a room, or as they called it "quarters" with either LTG Toldai or CPT Hegyes because there were only two available. There was no possible way that I could stay in LTG Toldai's room for obvious reasons, and I felt uneasy being in the same close vicinity with the man who looked like my almost rapist. "Sir," I told Toldai, "I will sleep in the car, the backseat doesn't look that uncomfortable," I suggested.

"Absolutely not, and Captain, don't even dare to volunteer to do it," LTG Toldai said. "It is freezing cold outside and even the sentries are inside the guard houses."

I made a face because I knew that the inevitable is going to happen, I had to share a room with the Captain I could not stand. "It's not like you two have to sleep in the same bed," he said jokingly.

"Thank God for small miracles," I remarked. Even the Captain grinned at my remark.

"Do you want me to put a sword in the middle of the room?" LTG Toldai offered with his usual blend of humor. We both shook our heads. "I trust you, Captain," LTG Toldai said and looked at the Captain firmly.

"Sir, to my honor as an officer, I respect Angie's privacy." He replied.

We bid goodnight and went into our rooms. "You want the left or the right bed?" Captain Hegyes asked.

"It doesn't matter, Captain, you make the selection and I'll take the other," I replied.

"Can I ask you a favor?" He asked with a smile.

"Depends," I replied as I put my travel bag on the bed at right side of the room.

"Can you call me Mark while we are in private?" He asked. I raised an eyebrow.

"You have a first name? I did not know that," I joked with him. He laughed and then he looked at me. "I have to go to the bathroom, do you want to come too?" He asked.

"I didn't think that you needed help," I said with a straight face but I was about to crack up.

"What?" He asked with another grin. "God, you are such a trip. I meant that since I have to go, perhaps you want to use the facility as well. I can stand guard while you are using the bathroom. As you know, there are no separate female bathrooms in the garrison." He looked at me and began to laugh. "I just don't know about you."

I grabbed my toothbrush and toothpaste and joined him at the door. "And you never will." I finally answered him.

We were back in the room several minutes later and after asking him if I could change into nightclothes in dark, he turned off the light. I put on my pajamas and warm socks, as the military quarters did not have my nice comforters, only blankets.

"Good night," Captain Hegyes said.

"Good night, Mark," I replied and I could almost see him either grinning or smiling.

I was rather tired from the long trip and fell asleep almost right away, just to be awakened some time later with a hand on my mouth. For several long seconds I thought that I was back in Kisegres and Joe was trying to rape me. "Ssss," I heard the Captain's voice. "It's me, Mark. I put my hand on your mouth because you were screaming. I am going to take my hand off now, okay?" He asked. I nodded and he did. "You must have had some terrible nightmare. You were tossing and turning and yelling, *no, Joe, no*."

I looked up at him in the semi darkness, there was a street underneath our room's window and the streetlight softly reached us through the blinds. I saw genuine concern on his face. "You want to tell me what happened?" He asked. I shook my head. "Does Andy know?"

"Yes, he was there," I told him. He looked confused. "Mark, it is a very long story," I said and touched my forehead, it was moist from perspiration. He left but returned a minute later and sat down at the edge of my bed and with a handkerchief he gently wiped my forehead and my face.

"Tell me only the basics," he suggested.

I briefly told him about an "old boyfriend" who could not accept that it was over, how he tried to rape me and how Aunt Lucinda and Andy just got there a couple of minutes later, after that I already hit Joe on the head with the porcelain nightlight. Mark shook his head. "I am very sorry that you had to go through all that." He said solemnly.

"I don't think about it often but I do once on a while, and in my nightmares, it plays out again and again," I confessed.

"Maybe someday it will go away," he suggested.

"I sure hope so," I replied and un-lady like I yawned.

"We better get some sleep, it will be morning before we know it," he replied and gently touched my face with the tip of his finger. He got up from the edge of the bed and then he turned around. "Andy is a very lucky man. I hope that he is aware of that." I did not reply and shortly after I was in a deep coma like sleep.

"Good morning, beautiful," I heard Mark's voice. I looked up and to my surprise; he was already freshly shaven and completely dressed in uniform.

"What time is it?" I asked.

"It's five thirty in the morning," he said and chuckled when I yawned. "If you need to use the bathroom this is a good time as the soldiers are out on their morning physical training. They should be back in a half an hour."

I jumped out of the bed in my pajamas, not thinking straight that early in the morning. He turned away, not that he could see anything in my winter pajamas. I put on my bathrobe and followed him to the bathroom/shower a few doors down the hallway. He went in to check if it was unoccupied and he confirmed it was when he returned. He motioned to me to make it quick. I was in an out less than ten minutes. I didn't dare to shower just did the essential cleaning and he escorted me back to the room, staying outside while I got dressed. Since his bed was already made, I did the best to imitate how he did his. *So what if it was not up to regulation?* I thought. *Are they going to court martial me?*

Mark knocked on the door and entered. He noticed my made up bed and smiled. He didn't say anything, not even a sarcastic remark; he just waived to me to go with him.

"The General is already in the chow hall," he informed me. "The interrogation will start at eight o'clock." I looked at him questioningly.

"Interrogation?" I asked in a lower voice. He nodded.

"We are not at liberty to discuss it in public, you know what that means?" He asked.

"Yes, I do." I replied as he let me in first inside the cafeteria the soldiers called "chow hall". Have you ever had a couple of hundred pair of eyes or more looking at you all at once? I was the only female in the entire place. We noticed LTG Toldai sitting in a more secluded area of the mess hall with a local Colonel. We nodded at each other as Mark guided me into the line of soldiers and gave me a tray. The soldier behind the food warmers who did the serving, semi-rudely asked me what I wanted until he noticed Mark, in his Captain's uniform. I had some scrambled eggs and ham with two slices of toast and orange juice.

Mark was looking for a place to sit when I told him that the General was waiving at our direction, he wanted us to sit with him and the Colonel. We walked to the table and Mark saluted them after placing the food on the table. LTG Toldai introduced me to Colonel Carter who shook hands with me, and just then I sat down next to the General.

"Would you like some coffee?" Mark asked before sitting down.

"Yes, please, some milk and two sugar cubes," I told him and smiled. I glanced at LTG Toldai who had a grin on his face.

"I am pleased to see that you two survived the night in the same room," LTG Toldai said and looked at Colonel Carter. "I had to explain to Colonel Carter why the two of you shared one room and I expressed concerns about a possible battlefield in there."

"There was no problem, sir," I told him. "Although I would appreciate if Andy would not hear about it."

"It is an excellent thought," LTG Toldai replied.

We ate quietly and quickly, occasionally glancing at each other as the two senior ranked officers were engaged in some sort to conversation I did not tune into. Eventually the two of them left the table leaving us behind, but not before telling us where we needed to be in a half an hour. When we finished eating,

Mark also took my tray where the dirty dishes were collected, and when he sat back down to finish his coffee, the way he looked at me made me wonder what caused him to change, what made him turn into a real gentleman.

Mark and I arrived in the designated area, which was at the Provost Marshall's office where the recently arrested man was held. Mark had to leave his service revolver with the Duty Sergeant on the first floor, and my purse and briefcase was searched for possible weapons. The subject was in heavy hand and ankle chains and it appeared that he had a sleepless night in his cell. While I am not at liberty to discuss what was going on in there and what happened later, in a nutshell, the arrested military personnel was caught at the border as he was about to cross no-man's-land, carrying military maps tucked into his shirt. I would not dare to ask what happened to his face or body for that matter, as I was sure that he was not "well" treated before he finally agreed to talk about his foreign connections.

One may wonder why a senior ranked officer such as a Lieutenant General himself wanted to be at the location of the interrogation, furthermore, he did the interrogation himself, the reason is simple. The captured soldier was not an ordinary soldier, rather, he was another local Colonel who worked in the intelligence field and had knowledge about things that I had no clue whatsoever. My job was to take the confession in short hand, then type it up at the Provost Marshall's office for the confessed man to sign it.

It didn't take me too long to type up the confession from the short hand I took, and by one in the afternoon we were ready to leave for home. The General insisted that we had lunch before we left and use the facilities if needed because it was a long way home. We did as he suggested and by one forty-five in the afternoon, we were on our way.

Just outside our city we hit heavy traffic which delayed getting home even longer, and I still had to go back to the office to drop off the signed confession and the office items I took with me, it could not be taken home under any circumstances. We dropped off the General at his home and we drove to our office. It was already late, and other than some workaholics and the security personnel, there was hardly anyone in the building.

I took the folder with the signed confession and put it inside the safe in the General's office. I put my briefcase behind my desk and I smiled at Mark that I was ready to go.

I was walking right behind him and when we reached the door he turned around. Mark looked at me with an expression on his face that I recognized from seeing it on Andy's face. Without a moment of further hesitation he leaned over and kissed me. I gently pushed him away, thinking about Andy, but Mark leaned over again and at time his hands were on my shoulders. His kiss sent a tingling sensation down on my body and I couldn't help it, I kissed him back when his tongue forced my lips open. The reality of what was happening dawned on me within a minute and I pushed him away. "I am sorry, I just can't," I told him.

"I know," he whispered and I could hear his breathing. "It won't happen again." Mark said and as I was trying to catch my breath, the tingling continued and I looked at him as his face radiated his desire for me. I leaned forward and my lips automatically opened for his tongue and we wrapped our arms around each other.

"Oh, my God," I whispered after the kiss ended. "My God please forgive me and you too, Mark, but this cannot happen again, you understand me?" I told him as he stood there, clearly not wanting to leave. I opened the door to step outside the long hallway. While he locked the door, I staggered along the walkway touching the wall and feeling dreadful about what happened, and guilty because I enjoyed it.

We didn't talk during the drive to my parents' apartment building. Once I pointed out where I lived; he pulled up to the curb to let me out. I was about to open the car door when he reached out and touched my arm. I turned to him and shook my head. I didn't wait until he left; I rushed inside the house and into the apartment. It was already after ten in the evening and I was surprised to see lights in the kitchen. Under normal circumstances my parents normally went to bed around nine, or nine thirty, sometimes even earlier and watched the television from there, while Andy and I laid on the opened up couch, naturally fully clothed, with no hanky-panky under the heavy supervision.

I opened the kitchen door and I found Andy sitting by the table reading a newspaper. "I have been waiting for you since six in the evening," he complained.

My mother heard the opening of the door and came out to see if it was me arriving at home. I kissed her and handed her my travel bag. I explained what I could about my day, leaving out what happened at the office. With Mark's passionate kisses still fresh on my mind, I turned to my mother.

"Mom, would you mind to give us some privacy, please," I asked, she nodded and closed the room's door.

"What is going on?" Andy asked with concern.

I stood in front of him as he was still sitting. "I want us to get married, now." I told him with a demanding voice. He rolled his eyes that made me very upset. "Andy, do not roll your eyes at me as if the subject was annoying to you." I told him.

"What got into you?" He asked not understanding what made me so demanding, not that I was not nagging him often about setting a wedding day.

"Do you love me?" I asked and tears began to gather in my eyes.

"I love you more than anything," he said. While I normally believed him, at that very moment I had difficulty accepting what I had been hearing for over two years, since we met. "I want us to get married now," I repeated my demand.

"Honey, please, you know the situation. We wouldn't have any place to live." He gave me the same excuse as always.

"If you love me, you would have found a place by now. Why am I getting the feeling that I am not as important to you as I used to be or I supposed to be?" I asked.

"I don't understand where all these coming from," he said and studied my face. "Did something happen on this trip?" He asked.

"No, but I had plenty of time to think. I love you very much and I want to be with you, is that too much to ask?" I wanted to know.

"I think that you are tired and need some sleep," he said completely ignoring a straight answer. "I should be going, I have an early start." Andy got up and kissed me, which I did not return. "I'll see you tomorrow." He said from the door.

"I'll be busy," I replied as he walked out the door. I locked the kitchen door and joined my parents in our room.

CHRISTMAS AND NEW YEAR'S EVE, 1967

THE FOLLOWING WEEKS were very tense in the office and LTG Toldai was under the assumption that perhaps Mark and I had another fight. Christmas came around and our department, ten offices on the eighth floor held a Christmas party that I helped to organize. We drew names to give presents, it was new to me as we didn't do that at my previous work location, but it was refreshing to see how well people got along. We all pitched in and ordered sandwiches and finger food. We could not bring hard liquor, wine or beer into the building, some Russian champagne, apple cider, punch and soft drinks were brought in.

The party began and everyone was there when I realized that I forgot my Christmas present for the person whose name I drew, so I had to go back to the office to get it. I was about to return to the party when Mark walked into the office and stopped me. "Angie, we have to talk," he said and he was more serious than I had ever seen him.

"I don't think we have anything to talk about," I replied, although my heart began beating faster. We had managed to avoid being completely alone in the office and I tried to looked everywhere in the office, but at him. It was difficult as there were no private discussions, only work related, just like after he arrived.

"I think you are wrong," he said. "You surely know and noticed that I have developed feelings for you." He waited because I didn't reply. He stepped closer but I took a step back. "You are waiting for something that is not going to happen. Andy doesn't want to marry you; otherwise he would have done it by now. I am not like him; I'll marry you in a heartbeat. Angie, I am in love with you," he said and for some reason, I actually believed him. Yet, I was disturbed by some of the things he said.

"You do not know Andy, so you don't have the right to criticize him. I love my fiancée, do you understand me?" I said to him angrily.

"The way you kissed me told me that you had doubts, and I know for a fact that you have feelings for me too," Mark said and looked at me with pleading eyes. "Don't throw us away, don't disregard me because this is genuine what I am offering."

He hurt me deeply because he pushed some buttons that he knew I was sensitive about, mainly about the lack of a wedding date, therefore, about my own unknown future. Yes, I felt something towards him but it was not clear what it was. I did know that I genuinely liked him, but ever since we kissed, I had nothing other than regrets about it.

Mark looked at me long and hard, and then he turned around and left me standing there. During the party he talked to people but he pretty much stayed to himself while his eyes followed me, or rested on me.

The New Year came around and my parents and I went over to Andy's parents' house. I was not even close to be in a celebratory mood because that very morning I found out that Mark requested and was approved for a transfer to an Army Garrison outside the capital city. He didn't tell me, I had to find out from LTG Toldai. Since I was on a three days leave, I wasn't there when Captain Mark Hegyes walked out of the office and I thought at that time, from my life.

Andy asked me several times during the evening if something was wrong as I looked upset. I told him that a friend of mine at work just transferred out and I didn't have a chance to say goodbye. Lucky for me he did not press the subject any further; I suppose he was just glad that he was not the source of my bad mood.

We had dinner around seven o'clock with Andy's parents, his brother Sándor and his wife, Ildikó. She had changed since they got married and I thought that she changed for the better. Naively, I did not realize at the time, that her different demeanor came from the fact she was not happy. Around ten in the evening some of the tenants arrived, I found out later that Andy's parents also invited all of the tenants which made the apartment rather crowded. I didn't mind the tenants' presence with the exception of one, Judy, the woman who did not hide the fact that she liked Andy too, a lot, I may add.

"Let's dance," she said to Andy when the radio was turned on and music was playing. Andy became nervous and shook his head.

"Thanks for asking, but no thanks," he finally replied.

"Oh, come on, she wouldn't mind," Judy asked nodding at my direction.

"Yes, *'she'* would," I replied. She made a stupid face at me and then she laughed. I looked at Andy and I shook my head. I really wanted to go home. My parents never drank, I certainly never did, but everybody else, even Andy had plenty to drink. Andy's mother who only had a glass of champagne came to sit with us and she told us that we should not be leaving because there were a lot of drunk people on the street and not that many streetcars were running that time of the night. While both were true and as much as I wanted to go home, I could not leave Andy who drank more than I have ever seen him drink before, not to mention that Judy was still there as well. I always believed that a drunken person could not say no to temptation, so we remained there until the early morning hours. In the meanwhile, the tenants left and so did Judy, but not before she managed to land a kiss on Andy's lips by saying that it was a "New Year's Eve" kiss. *Whatever,* I thought.

We left early in the morning and Andy said that he would stop by later and perhaps we could go out for dinner and a movie. I told him that it sounded great and I left to go home with my parents. I slept until the early afternoon, washed and got ready for Andy's arrival. He came by later than usual, he told me that he had to help his parents to clean up the party mess and he slept longer than he anticipated. Because he came late, we decided that we would go out for dinner and skip the movie that night.

He seemed somewhat somber during the first part of the dinner and I had to ask him repeatedly what was wrong. Finally, after a number of naggings, he told me that Ildikó, his brother's new wife tried to commit suicide in the early morning hours, probably right after we left. I told him that I noticed that she was not as flashy and talkative as she used to be. Of course, my next question was, why would she want to take her own life? I could read Andy's face as if I was reading a book.

"He cheated on Ildikó," Andy finally blurted out.

"What?" I asked with my jaw dropped wide open. Sándor, my future brother-in-law was a straight as an arrow guy and it was almost inconceivable that he would cheat on Ildikó. Despite her somewhat unpleasant personality, she was a very attractive woman, certainly a lot prettier than I was. If a man like Sándor cheated on a woman who looked like that, I could not imagine what other man would do.

"How is she now?" I asked.

"They pumped her stomach and they are going to keep her in the hospital for psychological evaluation," he informed me.

"Did she leave a suicide note?" I inquired. He nodded.

"Yes, that it how we know why she did it. Mom, dad and Sándor left for the hospital, that is why I ended up doing the cleaning," he said. I finally had the full picture.

"So what is going to happen now?" I wanted to know. Andy shrugged.

"She told Sándor and my parents that she was going to move back to her parents and that she wanted a divorce," Andy told me.

"Do you know who he was cheating with?" I asked and for whatever reason, I was not entirely shocked when he unwillingly told me.

"Judy," he told me.

"Gross," I said the first word that came to mind. He didn't say it out loud but he indicated that he didn't want to talk about it any longer. Andy was holding my hand over the table and I realized that while he was physically there, his thoughts were far away as his fingers absent-mindedly were caressing my hand. "I love you," I told him. He looked up at me a smiled.

"I love you, too," he replied and I noticed that he wanted to say something else, so I encouraged him. "I just was thinking how disturbing Ildikó's suicide attempt was. Sándor was obviously very upset when he found Ildikó unconscious with an empty bottle of sleeping pills next to her, but he became totally devastated when she told him that she wanted a divorce. What would you do?"

His question caught me by surprise and I had to do a quick check on my emotions. "Well, I would not try to kill myself for one, but it would be over between us," I replied and I added. "Luckily we don't have to worry about anything like that, right?" I asked. He finally smiled.

"That's for sure," he commented right away.

I thought about his brother and his soon to be ex-wife, and I had to admit to myself, I would have never imagined that a man with Sándor's character would cheat on Ildikó, while it was much easier to imagine that she would have cheated on Sándor. I concluded that one never know from just looking at perfectly normal people how they could hurt someone so deeply and maliciously. I tried not to think about it, but it was not as easy to overcome about what happened than I first thought.

A BIRTHDAY AND A SURPRISE

ANDY'S BIRTHDAY WAS two months before mine and I never failed to ask him each time we met what he would like as a present. I begged him to give me a hint but he just smiled, kissed me and said that I always get him interesting things; he wanted me to surprise him. It was an easy thing to say; yet it took me a few hours to come up with the idea for a present after some heavy patting and kissing session earlier.

Mrs. Horváth, Andy's mother told me when I stopped by one day after work that they were going to have a small birthday party for Andy, just for their family and of course, for mine, and then she asked me to pick up some items that she already ordered. She gave me the money to cover the expenses. I didn't understand why I had to do it, not that I objected because she was doing all the planning. She told me that she and Andy's father had to visit their former village because Andy's uncle was very ill and they did not expect him to live for more than a few more days. Andy's birthday party was still on for a week later, but they would not have time to pick up what she asked me to do. She also asked me to take care of Andy while they were gone, meaning to prepare some food for him and such. Technically Andy ate in my parents' apartment every single night, so that request was easy to fulfill.

As it happened, that very same week, my Aunt Elizabeth had a procedure done at a hospital near by our home and she had to remain in bed for a couple of days. We did have a problem as we only had the double bed where my parents slept and the sofa bed where I normally slept. Once the sofa bed was open, there was hardly any space to move about. Andy had an idea and when he told my parents what it was, they did not reply right away, they just looked at each other. Andy suggested that I could stay in his parents' apartment because they already left for a few days and the place was empty. When my parents did not reply, he took an offense in it and he told them so.

"After almost two years, you still don't trust me?" He asked with hurt in his voice. My parents, who loved him like a son, immediately agreed, yet they reminded him what he promised to them about waiting with consummating our relationship after we got married. Of course, Andy promised them again. Andy did, but I did not.

Friday night on our way to his parents' apartment, we stopped by the store and bought some food. When we got home, we found a note from his mother that she cooked for a couple days in advance, so there was plenty of food already prepared. We had dinner and watched television until I could not keep my eyes open any longer. I brushed my teeth and went to the freshly made bed where Andy was waiting. I noticed that he was sleepy too, so we kissed each other goodnight and went to sleep. I suppose that if I wouldn't have been so sleepy, I would have felt insulted by him ignoring me, but those thoughts only occurred to me later on.

It was a weekend and we didn't have to go work. I considered that a double heaven, no work and an apartment only to ourselves. We had a leisurely breakfast and went back to bed to vegetate. I would have difficulties to explain how it felt like being in Andy's arms. I felt completely warm, loved and secured; he was like an unfolded safety blanket. We left the blinds down and it created a moody atmosphere in the bedroom. I closed my eyes and rested my head against his strong chest with his arms around me.

"Can you imagine," Andy said. "We are going to have mornings like this for the rest of our lives."

"I like the sound of that," I told him and kissed his hand. "Unless the kids don't let us sleep in."

"Oh, yes, I forgot about the kids," he laughed. "How many children would you like to have?" He asked, although we had already casually talked about the subject a long time ago.

"Two would be nice," I replied and smiled. "Maybe a boy first, and a little girl a couple of years later," I replied.

"In that order?" He teased me but I confirmed it with a nod. I turned around and then I guided my hand down to his already erect manhood. "What are you doing?" He asked me with surprise but did not move my hands away.

"I thought that perhaps we could get started on that plan," I said sheepishly and pasted my lips on his and let my tongue due a quick search. I knew he loved that when I initiated something like that and I was not disappointed, well, at least not for the next few minutes. He was kissing my stomach area when he looked up at me just as I opened my eyes.

"Angie, we promised your parents that we would wait," he said and rolled off from me. I bit my lips so hard that tears rushed into my eyes. At the same time when disappointment cast it shadow over me again, I also began to feel ashamed of myself. Not because of my nudity, I way passed that stage, I felt that way because he seemed to be stronger than I was. I wanted him but he exercised control and stopped before anything could happen. There was a question that always came up when something like happened, or should I say, did not happen between us, and it was; did Andy want me at all?

I was told over and over by him how beautiful and desirable I was, and yet, he wanted to wait. Wait until when? I rolled on my side and quietly began to cry. "Please, don't do that," Andy said and kissed my back and my shoulders. "You know that I love very much, don't you?" He asked.

"I don't know," I replied while I was choking on tears.

"Angie, please," Andy said and got out of the bed. I didn't care what he was doing; I remained in bed and cried myself to sleep.

I woke up late in the afternoon and the smell of food tingled my nostrils; it was coming from the kitchen. I used the bathroom and washed my face. I didn't like what I was seeing in the mirror, both of my eyes were puffy and red from crying. I took a deep breath and joined Andy who was waiting for me. He already warmed up the food that his mother prepared ahead of time and the table was also set as well. Andy put the entire pot on the table instead pouring it in a serving dish, but I was not in a good mood, not even to criticize him.

"Is your food warm enough?" He asked seeing that I was picking on my perfectly tasty food. I nodded without looking up at him. "Are you alright?" He asked again and it began to annoy me. I nodded yet again, but I was not right at all. I wanted to scream and most of all I wanted to go home, but I wouldn't have any place to sleep as my aunt was using my sofa bed.

After eating I helped him with the dishes and I told him that I was going to take a shower. "You need any help?" He asked jokingly.

"No, I need space to prepare your birthday surprise," I replied without even as much as a smile.

"Okay," he replied almost cheerfully and that made me even angrier. "In that case, take your time."

I looked at the bathtub and the showerhead and I decided to take a leisurely bath, taking my time, letting the bath oil soak through my pores. I must have dozed off because I came to when I heard a knock on the door. "Are you alright?" Andy asked with some level of concern.

"Yes," I yelled back and by that time I was not in the mood to do anything, especially his birthday surprise, but I did it anyway. I got out of the bathtub where the water was already getting cold and dried off. From my overnight essential bag I removed a large and wide ribbon and huge bow. I know that probably looked stupid, but I wrapped the ribbon around myself and tied the red bow on my stomach. I slowly opened the door and yelled out. "Close your eyes, your surprise is coming."

I put embarrassment aside and walked into the bedroom where Andy was standing in front of the television. He turned around and dropped the TV Guide from his hand. His mouth opened but no sound was coming out. I walked up to him and pulled off his t-shirt over his head and pushed down his pants, he didn't have underwear on.

"Happy Early Birthday," I said and I curtsied him.

"Angie," he said and to my shock, he began to laugh. "You are so funny."

I stood there like a moron without a hint of humor or smile. "This is not funny. Andy, I am your birthday present." I stepped up to him and hugged him. "I am your special birthday present," I repeated. He hugged me and began to kiss me and then, he let me go. He pulled up his pants and after picking up his t-shirt, he also put that back on. I was totally shocked and utterly disgusted about what I had done, but at the same time I felt that same way about Andy's reaction.

"Angie, what are you trying to do?" Andy asked, seeing that I was fighting back my tears. He tried to hug me but I shrugged his arms off from my shoulders. I was no longer ashamed, I was becoming genuinely angry and I lost it.

"What am I trying to do?" I yelled at him. It took him aback; I have never raised my voice at him. "Just what is going on Andy? Why don't you want me?" I asked.

"Angie, please, you know that I want you more than anything," he said, trying to reason with me. I would not have it, not then and not again.

"In two months we are going to be engaged for two years. TWO YEARS," I said emphasizing those words. "We have come close to making love on more than one occasion, and now, when I am ready and willing to be with you, you are treating me as if I was this insane person who doesn't know what she wants. But I do, Andy, I want you to make love to me, right now, right here," I told him and stepped up to him.

He shook his head. "You are upset for no reason, no reason at all." He told me in a calm voice that irritated the daylight out of me.

"Oh, forgive me, you are so right," I replied and I changed my tune. "Is there something you are not telling me? Is there something physically wrong with you?" I inquired with a smirk on my face. It was time for him to get mad at me. He picked me up and carried me to the bed and dropped me on it, not very gently I may add. Andy was out his clothes in one second and he laid down close to me and began to kiss me hard, the way we liked it, and then his hands began its pleasure filled journey down on my body. I bit my lips, and I held him tight as he climbed on the top of me.

"This is what you want?" He asked between kisses. Both of us were short of breath and I wanted to believe that it was finally going to happen because he indeed wanted me, that is what he was saying for over two years, even before we got engaged.

"No," I replied, completely out of breath. "I want more."

He did not reply, he touched me like he did several times before and then he parted my legs and position himself between my thighs. "Are you sure, are you absolutely certain?" He asked.

"Yes, I am," I replied and held my breath. I could almost feel him, right there when his manhood belonged and then, it happened again. He rolled off from me and buried his face in his pillow. I glanced down and I noticed that he was still erect, so I concluded right there that it was not a physical problem.

I did not say a single word; I did not shed a single tear. I pushed myself out of the bed, grabbed a pillow and one of the comforters and went to the sofa bed at the opposite side of the room. I didn't have to open it; it was wide enough for me to lay on it comfortably. From my bag I took out my pajamas, slipped them on and went to sleep on the sofa.

I was confused and saddened, but most of all, disappointed. I fully understood that he wanted to wait with consummating our relationship after the wedding; I fully understood that he promised my parents that he would not try anything, but I refused to believe that it was not something else. It could not possibly be me, there were men in my past who wanted me, regardless my age or who I was. There we were, without any parental supervision for two whole days, and he stopped himself at the very last moments before he entered me. To me, it was maddening, if for no other reason but for not understanding why, because his reasoning no longer meant anything to me.

I woke up at five in the morning and as quietly as I could, I left for home. Andy was still asleep, even snoring a little bit, but I just wanted to get out of there. To my parents' surprise, I got home by five thirty. My mother took a look at me and she was not my mother for nothing, she immediately noticed that my eyes were still puffy and that I looked very unhappy. "What happened?"

She asked me as we sat by the kitchen table, not wanting to wake my father and my aunt.

I looked directly into my mother's eyes and I replied to her. "What did not happen would be a more appropriate question." She stared at me for a brief moment, but for the next half an hour, she was not only my mother, but also a woman who understood me.

"Maybe he is just scared because you are still a virgin," my mom suggested.

"Due to no fault of my own," I replied and it even surprised me how I dared to talk to her like that. "Mom, it has been over two years and we are getting steadily nowhere," I told her. "It's like he is hanging onto something what I can't see and I don't know anything about." It was all-new to my mother. She used to tell me stories about her ex-boyfriends who only wanted to have sex with her, nothing else, but she did not budge, she wanted to have her husband be the first man. She was thirty-seven when she married my biological father and to his surprise, she was still a virgin. He was so proud of her that to my mother's embarrassment, he told every friend and buddy he had.

"The truth is, I wouldn't have held on to it if I had someone like Andy," she confessed. "This got to be psychological, because like you said, it was is physical."

Around noon Andy arrived and I kept reading the magazine when my mother tried to usher him into the living room. My father wasn't home; he was escorting my aunt who left for her apartment, so Andy kept my mother in the kitchen for a few minutes. "Mama, did she tell you anything?" He asked with concern.

"Andy, she told me everything," my mother informed him. "May I ask you something?"

"Sure, anything," he offered.

"Why didn't you make love to her?" My mother asked out bluntly. I dropped the magazine to the floor. *Oh, my God*, I thought. *What is she doing?*

Andy was equally shocked. "Mama, you and papa told me not to dare to do anything, didn't you?" He reminded her.

"We said that because that is what parents say and do," my mother replied. "I would not just say this to any other man, but I know that the two of you love each other and that you are going to get married someday. So let's just say, I would not have killed her or disowned her if the two of you made love." When my mother said that, I had to cover my mouth from screaming.

"Well, I suspected that but I want to wait just the same," Andy told her.

"Hmm," the nurse kicked in my mother. "Are you alright, physically I mean?" She asked.

"I am perfectly fine," he replied with an offended tone of voice.

"Well, then for the world of me I cannot figure out when a girl like my daughter wants you physically, why are you refusing her? There is got to be another reason," my mother said continuing her inquisition.

"There is no other reason other than what I told her and I told you," Andy answered.

"Do you have someone who you are intimate with, having sex with that is?" My mother's question went straight to the point.

"I swear to everything that is sacred to me that there is nobody else," Andy said. "I feel like I am being ambushed just because I am decent person."

"No, you are not being ambushed at all," my mother replied in a soothing voice. "I just like to know why you made my daughter so unhappy in the past couple of few days," she said. "Go ahead and talk to her, she is in there." The door opened and Andy walked in. I casually looked up and I couldn't help it, I smiled seeing how red his face turned from the discussion with my mother.

"Hi, Angie," he said softly and hesitantly walked up to me. He bent down and tried to kiss me. I turned my head and his welcome kiss landed on my chin. "Are you alright?" He asked.

"Why shouldn't I be?" I asked him in return.

"I was under the impression that you were mad at me," he said and stared at me, seeking any kind of sign how my mood was.

"I guess you know me well," I replied and glanced at the magazine page in front of me.

"After you left, Ildikó came by and collected her belonging," he said, trying to change the subject.

"Is she alright?" I asked, as I really wanted to know.

"Yes, she actually looked much better," Andy replied. "She confirmed that she has filed for divorce from my brother." He added. I put the magazine down as something occurred to me.

"So what is going to happen with the apartment?" I asked. My questions surprised him.

"What do you mean? That is my brother's apartment," he said.

"Your mom said that they gave it to him as a wedding present, but he wouldn't be married any longer. Why can't he move in with your parents so we could get married and have that apartment? I think that it is a fair idea, don't you?" I asked.

Andy was lost for words. "I suppose, I could ask," he said eventually.

I took a deep breath and put the magazine down. "This thing, this whole thing needs to be taken care of real soon. I don't know anyone who was engaged as long as we are. I know that I am pestering you about the wedding date for a long time, but please, Andy, we either get married soon or I don't know what is going to happen."

"Angie, I have told you hundreds of times or more that I love you, and that you mean everything to me in this world. That is how I still feel. I want to marry you and live with you for the rest of our lives. I want to raise children with you, but I need you to give me time." He said in a pleading voice. It was the same speech that I heard almost from the time since we first met.

"Okay, Andy," I said and touched his face. "I want to do the same things as you, but you have to speed up things a little bit."

After that frustration filled weekend, things sort of went back into "normal". I picked up the things my future mother-in-law asked me to do and she indeed gave a small but nice party for their youngest son, Andy. He turned twenty-four years old, and although the celebration was toned down due to the passing of his uncle, we did have a nice time at their home. His brother, Sándor looked very unhappy, the way he was supposed to feel after what he had done and especially with whom.

Since my birthday was also around the corner, I gave strict instructions to everyone that I did not want anything, which included a party. It promised to be a very somber one for me because just a month after Andy's birthday, my professional life was turned upside down.

It was a Monday morning when I went to work as usual, I normally got there twenty to thirty minutes early to get the coffee maker going, so by the time LTG Toldai came in, I was able to hand his favorite cup filled with steaming hot coffee, black with one cube sugar, the way he liked it.

Arriving to the office I was surprised to notice that the door was unlocked. I was always the first one to arrive to open up, but when I pushed the handle down, it opened right up. I went inside and there wasn't anyone there, although the coffee was already dripping and the carafe was almost full.

I glanced at Captain Erdei's desk but there was no sign that he was in yet. There were four keys to the door, I got one, CPT Erdei, the new aid had the second, LTG Toldai had the third, and there was a generic key for the custodial crew that opened all the doors of the offices on our floor. So if I was not the first one in, and it was not CPT Erdei, it had to be LTG Toldai, because the custodial people cleaned during the night and they would not make coffee anyway. I put my purse on my desk and walked to the General's office door and knocked.

"Come on in," he said. I stepped inside. "Good Morning, Angie," he said and from his tone of voice I immediately knew that something was up.

"Good Morning, sir. You are in early," I said and stared at him. He stared right back at me, and then he smiled and shook his head.

"You know me better than my own wife," he said and nervously laughed. He was nervous? Now that was the first since I knew him, something big had to be happening.

"Sir, with all respect, I cannot function properly if there is something kept from me that I am also the part of," I told him stubbornly standing in front of his desk.

"Have a sit," he said and motioned toward one of the chairs. "Wait here," he ordered me and I stayed put. He disappeared into the outer office that I shared with CPT Erdei. I heard the Captain's voice as well and both of them walked through the door, LTG Toldai was carrying two cups of coffee, and the Captain had a cup in his hand. He said good morning and he took the other chair. The General handed me a cup, although it was not the first time, actually it was the second. When I saw his hand reaching out towards me with a cup of coffee, another episode, similar to that one played out in my head. I took the coffee and thanked him for it.

He walked behind his desk and after putting his coffee down in a safe place so the tons of paperwork accidentally wouldn't get coffee stained, he just sat there and stared at the desk in front of him, debating how to break the bad news, because it just had to be bad.

"Sir, did you get another promotion?" I asked. He looked up and he glanced at the Captain.

"Who told you?" He asked. I shook my head.

"The cup of coffee you handed me, sir," I replied. "The only other time you brought me coffee was when you told me that you are getting promoted to Lieutenant General, and that you were leaving," I replied.

"Indeed, you are correct," LTG Toldai agreed. "I am getting promoted to Major General, which of course means another assignment."

"Am I able to go with you there as well?" I asked but I was scared of his answer.

He lowered his head and he actually looked sad. "I am afraid not," he told me straight out. "I accepted a position as a Military Attaché at the Hungarian Embassy, in Washington, DC, in the United States. Those assignments usually two to three years long, and at this point there is no way to predict where the assignment after that will take me when I returned from America."

"Am I going to remain here, sir, in this office under another Commander?" I asked in a weak voice.

"I am afraid not. The incoming General doesn't trust civilians. You will be transferred to the Legal and Justification Department on the first floor. As for you Captain, you will remain here as an aid to the incoming General Soos." He informed us and did not say anything further, which meant that we were dismissed. I took my coffee cup and somehow made it to the door. I turned around and I saw the General staring after me, and then he lowered his head.

I was on autopilot for the rest of the day and I could hardly wait to get out of there. CPT Erdei was always very nice to me, he knew that the General and I went way back and I could even tell that he sympathized with me, the way I felt. I made it home in a daze and I barely walked through the door when I had total meltdown. Andy was in the kitchen helping my mother with cutting up vegetables and they could not imagine what have happened to me. I throw myself on the sofa and cried. My father just sat by the table staring at me; he knew that asking would not help me to feel better. My mom and Andy came into the room and Andy sat down on the sofa next to me and pulled me up to his shoulder. Let's just say, it took another half an hour before I was able to talk and told them what will happen in two weeks.

"Maybe you are going to like that other office," my mother suggested. I had to explain to her that is where people were sent as either as a form of punishment or in cases like mine, when a position was abolished. Andy kissed my forehead, and then he pushed me away so he could look at me.

"I have a great idea," he said and smiled. "There is a big office at the end of the hallway of our floor at work and they are looking for an office manager. There are four young women working there, just barely a few years older than you. Why don't I talk to the Section Chief tomorrow and maybe you could go in for an interview. They pay just a little bit less than what you are making now, but your travel time will be a much shorter." Andy suggested.

"So we would work together?" I asked.

"Well, sort of but not really," he said. "I am working where the mechanics station is, you would be at the end of the hallway, but only a few feet away. We could have breaks together and even lunch together. Wouldn't you like that?" He asked and hugged me tightly.

"Do you think that they would like me?" I asked with hope in my voice.

Andy laughed. "Love, only a dead person would not like you," he told me. He lifted my spirits somewhat and he saved me from a night of misery thinking about the situation.

The following day I asked LTG Toldai if he would be kind enough to write me a recommendation. He not only wrote one, he also attached my school's recommendation as well that he saved in my personal file.

My life changed dramatically in just two weeks. I said a teary goodbye to a great boss, Lieutenant General Toldai, who was promoted to Major General. What I would have never dared to do before, I hugged him, well, we hugged each other and I told him that he was a great person to work for. In return, he told me that my potentials are unlimited, and then he said something that I desperately wanted to suppress, as it kind of stuck in my mind for a long time to come. He said I should not waste time on any ongoing project that has no chance of succeeding. I could have translated that anyway I wanted to and he did not say anything further.

I was interviewed for the job at the same factory, at the same department where Andy worked, and to my surprise I was hired right on the spot after the interview, which I backed up by showing them my diploma and the letters of recommendations.

It was a good job, but it was not a great job. True to my nature, I turned the filing system upside down; luckily the girls who actually worked for me liked my system better. The factory where I started my new job was the second largest company in the country, and it had over sixty-eight thousand employees working in three shifts. Lucky for me, all administration offices only had morning schedules. Because of its size, there were companies within the factory due to the nature what they manufactured, which was from x-ray machine to lab equipment, all types of lighting fixtures, light bulbs to neon lights of all shapes and sizes, radio and television tubes (yes, tubes).

Our office handled everything from the shipping and receiving paperwork to correspondence and orders, and also doing personnel business as well, such as time sheets and payroll. We also updated personal information and in-processed new comers; basically it was a small human resources office and bookkeeping department. Each of my co-workers had their individual duties and when I started working there and had our first meeting, I found out that when one of them got sick, her work would be waiting to be completed while she was out.

This is where leadership comes in. I made a suggestion and put it to vote when we invited the Section Chief, who was my boss. I suggested that all of us should be cross-trained and rotate every three months. The girls were elated by my idea, as was my boss. As it appeared, all four girls were getting tired of doing the same work over and over, and by being cross trained, their job did not appear as boring and monotone as it really was. From my part, I had to learn everybody's job, as my signature was the next to last to go on every forms, invoices and timesheets. Once the Section Chief (my boss) signed it in the "approver's" signature block, they were dropped up at the central offices.

As I mentioned, each sub company had their own offices, just like ours was and there was a central human resources office that also handled the final payroll, including the money part. There were also two central accounting offices. Each Friday afternoon, before we left work, it was my job to make sure that all reports and payroll timesheets were forwarded to those two central offices. When I talk about the money part, in those days average Hungarian people did not have checking accounts, I am not sure if anyone else had really. We got paid once a month and the payroll came in individual envelopes. Once the financial clerk, escorted by armed security guards brought up the payroll into our office, it was our job to sort the envelopes by shifts.

Once that was accomplished, I would then go to the "floor" as we called the quality control department where I worked, escorted by one of my co-workers and then the employees would line up to pick-up and sign for their income.

If they had any problems, thank goodness they seldom ever had, we just went back to their timesheet and checked it, and if it was necessary, we made corrections. The majority of the time the employee simply forgot that they were late and even a couple of minute tardiness cost them a half an hour of deduction.

After a month I began to like working there and it helped that I got along well and became fast friends with everybody. Andy proudly introduced me to everyone who worked on the "floor", and as far as I was concerned, I was well received. And then, my eighteenth birthday arrived.

HAPPY 18TH BIRTHDAY TO ME (SORT OF)

WHERE I WORKED, the announcement that I was turning eighteen years old came as a surprise to everyone as the general consensus was that I was over twenty-one. It was not unusual as I always looked a few years older than my real age. Nobody was upset in a bad way, as a matter of fact, I was complimented how mature I was for my young age.

I told everyone that I didn't want any surprises or presents; truthfully, I didn't even want to celebrate my birthday. Becoming eighteen years old made me realize that I had officially became an adult and that I had to take a serious look at my life so far. I had Andy in my life for over two years and we were engaged almost just as long, take or leave a few months. The promises that he made yet to be fulfilled and the world of me I could not figure it out why he was unable to find an apartment for us. I didn't want much as I grew up with not much, a room, a kitchen and a bathroom would have been sufficient. When I mentioned to him that perhaps I should start looking, he took my offer not as help, rather, he find that insulting. I suppose it was a "manly" thing.

I would like to explain how I truly felt and how I was thinking in those days. No, I was not a sex starved young woman who desperately wanted to lose her virginity. It would have never been a problem; there was always some man who was willing to do that, but I only wanted to be with Andy, because we knew each other well, minus the sex part. We hugged, kissed, touched and give each other minor pleasures. All of those times, both of us worked ourselves up to the point of almost consummating our relationship, but it was always "almost". It caused me concerns because Andy always told me the same story, he wanted to wait with making love until we married so our honeymoon would be extraordinary, and that he made a promise to my parents that he would wait. The last part should have been scratched off from his list of excuses because even my normally very strict mother thought that there was enough holding back.

I suppose if Andy would come clean and tell me some other valid reason as to why he kept putting on the "brakes" in the last moments when he was about to make love, I would have been more patient or understanding. I often wondered if he was simply afraid from the fact that I was a virgin, was it a fear that perhaps he would be unable to satisfy me? I mean I didn't have anybody to compare him with and he always told me that he would teach me how to make love different ways, in different positions. I didn't know what his real reason was, but he certainly had a lot more will power than I ever had, that's for sure. But, there was that "but", I loved him and I could not visualize my life without Andy not being in it. I would be unable to recall a single day when I had not seen him since we were engaged, well, with the exception of course when I had to go out of town with LTG Toldai, which did not happen too often. Each day we told each other that "I love you" and I began to wonder if it was said just like a routine saying and that it did not mean anything. He didn't act any differently than before, so I could not even pinpoint or suspect anything out of the ordinary. But then again, there was that comment by my former boss, *"perhaps, you should not waste time on any ongoing project that had no chance of succeeding"*. Did he mean Andy? I would never know.

So there I was, turning all eighteen years old. I went home from work and Andy told me before I departed the factory that he would see me later. It was an everyday promise and he always kept it. When I arrived home, my parents were all dressed up and I asked them where they were going.

"The same place as you are," my mother said and pointed at the dress she put on the arm of the chair, so I would change into it.

"I asked not to have a birthday party," I said, not entirely angrily but not happily either.

"Andy's mother insisted," my dad said and I could not turn that down, right? They just wanted to be nice to me, that's all.

We took the twenty-minute streetcar ride to Andy's parents' house, they lived about two short blocks from the streetcar stop, so it was not a far walk. When we walked through the gate, I was shocked to see that there was a tent set up in the courtyard with two long tables with benches on the sides. *Just how many people did they invite?* I wondered.

Andy came out of their apartment with a big smile on his face. He kissed and hugged me, and then he kissed my mom's face and as usual he shook hands with my dad. As it turned out, from Andy's cousin and their families to all of my immediate colleagues and their families were also invited. Sándor, Andy's brother was there too, and he looked extremely unhappy. I found out from Andy that his brother got the notification from the court that afternoon that his divorce has become final. I could not help it, I began to wonder how I would able to talk Andy into convince his brother, now that he is single, to give up the apartment. It may seem like a heartless thing to think about at a sad time that he was having, but I just could not help it, it was constantly on my mind that I wanted to be Mrs. Andrew Horváth.

A nearby restaurant that Andy and I frequented catered the food, and as usual it was very good, even my mother liked it, she was just as picky with food as I was. I noticed a small table, standing by itself not far from the first long table; the top of it was full of presents. I genuinely hated to receive presents. I would have been a lousy actress because I could not hide my disappointment when I received something that I did not like, or if I found the present stupid. No, I was not a spoiled brat. I always believed that if you give a present to someone, you should make it meaningful; give something that they liked or something that they needed, not something that they had several of already.

There were a lot of odds and ends among the presents, mostly things that I was going to put away and never see again. A lot of people gave me books, I especially liked books about the Arts and Sciences, and nobody could ever go wrong with me by giving me something to read. My future in-laws gave me clothes, a matching set of sweaters and a half a dozen pantyhose that was hard to come by in those days, and I was certain that it cost them a lot of money. My parents gave me a beautiful twenty-four carat gold ring which had a sparkling pink stone that I had seen in the window of a local jewelry store, and which I mentioned to them months earlier. I was wondering how could they afford it, but I loved it and I was grateful for them of remembering what I mentioned to them.

At last, but not least, Andy waited until I opened all of the packages before he handed me an envelope with my present in it. "It is something that you mentioned that you wanted," he said and watched my reaction as I pulled out two first class train tickets, dated three months in advance. I smiled as I looked at it but I could not figure out what the tickets were all about. "Look at the destination," he pointed out to the bottom of the ticket, it read, "Balatonfüred". Indeed, I always wanted to go to the resort town by Lake Balaton, but for our honeymoon. Did the tickets mean what I thought it meant? I had to ask.

"Are we getting married? Is this for our honeymoon?" I whispered my questions to him. The look on his face made my blood freeze over. His confusion was so clear like a sky without a single cloud.

"Well, no, not exactly," he said, stuttering. "I, I just thought that you and I could get away for a week."

"Oh, I see," I said and I felt my heart sink lower than the Bottomless Lake in the City Park. I put the tickets back into the envelope and put it down on the table. "You hold on to it, will you?" I told him, and after excusing myself, I went inside his parents' apartment where I locked myself into their bathroom. I tried not to cry because when I cried my eyes became red and puffy, and there were at least thirty people outside celebrating my birthday, my lousy birthday.

"Honey," I heard Andy's voice outside the door. "Are you alright?" I washed my face, flushed the unused toilet and opened the door. He was standing there leaning against the doorframe.

"Why shouldn't I'll be alright?" I asked without humor. He grabbed me and pulled me to himself. His lips pasted themselves to mine and his tongue did its routine, forcing my lips open and entering my mouth.

"I love you so much," he whispered between kisses. He pulled me into the bedroom, locked the door and pinned me against it. Andy pulled up my skirt and reached into my panties and touched me the way he already knew I liked it and kissed me even more feverishly than he ever had.

"Andy, are you in there?" We heard his mother's voice.

"Yes, mom, I'll be right out," he yelled back and he looked at me. I was breathing hard and he was too. He pressed himself against me and I could feel that he was aroused when we heard his mother's voice again.

"Is everything alright?" She asked again. I threw my head back as I bit into my lips hard enough that it bled.

"Mom, I'll be right there," Andy repeated and he looked at me while he shook his head.

"We will be waiting," she said and left.

"Angie, you are so right," Andy said and he pulled up my panties while I tried to get a grip with reality. "This can't go on any longer." I looked at him wondering what he meant. "I am going to take time off and walk the city until I find a place to live. You were right all along. I want to marry you in the worse way, not just because of this," he kissed me real hard, even though my lips were bleeding from biting myself. "I love you and I want to make love to you every night," he said and I believed him.

"You just gave me the best birthday present by saying that," I whispered to him.

We checked out each other's clothes and used the restroom before we joined the crowd outside. "Is everything alright?" My mother asked seeing that I was putting a handkerchief on my lips.

"I accidentally bit myself," I told my mother. She smiled because she did not believe me, although it was true. I leaned to her and whispered the news that Andy is finally going to look for an apartment and not wait for a miracle to drop on his lap. Andy told me on the way back to the party that his brother did not want to give up the apartment, as simple as that.

It began to turn dark and although they had lanterns put up, next day was a workday so the party had to end before it got too late. I thanked everybody for the presents and for attending. I especially thanked my future in-laws for throwing the party for me. When everybody left, my parents and I gathered the presents and we were about to head home as well. I looked for Andy and I saw him talking to his brother. They both looked in our direction and then Andy walked up to me.

"Angie, honey, would you terribly mind if my brother and I go out for a couple of drinks? He is pretty upset about his divorce becoming final and he wanted to wash away his sorrow with a drink or two," he said. I did not like that idea at all, but what could I do? I could not possibly prevent him with socializing with his own, apparently depressed brother.

"Just don't do what I wouldn't do," I told him jokingly. He escorted us to the streetcar stop and waited until we got on the next one. We kissed a few times when we saw it coming and I wished him a good time, to which he replied, that it was going to be one or two drinks and go home to sleep.

"I'll see you tomorrow," he said and kissed me one more time.

... AND THERE WAS NONE

ON THE MORNING, following my birthday, the teasing in my office was on because of Andy and my disappearance after he gave me my present. I laughed it off by saying that we were only gone for ten minutes and who wanted to do something for only ten minutes. I said that as if I knew what I was talking about. Our first daily break was for fifteen-minute at nine thirty, and another one at eleven thirty for lunch. As usual, I poured a cup of coffee for Andy and placed a piece of leftover birthday cake on a small plate and then I went to his work station which was a few feet away from my office, just around the corner, well exactly in the corner.

We usually met halfway, but that morning I just couldn't find him anywhere. It was not entirely unusual, sometimes he was called into another building because he was familiar with variety of machinery and his boss loaned him out. Usually Andy stopped by to tell me that he would be in another other building, so I would not wait for him. Mickey, one of Andy's co-workers noticed me as I stood there scanning the length of the floor where machines lined up the room on both sides, but I just couldn't see him.

"Hey, Angie," he yelled to me.

"Hi, Mickey," I nodded towards him because I was holding the coffee in one hand and the piece cake on the plate in another. "Did you see Andy?" I asked.

He didn't want to yell, he got up and walked up to me. "He called in sick," he told me. "Can I have what you have there?" He asked. Before I surrendered the goodies, I had to ask him.

"What is wrong with him?" I asked with concerned.

"He said that he got food poisoning last night and he felt sick enough to go to a doctor," he told me. I didn't reply I just handed him the food and drink. He thanked me and returned to his workstation.

I walked back to my office deep in thoughts. I had known Andy for years by then and I could not remember a single time when he was sick. He had no known allergies, he never caught cold or flu, and he never had stomach problems, well, apparently not until last night. He ate the same thing as all of us did and nobody else got sick. My mother has a sensitive stomach and she got a stomachache from anything unusual or too spicy, you name it, and she was not sick at all. It had to be something else. As I sat back down at my desk and stared at the two huge piles of documents that waited to be reviewed, it occurred to me that perhaps it was not the food that got him sick, rather the drinking with his brother after we left.

I took a deep breath and began to concentrate on my work. After I left work, instead of going straight home, I got off the streetcar near where Andy lived and I stopped by to visit him. I knocked on the door despite the fact that by then I had my own key to my future in-laws apartment. I made a point to only use the key when they were not home. Andy's mother opened the door and I was shocked to see that her face was puffy from crying. When she saw me, she immediately gave me a big hug. Fear rushed into my heart, did something terrible happen to Andy? That is why she was acting in such a way, not that she did not hug me each time we saw each other, but that hug, on that day was different, that is how it seemed.

"Is Andy okay?" I asked with concern. She began to cry again and pointed at the direction of the bedroom. Before I opened the door, I imagined him lying in bed and moaning from pain with a priest standing by his bedside giving him his last rights, but instead, Andy was sitting on the sofa and was watching a football game. He looked up and gave me a smile that I could not interpret. I set down next to Andy and kissed him. He returned my kiss and wrapped his arms around me. "How are you feeling?" I asked.

"Well, most certainly better than last night," he replied. His mother walked in and sat down by the table under the window.

"How late did you stay out?" I asked quietly. He shrugged.

"Around two in the morning," he confessed and I noticed that he glanced at his mother who was still crying.

"Oh, my God, Andy, what were you thinking?" I asked and I pinched his arm.

"I am sorry, honey," he said and kissed my hand. "Do you mind I am not coming over tonight?" He asked. *Now that is unusual,* I thought, but I told myself that perhaps he was still not feeling well. One thing was for certain, it was not food poisoning, rather, he probably had too much to drink, that is what made him sick.

"No problem," I told him. "Just get well for me, alright?" I asked him.

"I love you very much," Andy said and escorted me out after I said goodbye to his mother.

After I got home I told my parents what happened, both of them agreed that it was rather unusual behavior from Andy's part. He had never missed a day of work; he was never late for work in his life. Although it bothered me what happened, I did not entirely blame Andy for it. His brother was the instigator and he was the one who asked Andy go with him. Sándor was already on my new "*I don't like*" list for not giving up his apartment for Andy and me. If he was to marry again, I could understand it, but according to Andy, his brother did not even go out with anyone since Ildikó tried to take her own life.

Andy returned to his normal self on the following day, and a month later, when there was a three-day weekend due to a national holiday, he and I took two extra days and went apartment hunting together. It turned out to be a sheer nightmare. Since Budapest had twenty-three districts, we lived in the fourth district, called Újpest, we tried to find an apartment in our vicinity, but eventually we extended our search to the fifteenth and the thirteenth districts, which bordered ours.

The apartment hunting was depressing, because while we found places to live, they were out of our affordable price range, or was only one room, or the room was big but the owner had to walk through it to get to the bathroom, or the place was so small that only a single bed would fit in there, simply said, it looked hopeless. I began to get angrier and angrier with Andy's brother because he lived in a large apartment by himself, in an apartment that was big enough for an entire family. It had a nice size kitchen, bedroom, a small living room and a bathroom.

During one evening when I was over at Andy's parents for dinner, and Sándor was there too, I began to talk about how desperate Andy and I are becoming because we could not found any suitable place to live so we could get married. I said those words while I looked at Sándor who gave me a sarcastic smile; he knew exactly what I was getting it. "I know exactly what you mean," he said and that was it, he exhausted all of his sympathy for us. My future in-laws expressed their concerns as well, and they said that they hoped that maybe one of the tenants would move out sooner or later. The only question was, when?

Two months had passed since my birthday and when I left for work on that particular day, I couldn't help but thinking about the dream I had. While I ate my usual breakfast, a couple of pieces of toast, I told my mom who was an expert in interpreting dream that I was wearing a beautiful long wedding gown and my flower bouquet was simply beautiful. I was so happy in my dreams that I was laughing from joy. My mother's face became very serious, even worried, and while I had to rush off for work, I begged her to tell me, at least briefly what my dream meant. "Not good," that was all that my mother said.

As I was walking towards the streetcar stop, about four blocks from my parents' apartment, it began to drizzle, and by the time I made it to the stop, the rain was coming down like crazy. I was already drenched when I got off the streetcar but I still had a ten-minute walk to my building. As I mentioned earlier, it was a huge factory, the second largest in Hungary. While I was still on the streetcar, I looked for Andy, he usually caught the same streetcar in the mornings, but I could not see him.

It poured all day and the sky was so dark that we had to turn on our desk lights as well; the overhead neon lights were just not enough. We all kept looking at our office windows, and Emma, one of my co-workers remarked that she was unable to recall such a dark and rainy day for years back. There was no argument about it and the darkness of the day also reflected on people's mood and behavior.

As usual I went to see Andy during the first break, taking him his second cup of coffee of the day, just to found out that he was working in another building, which he failed to let me know. I was not mad at him, things could happen, he was probably told to go immediately and he didn't have a chance to tell me, so I told myself. Again, I went to look for Andy at lunch but he was not back yet. I was about to leave work at the end of my day when Andy called me on the phone. He told me that regardless of the weather, he was coming over that night, which of course I was pleased to hear.

I could hardly wait to get home and put on dry clothes, everybody was miserable at work and we borrowed some robes that the women who worked on the machines wore over their clothes, so we could get out of ours to dry them as much as possible.

My mom was preparing dinner and asked me if Andy was coming over so she could make some extra food. I told her that he was coming and I even mentioned that if it not stop raining, I may not let him go home. Neither my father nor mother had any problem with that, as my mother said; she was even surprised that he was coming over at all.

"Now that is love," my mother remarked with a smile.

Andy came by around six o'clock and he looked absolutely terrible. My mother immediately handed him a towel. Andy thanked her but declined. He looked raggedy, as if he hadn't slept in days and he stood by the door, dripping water from his raincoat. His thick wavy blonde hair was also completely wet. He had difficulty looking at my mother or me; my father was in the bedroom.

"We could eat in a half an hour," my mother said and nervously looked at me.

"No, thanks mama, I won't be staying for dinner," he said quietly. *What got into him?* I wondered. He cleared his voice. "Mama, if you don't mind, I would like to speak with Angie alone," he said in a grave sounding voice. My mother nodded, put down her apron and walked by me into the bedroom. She stopped and looked at me.

"Your dream was a very bad dream my child," she said and left us alone. The only time she ever called me *'my child'* was if she had bad news for me, like when my father died, or when her brother, Ignác died.

Once we were alone, I stepped up to Andy and wanted to kiss him but his lips barely touched mine. I was never more frightened in my entire life than I was in those moments. "What is going on Andy, you are scaring me," I said to him fighting my nausea back. I sat down on one of the kitchen chairs. "Have a seat," I told him. He hesitated and finally sat down.

"We need to talk," he said the obvious, but I didn't want to rush him because he was in such bad shape.

"You can tell me anything," I assured him but I was not so sure about that myself.

"I did something very bad, something terrible against you," he said and stared at the floor in front of him. I waited, and waited, but he did not continue until I asked.

"What have you done?" I asked.

"I cheated on you," he blurted out. A cold chill ran through me. He did not want me but he was having sex with another woman? I told myself that this was not happening.

"When?" I asked because I couldn't imagine when he had time to stray from me.

"That night, when Sándor and I got drunk," he told me.

"Do you mean on my birthday, two months ago?" I asked with shock in my voice. He nodded. *On my birthday,* I thought, and then something came back to me. On the following day of my birthday party, he called in sick and when I went over, his mother couldn't stop crying. "Did you mother catch you?" I asked and held my breath. He began to cry. I have never seen him so upset.

I loved Andy so much and all the things that we went through, in the village where we met, my almost rape by Joe, our touching and kissing and how we tried to please each other without consummating our relationship. He had that dream to make love for the first time on our honeymoon, so we could tell our children and perhaps our grandchildren about the magic of those first days of marriage. I looked at his devastated face that was soaked with not only by rainwater but with tears too. My heart was beating so fast for Andy, the man who belonged to me, and who without my life would be worthless. I just could not let him go. He was at least honest with me and told me the truth that his parents taught him to do. I got up, walked up to him and knelt down in front of him. I took his hands into mine, and then I pressed his hands to my burning and tear soaked face.

"Andy, you are the love of my life and I cannot live without you. You were honest with me and I appreciate that, for that I love you even more. I found it in my heart to forgive you because I am sure that you learned from this mistake and that because you love me," I told him while I looked up at him. He pulled his hands away from me and began to sob. It was not a good sign. I got up and stood in front of him. *Was there more?* I wondered.

"She is pregnant and we are getting married this Saturday," he said quietly between waves of sobs.

"Who is she?" I asked with calmness that equally scared me and surprised me.

"Judy," he said the name of the person whom I not only greatly disliked, but whom I hated. I began to feel nausea rising in my stomach.

"The same Judy who your brother screwed, the same Judy who almost caused the death of Ildikó, the same Judy whom you called a slut?" I asked. I was very close to vomiting. He nodded. I barely made it to the sink and lost my light lunch and the two cups of coffee I had that day.

My parents heard every word. The door and walls were paper-thin and when my mother heard me retching, she came out of the bedroom and rushed to me. I rinsed my mouth in cold water and brushed off my mother's supportive hands.

"Andy, you better leave," my mother said the words I had no energy to say.

"Mama, I am sorry," he said in a quiet voice as he went to the door.

"Don't call me mama again, and you are telling the wrong person that you are sorry," my mother said in a firm voice. "You are no longer welcome in our home."

"I am so sorry," he mumbled and opened the door.

"Wait," I yelled after him. I pulled off my wedding band from my left hand's ring finger, it was also my engagement ring, and throw it at him. It hit his raincoat and bounced to the floor. He bent down and picked it up.

"I am so very sorry," he repeated, but I turned my back to him and walked in the bedroom, followed by my mother. We heard the kitchen door to the outside closing. Andy was gone, leaving me there feeling numb and cold, just like the rain was outside.

THE HAPPY COUPLE

MY MOTHER LOCKED the kitchen door as soon as Andy left. My father, my stepfather really, who raised me since age nine, was a man of few words. After I sat down on the sofa in a catatonic state, hugging a pillow as it was a child, he got up from the table and stepped in front of me. I looked up and I knew that he wanted to say something, but instead, he bent down and kissed the top of my head. He had never done that and his action spoke clearer than any words he could have said out loud.

My mother was crying by the time she joined me on the sofa. "He didn't only leave you, he left us too," she said, and I prayed to God that she was not going into a long speech that Andy did not deserve me, or that someday I will find the right person for me. To my surprise, she didn't say anything; she just cried quietly while she held my hand.

"Mom, please translate my dream to me," I asked her. She wiped her face and took a deep breath.

"Dreaming with a wedding dress means sadness and unhappiness, laughing in your dream means tears in real life," she explained. *So my dream, or more precisely nightmare did come true,* I thought.

I was certain that I would have difficulties falling asleep but the contrary happened, the moment my head hit my pillow, I was out. Waking up the following morning was an entirely different story. I sat up on the sofa bed where I slept and I asked myself the question, was that a nightmare about Andy or was it real. I looked down on my left hand where the engagement ring 'used' to be and my heart sank. No, it was not a dream or a nightmare, it really happened, I no longer had Andy in my life. I understood that but my heart and my brain refused to believe it or accept it. How could all this happen? What was about that woman, Judy that I didn't have? Andy could have had me at any time, I virtually threw myself at him and yet, he impregnated a woman whom he called a slut and a whore, and who destroyed his brother's marriage. So what if he was drunk and could not resist her advances? Besides, what was she doing there where Andy and his brother were, or did she take the opportunity and seduce him?

It did not really matter, she had Andy and I was deceived and abandoned, and that was my reality. I got up and readied for work. My mother cried most of the night because she and my dad also felt betrayed by Andy who was considered by them as their son, and they loved and adored him as such. While I ate my two pieces of morning toast and drank my first cup of strong espresso coffee, just like on most mornings, mom quickly French braided my below the waist long hair. Tears rushed into my eyes remembering how Andy loved my hair, how he loved to brush it over and over, how he loved to run his hands through my hair. I had to stop myself from those thoughts and concentrate on getting to work on time.

The streetcar stopped at corner where Andy usually boarded the streetcar and looked for me. He was there, but the moment our eyes met, both of us looked the other way. *Sure,* I thought. *Go ahead and just shoot me dead, why don't you?* That is exactly how I felt. I considered the situation worse than if I had lost him forever in an accident or due to illness. That would have been devastating as well, but I would not have to see him every single day with the exception of weekends, day after day, month after month and perhaps even longer.

As always, I was the first one to arrive at the office. I turned on the lights and made a pot of fresh coffee. My co-workers, who technically worked for me but I always treated them as equals, arrived one after the other. First Monika, than Judith, Adele and Edith came together as they were roommates in a rented room. I was standing by my desk and waited until they poured their coffee and got situated. Edith asked me if everything was all right because I looked rather pale. I walked to the door and closed it, just like we always did when we had a meeting. I gathered them together and looked at them one by one.

"As you know, I don't do gossip and I don't like gossip. What I am about to tell you, I am telling you as my friends as the news will eventually get out, due no fault of my own," I began.

"You are scaring me," Monika said with concern.

"I am sorry, it is not my intention. I want you hear it from me first. Something terribly bad happened last night and without going into much details, I want you to know that Andy and I broke up," I finally told them with my voice chocking back tears.

"Oh, my God," they said almost in choir.

"What happened?" Edith asked. I considered her as one of my closest friends. I debated long and hard should I tell them the whole story or not, but I went against it. I knew that they would not rest and will torture me with innuendoes until I tell them something, so I compromised and gave them the basics.

"He is marrying his pregnant girlfriend this Saturday," I blurted out.

"What? Are you kidding?" They all asked me and they were getting upset too.

"Please, guys, be a good friend to me and just let it go, promise me," I pleaded with them and while they promised, they went back to their desks with shaking heads and exchanging disgusted looks. I opened the door and began to prioritize my workload, a never stop project on my desk.

When the first break came I almost got up from my desk to take Andy his coffee. It was such a morning routine and every cell of my body wanted to do it, to see him and hear him to say that last night was only a test, nothing else, but I remained seated, fighting back tears throughout the day. At lunch, we closed the office and my four co-workers/friends, escorted me to the cafeteria for the first time since I began to work there. They acted in a very protective mode and when a man wanted to sit down at the table where we sat, which seated ten, they would not allow anybody, other than women to sit with us.

There were two more days until Andy's wedding and I had no idea how I was going to handle that day. I thought about taking a couple of sleeping pills and just sleep through both days, but later I ditched that idea as stupid. Why should I waste two precious days when I didn't have to get up early and go to work? On Friday afternoon I called the Fourth District's City Hall and asked them about their hours of operation on Saturday. I was informed that they would be open from nine o'clock until noon.

On Saturday morning I got up at seven-thirty and over my parents' objection, I took the streetcar to the City Hall. I was not planning to cause a scene and I was not planning to interrupt Andy's nuptials, I just wanted to see that with my own eyes if he was really going through with it. I stationed myself next to a newsstand just across the City Hall's building and waited. The woman who was selling newspapers and magazines asked me if I was all right because I stood there motionlessly for a long time. I asked her if I was in her way, but she just waived that I was not. Customers were still rare at that time on Saturday morning so she began to talk to me about her daughter. I apologized to her and I told her that I was not being rude; I was just there to watch my former fiancée to marry the woman who came between us.

"Oh, you poor child," was the only thing she said and finally left me alone.

At ten o'clock I noticed a taxi and Sándor's car as they pulled up to the parking lot, a minute walk from the building. Andy arrived with his brother and parents, while Judy and her parents travelled in the taxi. Andy completely ignored his future wife, he was talking to his mother and she began to walk towards the City Hall's entrance, followed by Andy's father, brother and finally Andy, not waiting for Judy and her parents. Andy was wearing everyday clothes, and so was his brother, Judy wore a pale pink dress with a small bouquet of flowers. It didn't take long, by ten thirty they left the building the same way as they arrived with the exception of Judy and her parents who had to wait for a taxi. I suppose the way Andy acted toward Judy was an indication of the kind of marriage they were going to have. I felt weakness in my knees and I thought that I was going to collapse. The lady working at the newspaper stand pushed her folding chair underneath me and helped me to sit down.

"Rest as long as you want too," she said without asking me any questions.

After a half an hour, I thanked her and I headed home. *Seeing is believing*, I told myself and tried to avoid looking at anyone on the streetcar during my ten-minute ride to my stop. Arriving home, my parents who were in the kitchen having lunch took a look at me and they did not have to ask me any questions, they knew that it happened, Andy married the ex-lover of his own brother.

I stayed indoors and when I looked out on the window, across the yard, I wished that my old friend, Steven was still living there, but they moved almost a year earlier and I never saw him again.

A week after Andy and Judy's wedding, Monika, who worked on updating our employee's personal profile and in-processing newly hired employee's paperwork called out to me. "Angie, what is the name of you know who's new mother-in-law?" She asked.

"Gertrud Szücs," I replied.

"A woman by the name of Gertrud Szücs was hired for the lead position that became vacant a couple of weeks ago," she told me with concern.

"Oh, well," I said sarcastically. "I suppose she wants to keep an eye on her son-in-law." I purposely tried to avoid saying Andy's name out loud and my friends and co-workers tried to do the same. Since it was part of my job to know everyone who worked on the so-called 'floor', I gathered my strength and walked out to introduce myself.

"You look familiar," she said a second after we shook hands. "Have we met before?" She asked. It hurt me like hell but somehow I managed to smile at her.

"As a matter of fact we did at the Horváth's New Year's Eve party last year," I said. She stared at me and then recognition clicked in.

"Oh, yes, I remember now," she replied and nervously looked around.

"I won't hold you up, but I always introduce myself to the new employees. Welcome, and hopefully you will enjoy working here," I said and unceremoniously walked back to my office. As I turned by the corner where my office was located, a few steps away my eyes locked into Andy's for an ever so brief moment until I was out of his sight. Inside my office I could barely make it back to my desk, I could hardly breathe. Adele brought me a brown bag and I began to breathe in and out by using that.

I was facing a major dilemma and I had no idea how I was going to solve it, it was completely out of my hands. How was I going to face Andy and his mother-in-law every single day, and sometimes more than once as I had to walk by the mechanics and technician's station if I wanted to go to the restroom, or the changing room where our lockers were located. Even if I wanted to go to the cafeteria, the stairway was around the corner where Andy worked. I could not afford to quit and I certainly did not want to look for another job. When I thought that the situation could not get any worse, it did.

One particular morning I was rushing to work, I had a lot of work to do and I did not want to wait for my mother to braid my long hair, so I just did a quick brushing and left in a hurry. By the time my co-workers arrived, I already made coffee and finished reviewing and signing a lot of paperwork in the "reviewed by" signature block. Around ten o'clock I was on my third stack of documents and I was pleased that I was catching up, when I noticed that someone just stopped in front of my desk. I was busy and I didn't look at the doorway until I saw the person standing there. It was strange that the office became deadly quiet. I looked up; Andy was standing there nervously with several invoices in his hands for the time he worked in the other buildings.

I did not say anything; I was staring at him waiting for him to say something. "Good morning," he said in a quiet tone of voice.

"Good morning," I replied and waited for his next sentence. To my shock and anger, he actually smiled at me.

"Your hair looks very nice," he said and with that compliment he brought back painful memories. I have no idea what got into me, but I removed the scissors from my desk door and I grabbed the left side of my hair and cut it, and then from the right side, all the way to my ear. I also I pulled my hair from the back and cut that too. Monika screamed and Andy took two steps back in total shock. I calmly gathered my long and cut off hair, put a rubber band around it and I handed to him.

"Here," I said calmly. "Take it as a souvenir." My anger was so evident that I was noticeable shaking and Andy's eyes were filled with tears. He quickly dropped the invoices on my desk and ran out of the office. I sat there stunned at what I had done and then I smiled, my hair will grow back but he would never have me. Interestingly enough, I never had long hair again in my entire life. When I turned around I saw four totally shocked faces looking back at me. "What?" I asked. "You never had your hair cut off?"

"No, not like that, I didn't," Edith replied. "Honey, you would never make it as a hair dresser." I couldn't help it, I laughed along with the girls. Adele went to the door and closed it. Being a hairdresser before she got the job in our office, she trimmed my hair properly and later on when I looked in the mirror, I happened to like my new short hair. It was not a pixie cut, but Adele actually managed to trim my remaining hair in a fashionable style.

"I wouldn't want to be your enemy," Monika remarked as I was cleaning the hair off my desk. I put my cutoff hair into a large envelope and took it home after work. I eventually found a doll maker in town and I sold my hair to him for a good price.

Life's gifts kept on coming. One day we had a newly hired employee that walked through our door to pick up her nametag and a timecard. When she walked in, I almost fainted; it was Judy, Andy's new wife. Evidently there was an opening in the evening shift and her mother told her about it. Needless to say she got the job, but lucky for me, if one could call it luck, I was leaving every day for home when she arrived to work, at least every other week. Although there were no rules that relatives cannot work together, however; if one of the employees was in a supervisory or lead position, the other family member had to work on a different shift. The unfortunate part was that the shifts rotated, those who worked the morning shift one week, worked the evening shift on the following week. Our particular area of work did not have a night shift, although if anybody wanted to work double shift as overtime, it was available.

"Hi," she said cheerfully. I looked up and smiled politely.

"Hi, how may I help you?" I asked.

"I was hired effective today, and I was sent here to pick up my nametag and my timecard," she said, relatively friendly.

"And what is your name?" I asked. She acted surprised, and then she caught on what I was doing, except that I had the upper hand.

"You know my name," she said sarcastically. I nodded.

"The name I know you by would be impolite to say it out loud in public, besides, my colleague here would need to know as they handle many aspects of your well-being here," I explained and turned away from her. I blinked at the girls who by then guessed the name of person.

"My name is Judy Horváth, I am Andy's wife," she said with a smile. "We got married a couple of weeks ago."

"It must have been a joyful occasion," I said and chuckled. She didn't know what I meant and I didn't give her an opportunity to say anything further.

"Edith, my sweet, would you mind to take care of this employee," I asked and got up from my desk. I casually walked up to Adele's desk which was located further back in the office. I sat down on the chair that stood by her desk, my back to the door and Judy. Edith went to my desk and from the middle door she took out what she needed to hand over. I turned around. "Edith, please make sure that she signs for them." Adele covered her mouth so she would not laugh out loud.

The whole scene played out in less than five or six minutes, and then she was gone. I thanked Edith for assisting me and I sat back down at my desk, Adele who was about burst out laughing remarked. "Does Andy have anymore family members who doesn't work here yet?"

I laughed too, but deep down inside I felt very sad. She stood there with her hand on her stomach as if she was trying to make a point that she was pregnant. I was so upset for the rest of day that I skipped lunch and worked as hard as I could to take my mind off from her working there. In the early afternoon, after most people were returning from their half an hour lunch break, all five of us were still standing around talking about miscellaneous things, when Monika poked me on my side and nodded towards the door. Andy was standing there, and then he hesitantly walked in. I whispered to the girls not to leave me, so they just stood behind me as I turned to him.

"What can we do for you?" I asked politely.

"My wife," he swallowed hard after saying that. "Judy was here earlier and she came to tell me that you were very rude to her," he said. I was stunned down to my bones.

"And you are here for what reason?" I asked.

He stared down to the floor. "She wants you to apologize to her." I began to smile and then laugh. I turned to my co-workers.

"I have four witnesses that I was not rude to her," I said to him.

"She said that you seemed very upset with her," he commented, still not looking directly at me.

"First, at least have a decency to look at me when you are talking to me. Secondly, if I were truly upset with her, she would not have made it out of here alive. That is all I have to say about that. Is there anything else?" I asked. He looked me in the eyes and a sharp pain grabbed my heart. I had never seen so much pain in anyone's eyes as I saw in Andy's.

"Thank you for your time," he said and left.

I stood there and I wanted to cry so hard that I could taste the salty tears in my mouth. All of a sudden, four sets of arms embraced me; we had a group hug that I cherished for a long time to come. When we separated and went back to our desks to work, all of us had tears in our eyes. Evidently, I was not the only one who noticed the sadness on Andy's face; all of my co-workers did as well.

Two more weeks passed by and those comments given to me by my parents and my friends, that my break-up was comparable to grieving, therefore time will heal all wounds, they were all wrong. Each morning I saw Andy and Judy on the streetcar as they also headed to work, unless Judy worked the evening shift, each of those occasions basically reopened barely closed wounds over and over again.

Two weeks after Judy began to work on what we called the "floor", basically it was a very long large room, from one end of the building to the other, with the stairway in the middle and both sides of the floor had quality control machines where the girls worked in pairs, Andy paid another visit to my office.

I was talking to Monika at the time with my back to the door when Adele motioned that I had a visitor. I turned around and my mind went back almost three years. Andy stood in the doorway in military uniform. I walked up to my desk and sat down. "What can I do for you?"

"May I sit down?" He asked. I nodded that he could. He had a briefcase with him and from there he removed several pages, one of them was an order that recalled him to active military duty, mainly they sent him to a military school so he could be more familiar with the new military hardware that was updated from time to time. I read his orders and I asked him if he wanted a copy, to which he replied that it was my copy. I pulled out several forms from my desk drawer and asked him to fill them out. I gave him the option to fill them out in our office, we had a small table with chairs for that, or take it home and bring it back later.

"If you don't mind, I would like to fill them out here," he said.

"That would be fine," I agreed and gave him a pen.

It was hard; it was so incredible hard being a few feet from him and being unable to touch his thick blonde hair that would be cut when he reports for duty. I wanted to hug him and smell his aftershave that I liked and what he used cautiously so it would not make me sneeze. I watched his hand as he was filling out the forms and I thought about how those hands touched my skin and gave me unspoken pleasures. He looked up and saw that I was watching him. "If you have any questions, please feel free to ask," I told him.

"Thank you," he replied.

I was unable to concentrate on my work when he was sitting only a few feet from my desk. Memories, like a tsunami rushed into my head, the wedding party where we met and what we talked about when he escorted me home, shadowed by Joe all the way to Lucy's house. I touched my lips with the tip of my finger and recalled our first kiss when I thought that perhaps I would never see him again.

He picked up his briefcase to take out an ID card and when he put his briefcase back down, he looked at me and gave me nervous smile. I did not smile back, I just couldn't. He finished a short time later and I gave him copies of the forms. "Thank you for your help." He said as he headed for the door.

"Andy," I could not help calling after him. He turned around in surprise. "You take good care of yourself." I said to him. He smiled again and nodded.

WHAT COMES AROUND, GOES AROUND (MAYBE)

SINCE ANDY WAS gone for three months, I had one less thing to worry about, seeing him that is. I was torn because even if I was unable to talk to him and being with him, I was so depressed about losing him that even just seeing him at a distance calmed me down with a side effect of pain. If were not for the four wonderful women I worked with and the loving parents that I was fortunate to have, I don't know how I would be able to survive what happened. Did I stop loving Andy completely? No, I did not. Did it still hurt what he had done to me? Absolutely.

A month into Andy's absence, Monika, who handled the timecards that she translated into timesheets, stopped by my desk and placed Judy's timesheet and an excuse from work note written by a doctor on my desk. I shrugged and I looked up at her. "What am I suppose to be looking at?" I asked. She sat down on the chair in front of my desk.

"Dr. Papp is a gynecologist, he is specializing in doing abortions," she said in a low voice. I couldn't believe what she was telling me.

"Monika, what are you saying? How would you know?" I asked her.

"Honey, I have two children and let's just say, my husband and I didn't want a third one," she said and smiled sheepishly.

"What if she just lost the baby and had to go for follow up surgery?" I asked.

"She would have to go to her assigned OBGYN," Monika replied. I gave some thought and calculations.

"Would they do an abortion if she is the fourth month?" I asked. She nodded.

"If she had a strong reason, like if her husband abandoned her or abused her," she said. "Besides," she added. "You only get a day off after a regular abortion without complications, if you lose a baby, you get a week off." I sat back in my chair. Monika leaned forward. "She is working the morning shift." She whispered.

"Are you up for a task?" I asked.

"What do you have in mind?" Monika asked.

"We haven't checked the daily logs for a while," I replied with a smile. She looked at me with a puzzled expression on her face.

"Is that our job?" She said. "I didn't know that."

"Well," I replied and got up from my desk. "Today, we are going to "spot-check" daily logs, just in case we have a surprise audit."

"Oh, yes, the audit," she repeated with a grin. I turned around.

"We will be right back," I told the other girls who barely looked up. Monika and I began our walk in the department called "aging". There were walls and walls of adapters and in them manufactured radio and television tubes were inserted. Each type of tube required different burning, or called "aging" time. Once the time was up, the employee removed the aged tubes and put them in wooden boxes, one hundred at the time. Once they were in those boxes, another employee took them to different workstations, but not before they were logged in a ledger by the Shift Supervisor. The women working in pairs did a quality control check and sorted the tubes that passed the inspection, from what needed more aging, to the ones that did not work at all. Each workstation had daily logs that employees kept. In that log, they registered the cases they worked on during the eight hour work shift by writing the batch numbers in the log and noting how many worked and was forwarded for shipping, how many went back to the aging department, and how many were thrown into what was called the "zero box".

We approached Mrs. Palotás, that week's morning shift's supervisor and asked her if we could borrow the log. Thank goodness we liked each other and she smiled as she handed her daily book. She blinked her eyes and whispered to me. "Auditing is coming up?" I was surprised to learn that auditing actually existed, but I blinked back at her and put a finger on my lips. It appeared that it was going to be our secret.

Her daily log had to match the log at individual workstations and Monika and I read out dates and numbers of each to check. We said *"hello"* and *"thank you"* to employees at several workstations until we finally got to Judy's. Monika, obviously being more experienced in child bearing than I was, walk behind Judy and reached over her shoulder for the log. I stood outside the area with the supervisor's log.

"What happened, Judy?" Monika asked her innocently. "You look great, are you on some kind of diet, God knows, I need to do something," she said.

Judy shook her head and glanced over at me. I could feel her stare but I was too busy with the daily book. "No," Judy replied. "I am not on a diet."

We checked two more workstations just for good measure, and then we returned Mrs. Palotás' book assuring her that it looked good to us. Walking back to our office, Monika said firmly that Judy most certainly had an abortion. Well, the way I looked at it, I was not happy about it either way, if she lost her baby or if she had an abortion. The fact that Andy was tricked into their marriage and she was nothing but a liar, no longer mattered to me.

On a nice sunny Monday morning Andy returned and came into our office with his military discharge papers. At that time I only had two forms for him to fill out that didn't take more than a couple of minutes. "How are you doing?" He asked in a soft voice.

"I am fine, thank you for asking," I replied and smiled. Andy nodded and he headed towards the door when he stopped and walked back. He leaned over my desk and whispered.

"I am very sorry about your hair," he said. I smiled up at him.

"Actually, you did me a favor. My new hair style became a symbol of my new life." I replied. His smile was gone and he quickly walked out of the office. "I don't want to hear it." I said it out loud for the girls to know that I didn't want to hear any comments.

Two months after Andy's return from military duty, my boss, Mr. Martin called me into his office. It almost never happened unless there was a disciplinary action or someone was about to get fired; he normally discussed the cases with me, at least the basics of them. My job required knowing who was coming or going because we had to send recruitment request forms to the central HR office for authorization to hire, more likely to replace departed personnel.

"Mr. Martin, you called me," I said to him as I walked into his office.

"Have a seat," he said and for a moment I thought I was in trouble, although I could not imagine why. Without any further delay, he handed me two letters of resignation. I quickly read them and I was somewhat surprised to learn that Andy's wife Judy and her mother, Mrs. Szücs, both resigned. I looked for the reason of resignation but I did not see it written down.

"May I ask what happened?" I inquired from Mr. Martin.

"You have not disappointed me yet and obviously I trust you, so I am going to tell you what happened. As you probably know, Judy Horváth was the wife of our Andy, who is well respected by all of us. Well, she was caught stealing two television tubes, and if I may add, two of the most expensive kind. Her purse was searched at the gate when she was heading home and that is how it was discovered." He explained. I suppose there is an explanation in order.

All of the gates had heavy security with armed guards and unarmed women in the gatehouses. The factory had four smaller and two large gates in various locations. Before an employee was able to leave the factory's premises, he or she had to push down the arm of a box, which had red and green lights while a security personnel was watching the procedure. Once the arm of the box was pressed down and the light was green, the employee was free to leave. If the light was red, they had to go into the guardhouse where female security personnel asked them to empty their purses or/and bags. Naturally there was a male security person for male employees. If there was further suspicion, there was a small changing room where they had to take off all of their clothes. It seldom happened though, but search of purses and bags happened rather frequently, including several times with me too. Supposedly, when the arm on the box was pressed down, a sensor recognized trembling or shaking of the hand and clicked on the red light. So that is how Judy got caught.

Radio and television tubes were very expensive in those days, it was way before transistor radios and modern television sets became available. Because the radios and televisions were rather poorly manufactured, the tubes had tendencies to burn out, sometimes frequently, and then the owner had to call for service or take the entire radio or television set in. In later years, there was a lot of private television and radio repairmen around and getting hold of stolen tubes meant big business. Luckily, the department where I worked only had a couple of cases since I began to work there; Judy's was the third.

"What about her mother?" I asked. "She wasn't caught stealing or anything like that, was she?"

He shrugged. "I suppose she resigned from embarrassment," he commented and gave me two blank but already signed forms. He always did that, signed it before I completed it, from his part it as a sign of trust. I told him a couple of times that I preferred to bring him the completed form for signature, but he continued doing it his way and each time he told me that he had full trust in me.

One would think that I felt elated or even happy for the way things were turning out, but I was not. Although I had never been a vindictive person, I knew that I had in me, and yet, many ways I felt more pity than satisfaction for the firing of Judy, and the resignation of her mother. However, I would lie if I say that I did not feel relief for not having to see either of their faces, especially Judy's.

As I walked back toward my office, a very brief distance with the two signed separation forms in my hand, I recalled the payday when Judy got her very first pay. I mentioned this earlier, on paydays, individual envelopes with earnings, which were prepared by the central payroll office, were brought to us under guard. Once we sorted the envelopes by shifts, two of us took the envelopes with the money and the signing sheet to the department floor, it usually happened around one thirty in the afternoon as the morning shift ended at two, when the evening shift began as well.

We took seats at the supervisor's desk and one of us gave the envelope with the money to the employees, while the other person watched as they counted their earnings, and then the employee would sign his/her name on the roster. I usually took Edith with me, or whoever was not super busy. Traditionally, and for the record, we always asked everybody's name, although we knew every single employee's name by heart. So it was Judy's turn and I asked for her name. She surely heard us while waited in line that we asked each and every employee his or her name, but she was either in a bad or mean mood, because she turned ugly on us, especially on me. "What is your name please?" I asked.

"You should know by now that my name is Mrs. Andrew Horváth, or did you forget what happened?" She barked at me.

"I think that it would be very wise of you to remember that we both know exactly what happened. So if I may suggest, you should get off from your high horse before you fall off." I told her and asked for the next person to step up to the desk. It was Mici, one of the longtime employees. She told me her name and went through the procedure without an incident. She counted her money and after putting it back into the envelope, she leaned closer to me.

"Honey, we all know what happened and we are all on your side," she smiled and went back to work. Edith was just all smiles after the incident.

"I love your style," she complimented me. "You never lost your cool."

"That maybe true, but I am dying inside," I replied and she nodded that she understood.

And then, that part was all over, and I didn't have to see the smirk on Judy's face anymore. I couldn't say anything bad about her mother, Mrs. Szücs because she was always respectful towards me, perhaps, deep down, she even felt sorry for me. I have no way to know that for certain as I never had a private conversation with her.

IT'S CHRISTMAS TIME AGAIN

TIME FLIES WHEN we are having fun, right? Christmas came around and yes; it was still not celebrated in our home. Of course, to be fair to other religions, we didn't celebrate Hanukkah either.

Christmas Eve arrived and my parents and I were having an early dinner so we could watch the holiday programs on the television when we heard knocking on the door. My father got up and opened the door and then he just stood there. My mother yelled at him that he either goes out or comes in but he was letting the cold air in. He opened the door wider and I dropped my fork when I saw Andy entering the kitchen.

"What are you doing here?" My mother asked.

"I just wanted to come by to wish all of you a merry Christmas," he said nervously and tried to catch my eyes, which I kept on my food.

"Andy, have you forgotten that we are Jewish and we do not celebrate Christmas?" Mom asked him again.

"I know, but still, it's a holiday season for everyone," he replied.

"Have a seat Andy," my father said to him. I could not believe that my dad actually invited him to stay.

"Thank you for dinner, mom," I said and got up from the table the same time as Andy sat down. I went into our bedroom and closed the door. I heard them talking so I turned up the television real loud to block out the voices. About ten minutes later the door opened and my dad walked in with Andy right behind him. "Dad, I don't have another room to go to," I said angrily and went back into the kitchen. I put on my boots and my coat, and after shaking my head at my mother I left the apartment.

I got as far as the outside of our building's gate and stopped. I had nowhere to go, it was Christmas Eve. Everything was closed because people were spending possibly happy times with their families. I was not getting sad by any means, I was becoming angry, mostly with myself. Why should I leave my parents' apartment? I was home; it was Andy who should be leaving. I turned around and the way I stormed out, I stormed back in.

"You have to leave," I said to him. He got up from the sofa.

"Angie, please," he pleaded with me.

"Honey," my mother interrupted him. "His parents would like to see you, his mother is not feeling well and it's Christmas for them. Why don't you go with Andy and pay a visit to Mrs. Horváth, she always loved you and you loved her."

"Are you suggesting that I go his parents' apartment with him?" I said to my mother as I couldn't believe what she was asking of me. I looked at my dad and he was nodding too.

"You two should talk," my mother suggested. I shrugged and looked at my mom.

"We have absolutely nothing to talk about," I said firmly.

"I believe that we do," Andy said quietly.

"Angie, out of respect for his mother, please go with him," mom pleaded with me. I sighed and motioned to Andy to let's go.

"But I will only stay for a few minutes," I told my parents.

It was very cold outside and I walked as fast as the ever-growing snow on the ground would allow me. The night was actually quite beautiful with the snowfall, which made the streetlights glow even prettier. The streets were almost completely deserted, as most people were already indoors to begin celebrating the birth of Christ on Christmas day in the town of Bethlehem, in the faraway country of Israel.

As we walked in total silence, I took some pleasure seeing decorated Christmas trees with lights through windows that had their draperies or curtains open. We reached the main street, four blocks from where I lived and where the streetcar stop was located. The store window behind us reflected nothing less than joy for those who were able to afford their merchandises.

It seemed forever for the streetcar to arrive as obviously there were a limited number in service and it was almost completely empty as we got on. The seats were across from each other and when Andy set down where I took a seat, he was facing me. Instead of changing seats, I made sure that I looked everywhere but not at him. I could still not believe what I was doing and I was still angry with myself for letting my parents talk me into going to Andy's parents' house. The only reason I agreed because I indeed missed them and I never stopped liking, even loving them. They were not responsible for their son's deed and I recalled how his mother was stressed out after that particular night when he got drunk. Only I did not know at that time that his mother cried because she caught him and Judy having sex in the gateway of the house, out in the open.

We walked into the yard and then turned left toward their apartment. I was somewhat surprised that there were no lights on in the kitchen, but there was a faint light visible so I assumed that they were probably in the bedroom. Andy unlocked the door and turned on the light so I could walk in without bumping into anything.

"Let me take your coat," Andy suggested.

"I won't be here long enough," I replied.

"Please," he said again. I made an unhappy face and let him take off my coat. "Come on in," he said and opened the door to bedroom. I stepped inside and my jaw dropped, other than us, there was nobody else in the apartment. I turned around to leave but Andy blocked the door. "You can't leave until you hear me out." He told me and his tone of voice was very serious and very demanding.

After taking a deep breath, I took a seat on the sofa; he sat down across from me on a chair. "I love you," he said and I noticed that his hands were trembling. I stared at him without expressing any emotions. "I have made possibly the biggest mistake of my life when I left you for that woman. I am willing to bear the consequence for what I have done, except of losing you forever. I was tricked and played for a fool that I was. I have never loved that woman and I have never lived with her, not even for a day after we were married. I never had sex with her after that one time, when she got pregnant. I am telling you, she meant absolutely nothing to me." Andy told me and in a way, I believed him.

"What about the baby?" I asked.

He shook his head. "She got a late abortion while I was on active duty." He got up and from the small desk in a corner; he picked up an envelope and handed to me. I did not take it.

"What is that?" I asked instead.

"This is my divorce decree, I am officially divorced," he told me. I still felt nothing, nothing at all.

"Is this supposed to mean something to me?" I asked without any humor.

"Have you listened to what I am telling you?" He asked on a raised voice. *Big mistake*, I thought.

I leaned back on the sofa and looked him in the eye. "Do you have any idea what you have done to me, what I have gone through? Do you?" I asked.

"I felt the same way," he said quietly.

"What did you say?" I inquired as if I didn't hear him clearly. "I watched you from a distance as you went inside the City Hall to get married, because I wanted to confirm that my life as I know it was over. You assured me for years that I was loved by you and meant the world to you. In return for my unconditional love and trust in you, you betrayed and abandoned me for a liar and a cheater, as I meant nothing to you. Could you clear consciously say that you felt the same way as I did?" I asked him in a quiet tone of voice. I was no longer upset, but I felt that what troubled me since our break up had to be told. "For a while after you told me that you were leaving me, I woke up each morning thinking that perhaps it was just nightmare. Seeing you every day, and then seeing your wife everyday was just another stabbing in my already broken heart." I took another deep breath. "I suppose I just wanted to know why did you have to marry her? Moreover, in the first place, why did you have to have sex with her? I was always there for you. I virtually threw myself at you and you didn't want me, and don't you dare to tell me that you did."

"I only married her because she was pregnant," he mumbled.

"Ah, she was pregnant, that is why you threw me away?" I said bitterly. "You could have paid child support and be a part of the child's life, but you married her Andy, the woman who was your brother's lover first and whom you called a slut and whore. You married her, Andy and not me." I repeated.

"Angie, I can only tell you so many times that I know that I made a terrible mistake and that I am very sorry." He replied. "I have never stopped loving you and I want you back in my life. I am never going to let you go."

I wanted to laugh with sarcasm but I was too tired and depressed to argue any further. "Just one thing, why did you lie to me about your mother?" I asked.

"Because I knew that you would not come with me." He confessed. I got up, grabbed my coat and walked out of the bedroom. I tried to open kitchen door but it was locked.

"Open this door," I told him but he shook his head. "Do you really think that keeping me here will change my mind?" I asked.

He walked up to me and stopped, looked me in the eye what seemed like a very long time and all of a sudden he bent down and kissed me. I pushed him away and just stared at him unable to believe his audacity when he pulled me to himself and his lips came down hard on mine. As if I was on autopilot, my lips opened up to him and I kissed him back with a fury of a tornado. "God, Angie, I missed you so much." He whispered. Off came the coat again, and then my sweater and my pants, and his did too. With my boots still on, he picked me up and gently placed me on his parents' bed. His lips covered my breasts although I did not let him unhook my bra or remove my panties. He was naked and erect, and under normal circumstances it would have been the night when we became one in passion, but it was not a normal night and there was nothing normal about the circumstances. Andy was about to move his hands toward my thighs when I stopped him.

"Oh, I am so sorry, but I have to use the bathroom," I whispered as if somebody else was in the room too.

He sighed. "Please hurry back," he said breathing hard.

It was darkness in the room; I tried to remember where I dropped my clothes. I grabbed them as I was passing them, including his jacket where I was certain he put the key to the kitchen door after we walked in. I went to the bathroom that opened from the kitchen and quickly pulled on my pants and my sweater, my coat was by the kitchen door where it fell after he took it off from me. The apartment key was indeed where I suspected it would be, inside his coat's pocket. I quietly opened the door and dashed outside. I ran all the way to the streetcar stop while I prayed that one of them would come shortly. My heart was beating very fast, and then I noticed two things. One was the streetcar that headed my way, it was about twenty yards away, and a person, probably Andy was running down the street to where the streetcar stop was.

Since there were only a couple of passengers, streetcar number 10 stopped, I got on quickly and it departed, all within 1 minute. I have never walked so fast in my life as I walked from my stop to my parents' apartment building. Christmas Eve or not, I did not care. When I walked through my parents' apartment door, I was breathing fire. Both of them were rather surprised to see me. One look into my direction, I knew that they embraced themselves for what was coming.

"I love you both," I said and I had extreme difficulties controlling my temper and to keep my fire inside of me instead of burning them with it. "You are my parents, but whose side are you on? You helped him to trick me into his parents' apartment so we would make up, to finally do what you taught me not to do without getting married first? It feels like you threw me to the wolves when you knew how I felt." I told them. My mother tried to hug me but I pushed her away.

"Angie, he is still so much in love with you and he sincerely regrets what he had done. I think that your dad and I could forgive him." She said with hurt in her voice.

"Well then," I turned to my mother. "Go ahead and marry him." They looked at each other with a puzzled look on their faces.

"We thought that you still loved him," my mother said quietly.

"No, I do not. What I feel towards Andy is bitterness and sorrow. There is no more love left for him," I told them.

"It has been over two years that you invested in him, when you loved him with everything you got. Are you honestly able to close that chapter of your life on him?" My mother asked.

I did not reply right away, I got the sofa bed ready for the night. Once I was all tucked in, I looked at my mother who stood there, still waiting for my reply. "Mom, I need you and dad to acknowledge that it is over. Please do not let him in if he comes here again, I do not want look for another place to live."

That night, I had the best nights sleep in a very long time. When I woke up in the morning, I felt very good and finally free.

A NEW LIFE

ONE MAY THINK that after what happened on Christmas Eve would put an end of whatever Andy had in mind. It caused the opposite effect; so much so that I had to seriously consider making changes in my life. Each day when I went to work, there was a fresh bouquet of flowers waiting. On the weekend, it was delivered to my parents' apartment. When I am saying every day, I mean every single day. They were not big bouquets but big enough to be noticed, so it became my daily routine to give the flowers to the girls in the office and to the ladies working on the production floor. It happened in front of Andy's eyes, but he just smiled at me although I never smiled back.

In the mornings he always got on the same streetcar that I was travelling on and he always tried to get as close to me as was possible. However, getting close to me on the streetcar with one third of the people in our district working at the same company and using the same streetcar schedule made that difficult for Andy. At the end of January 1969, I went to talk to my boss, Mr. Martin, and I asked if it was not too much trouble, I wanted to change my work schedule from six AM to two PM, to seven AM to three PM. I figured that if I was to go back to school again, which I dropped out of when we broke up, I would still have time to study and get to my classes as most of them started around six in the evening. Mr. Martin had no problem with it and neither did my co-workers as Edith always worked the same hours as I did, so there was someone there when the morning shift for the department started in case there was an emergency.

A month after the first flowers arrived, cards and love letter campaign began. Addition to that, frequent stops in the office with various questions about rules and regulations, and *"what if"*, questions also followed. Frankly, instead of warming up to Andy again, he began to irritate me more than I ever thought that he could and I did not know what to do. Each time a note or a card came, I tore it up without reading it first, and on my way to the restroom I dropped it in his in-box on the technicians' station.

After work I could hardly wait to get home, and eventually my parents came to the understanding that what Andy was doing was no longer cute or nice, rather it was borderline harassment and stalking. I could only say to him so many times, "Please do not send me anymore flowers, notes, cards or anything". My pleading fell on deaf ears.

And then, with a blink of an eye my entire life changed. It was a Saturday morning and although I got up late, I was already fully dressed. I suppose it was around eleven o'clock in the morning, we were just sitting around the kitchen table drinking coffee, when we noticed through the kitchen door, which was a French door with a light curtain on the glass part for privacy during the day, and heavy curtain at night, that a tall man stopped and was looking at the name plate on the door. My mother went to the door when the man knocked and he took off his hat when she opened the door.

"Can I help you?" She asked.

"Good morning, Ma'am, I am looking for Angelina Aranyi," he asked politely.

"She is my daughter," my mom informed him. "May I ask why you are looking for her?" The tall man smiled and I tried to figure it out why his face looked so familiar. I went to the door too.

"I am Angie Aranyi, and you are?" I asked. Although he most certainly was familiar, I was sure that we had never met.

"My name is Colonel Nicholas Toldai, I am General Toldai's younger brother," he introduced himself. I smiled and opened the door as a sign of inviting him in. He nodded and stepped inside. I introduced him to my dad and my mom, and I offered him a seat while my mother offered him espresso coffee, which he accepted.

"How is my favorite general doing?" I asked.

"Well, apparently he is enjoying his new job and the area where he lives. His family also loves Washington, DC. He often mentions you in his letters by saying that he could have used your *"legendary"* organizational skills. Frankly, that is the reason why I am also here," he told us.

"I appreciate the compliment," I replied.

"The purpose of my visit is basically rather simple. I would like you to come and work for me, to run my human resources office," he announced.

My parents and I exchanged looks, which he noticed. "Forgive me for being forward, I didn't even tell you where I work and where the job is, and how much it pays." I nodded. "Would you be interested in change of scenery?" He asked.

"Yes, actually I am," I replied.

"I am the Commandant of the Gödöllö Military Academy, and the personal office, or as nowadays is called Human Resources Office, which normally has eight employees, well, one quit to go to another job in the city, and another just had a baby and informed us that she won't be returning. I need a fresh set of eyes and new ideas in that department because frankly, I am not entirely happy about the way it has been run. I am offering you the Supervisory Office Manager position, with the salary of four thousand forint a month," he told me. At my current place of employment, I was making little bit over two thousand.

"Colonel Toldai," I said with a smile. "The job offer sounds great, but you do understand that I am not even nineteen years old, right?" I asked, just to be sure.

He nodded. "Yes, I am well informed about your personal matters from my brother," he told me. "By the way, he wanted to know if you have gotten married to Andrew. What can I tell him?" I have no idea about my facial expression that he noticed, but he nodded a couple of times. "I am sorry about that." He commented.

"Where is she going to live?" My mother asked the very good question. He smiled.

"Well, I am going to make you an offer that you cannot refuse," he said, addressing me directly. "I have a small but efficient apartment at the academy, but I also own a house in the city because my wife and three children are living with me. I don't think that I stayed in that apartment twice since I have become a Commandant seven years ago."

"You wouldn't be in any trouble if I move in there?" I asked. He laughed.

"Who are they going to complain, to the Commandant?" He asked, but then he added. "But seriously, I have permission from the government to house anybody who holds an emergency essential position at the academy, and the job I am offering to you is such." He replied.

His offer sounded like an answer to my prayers. "Do I have time to think about it?" I asked. He nodded.

"Yes, the next five minutes, because my train is leaving in two hours and I have to get to the station," he answered. I looked at my parents and my mother opened her arms as a gesture that I translated as that the decision was up to me.

"I'll be pleased and honored working for you, sir," I replied and got up. He left me a brochure with instructions and maps where to find certain offices and the aforementioned apartment, which was located on the upper floor of the building where I was to work. How is that for treatment? *It would be a good start,* I thought. *At least until I would be able to get an apartment of my own.*

Before he left, Colonel Toldai asked me to sign a position acceptance form, which stated that I was obligated to report to work two weeks from the following Monday. It was actually a reasonable amount of time to turn in my resignation. After the Colonel left, I sank down on the sofa and thoughts like tidal waves rushed through my head. I have made a decision not to tell anyone where I was going to move and work, of course with the exception of my parents. The girls in the office will only be told that I got job at another place in downtown Budapest. I wanted to disappear from the scene for a while; I thought that new surroundings would do well for my self-esteem and my disposition in the world. My parents already missed me, but Gödöllö was only a thirty minute ride from the city, and I promised that I would visit them as often as I could, a promise that I intended to keep.

I was dreading Monday morning that came mercilessly way to fast. I arrived several minutes earlier to work and typed up my resignation. I did not give any clues where my future job was. I wrote that with a breaking heart, I would be leaving a great boss and supportive staff/friends behind. While I enjoyed my time working there, my new position will be a great challenge with a substantial monetary increase, a job that would have been a big mistake to let pass without accepting it.

Mr. Martin just stared at my resignation and then he finally looked up at me. I was not certain what to expect, I thought that he was going to scold me for being ungrateful and unappreciative, but instead he stood up and wanted to shake my hand. I was pleased and surprised at the same time.

"Mr. Martin, I am glad that you are not mad at me," I said emotionally.

"Mad? I am pleased that my prediction came through. When Mr. Postás and I interviewed you for the job, both of us said to each other that the only drawback about hiring you was that you wouldn't last too long. You gave us the impression that you have vast knowledge, that you are organized, ambitious, but most of all, that you were reliable. We knew then that it was just a matter of time before someone else recognizes that you would be a great asset to their workforce, and would make an offer that we could not match. Speaking only for myself, I am wishing you best of luck and if you should change your mind someday and would like to rejoin us, I would find a place for you." He told me. I just couldn't help it. I broke down and cried. He handed me his handkerchief and I used it to wipe off my tears. In an unprecedented move, he gave me a hug, something that was completely out of his stern character. It took me a few seconds before I told him how touched I was by his words and how guilty I felt about leaving when I loved my job and my wonderful colleagues as well.

"People like you are rare, and no matter what you will be doing, you will leave your mark because you will always love and care about your job and about the people around you," he said as he escorted me to the door. As I made my way back to the office, around the corner I bumped into Andy and he saw my sad face. He tried to stop me but I walked around him. "Are you all right?" He called after me. I waived at him to leave me alone.

I took a deep breath before I entered the office and closed the door behind me. All four girls, women really, looked up and saw my face puffy from crying. "What happened? Was Mr. Martin giving you a hard time?" They all asked. I shook my head and asked them not to be upset regarding of what I was about to tell them. I took a deep breath and then I told them that I have put in my resignation. There was a stunned silence after my announcement, and as if they were in some sort of shock, without saying a single word or asking any questions, they returned to their desks and let it sink in.

I just stood there and watched as my co-workers and friends' faces grew darker, sadder. "I need you to promise me that you keep my departure a secret, at least for awhile." They all nodded as they knew the reason behind my request.

The two weeks flew by real fast and I spent that time cross training and bringing the girls up to date on all issues, mostly on pending cases and bookkeeping issues. I promised them daily that I would be in touch, if no other way, but by letter and phone calls. My promises had a calming effect on all four of them, because they knew that once I gave my word, I would keep it.

On my last day, on Friday, Mr. Martin called me into his office and presented me with a letter of recommendation and an award of appreciation, which was a small medal along with a diploma like certificate. I wanted to get back to work, but each time I got up to leave, he asked me various questions about my future job, which I described without mentioning the location. He only stopped asking questions when his telephone rang. He smiled after answering it and then he got from his desk. "I'll escort you back to your office." He declared and we walked back to my office.

I immediately became suspicious that something was going on when I noticed that the door to the office was closed, and when Mr. Martin gentlemanly opened the door for me, a surprise party was waiting. I saw faces there from both the central accounting and from the main HR office too. There had a nice cake for me with "good luck" written on the top with chocolate and there were many small gifts placed on my desk. With the door closed behind us, Mr. Martin made a brief speech, and then he presented me with an envelope with three thousand forint inside. He informed me that everyone in the central HR office pitched in, and of course my office did as well. That probably included him and the director of the entire quality control department, Mr. Postás too. I was touched and grateful.

There were hugs and well wishes, and then we cut the cake, one of the women served non-alcoholic punch. We were just chatting away when the door opened and Andy walked in with some paperwork excuse. "I am sorry, I didn't know that there was a party going on. So what's the occasion?" He asked.

"It's my birthday," Mr. Martin said to everyone's surprise. Andy nodded, mumbled a "Happy Birthday" and left without saying another word. I shook my head and whispered *'thank you'* to Mr. Martin while the others were laughing. I guess I stupidly thought that Mr. Martin was not aware of Andy's daily routines, the flowers and the notes, but evidently he knew.

I began to prepare for my move by packing work and leisure clothes, shoes and everything that was needed to last me for a while. It was not like moving into the woods, the city of Gödöllö had many stores and restaurants, well, it was just like a big city in a smaller scale. I managed to pack three suitcases, although I had to borrow one from our next-door neighbor who was nosey enough to loan one in exchange for the news that I was moving. I ask my parents not to tell others where I was moving, in case Andy would snoop around in our apartment building. We told everyone that I am moving into the downtown area, closer to my new job and where I found a small apartment with a rent that was reasonable. They seemingly accepted the fact that I was moving out and that they had a new subject to discuss.

It almost took longer to get to the railroad station than to take the train to Gödöllö. The city itself had more than one university and various higher education institutions, not to mention the beautiful Grassalkovics Palace, a favorite visiting place of King Franz Jozsef and his much beloved wife, Elizabeth, also called, Sissi. I knew from available statistics that the population was around 34 or 35 thousand, a big change from the population of Budapest, which was around two million at that time.

I found out later that the city also had museums, one of them was called "The House of Art" and the "Arboretum" which I planned to visit someday. Other than the Gödöllö Military Academy, as I mentioned earlier, there were other universities, such as the St. Stephen Mechanical Engineering University, the Institute for School and Speech Therapy, and among others, the Frederic Chopin Music School.

I had so much to learn, to become familiar with my new surroundings, but I knew that it would be a while as I had to focus on my new job first. As my parents and I arrived, they came with me at that time to see where I'll be living and working, to our surprise, Colonel Toldai himself was waiting at the railroad station with a jeep and with his own personal vehicle. His driver helped me and my parents with my suitcases, and then he departed to deliver my belongings to my new residence. I felt welcomed right away and as soon as we boarded his car, the Colonel gave us a mini tour of the city by driving around, pointing out major areas, which was like, one, not counting the other educational institutions and other tourist places I mentioned above.

Within minutes we arrived to the main square called Szabadság Tér (Freedom Square) where the Colonel slowed down so he could point out some of the other streets and buildings I may wanted to get familiar with right away. To the right from the Dózsa György Street stood the Queen Elizabeth Hotel, which used to be the Old Town Hall, there was also the Reformed Church, the New Town Hall, the Hamway Mansion, the Town Museum and the Town Market, just for starters. I concluded that I would probably be able to walk all around town, when I will have time.

My parents seemed to like the city and when we drove up to the huge L-shape building of the Gödöllö Military Academy, they were speechless. We drove directly to the main building where the apartments were also located. As it turned out, there were ten apartments, and with the Colonel's apartment, his secondary home really, all had temporary and at times long term occupants, mostly officers who actually taught at the academy.

The apartment consisted of a small kitchen without any stove as it was illegal to cook in the building, which sounded kind of funny having a cafeteria on the second floor, but it had a medium size refrigerator, microwave on a stand, a kitchen table and two chairs, some cabinets with a few dishes in it, and a bedroom and living room combination, just like at home. However; unlike at my parents' apartment, it had a private bathroom, just a shower, a toilet and sink, perfect really as I seldom had time to soak in a tub of water. Most people I knew did not have a bathtub, only a shower, and it was considered a luxury. Fortunately that part of the building had an elevator as the apartments were on the top floor of the eight story building.

The first thing I did was sat on the sofa bed that was not opened up and I found it comfortable enough. There was not a lot more furniture in there, but there was certainly enough not to be able to call the apartment Spartan. I stared at the television, it was an older model and when the Colonel noticed what I was looking it, he assured me that it was still in perfect working condition. I smiled and nodded.

I thanked him again and I assured him that as soon as I get my feet on the ground, I will be looking for other accommodation. He just waived, meaning not to worry about it. As for the kitchen, he apologized about the refrigerator for being so small, but he showed me that it had some essential food in there that his wife asked him to bring for me. It was then that he informed me that

I was also invited for dinner at his house, and out of politeness he also invited my parents as well. They thanked him but they were anxious to catch the local train, that was called HÉV by the Hungarians.

Colonel Toldai informed us that his driver was going to take my parents back to the train station, and that if it was alright with me, he would pick me up at six thirty in the evening. I thanked him again for everything, and then I said goodbye to my parents and I promised them that I'll come to visit as soon as possible. Of course my mother cried and my father made funny faces that made me smile.

It was just barely after noon and I had nothing else to do but to leisurely unpack, get a little bit organized, and at the same time get familiar with the place, which did not take more than a half an hour. I walked around the small but clean apartment, the very first place where I would be living all by myself. Since I did not have lunch, I made a salami sandwich from the meat I found in the refrigerator and took the food back into the living room, something that I would have never done at my parents' apartment, except when I was sick. I turned on my radio while I laid down on the sofa.

At first I wasn't certain if I heard correctly or not, but there was a knock on my door. I knew that it was not the Colonel as it was much earlier then the agreed time to pick me up.

"Hello," said the movie star standing in front of my door, looking at me with beautiful blue eyes. "I am your neighbor, Captain Attila Bartha."

"Hi, I am Angelina Aranyi," I introduced myself politely.

"May I come in?" He asked with a smile that took me back a few years and that made my blood run cold.

"What for?" I asked with a smile on my face. He made a silly face.

"I saw you from my window when you arrived and I thought that I would like to know you better," he said and turned his head sideways as if he was trying to measure me up from the narrow vision that the crack of the door allowed.

"I guess you will have to wait until the movie or book comes out," I replied and closed the door, turning the key twice in the lock. I heard him murmuring something but I could not make out the surely not praising words. *How typical is this?* I thought. *Here is this gorgeous guy and he had to turn out to be a jerk. Oh, well, life goes on.*

I had an unspoken and unwritten rule that I made when I began to work at the garrison where the first Colonel Toldai was my boss. The rule was that I would not date anyone I work with or from the environment where my job was located, meaning other departments as well. A place like a military academy where only few of the teachers, the administrative personnel and the cafeteria including the kitchen staff had female employees, there were a lot possibilities for finding a date, or worse, getting hurt by dating someone in the vicinity. Also, there was a possibility of a bad romance, and then what? The entire academy would have known. It was my philosophy, right or wrong, I stuck to it even when I had chances at all of my previous work locations too.

Colonel Toldai's driver picked me up and drove me to a beautiful family home, a short ten minute drive from the academy. The driver, a civilian did not speak a word to me and it was fine. I couldn't say that he was rude, but he was just that, a driver.

The Colonel, wearing civilian clothes came down the few steps that led up to a garden and the main entrance of the house. One of his children, a five year old gorgeous little girl who came outside with him took my hand as we walked to the door. Two other children, one seven year old boy and a nine year old girl were standing inside the doorway, curious about their new guest.

He showed me inside and called out to his wife that I had arrived. A woman in her early thirties appeared, and when I stretched my hand out for a shake, she actually hugged me. "I am Terri," she introduced herself and then she added. "I am so pleased that you have accepted our invitation," she said and motioned to the couch and the chair, so I could pick where I wanted to sit. I sat down on the couch and the little girl, whose name was Zsofia curled up next to me. Her mother asked her to leave me alone but she just shook her head. I assured Terri that Zsofia was not bothering me at all, and that I liked children. "What would you like to drink? We have red and white wine, and two different kinds of beers," she offered.

"Thank you so much, but I don't drink," I told her. The Colonel turned around from the bar cabinet.

"Never?" He asked with surprise.

"No, sir, never," I confirmed.

"Not even on special occasions?" He pushed on. I laughed.

"No, sir, not even then," I said again.

"We do have soft drinks too," Terri suggested and I told her that any soft drinks would be fine.

"I have never met a person who did not drink at all," Colonel Toldai remarked.

Terri returned and handed me a strawberry soda, which happened to be one of my favorites. I thanked her. She also sat down and the Colonel repeated his remark to her that I was the first person he ever met who never drank.

"Sir, it actually gets funnier. My paternal grandparents owned and operated a tavern in the city of Mátészalka, and my maternal grandparents owned a brewery and a distillery. Interestingly enough, my mother also never drinks and neither does my two living aunts," I told them.

"Angie, while we are in a private surroundings, you can call me Nicholas," the Colonel offered.

"Thank you sir, but I would rather not." I replied politely. "Your brother also offered me to call him on his first name in private, but I need to set up some boundaries. Naturally, while I like to remain on friendly terms with you, I would still prefer to call you sir, or Colonel Toldai."

"Yes, my brother told me about your work ethics, no dating with co-workers, not going out with anyone from where you work, do those rules still exist?" He asked. I nodded.

"A place like the academy sir, more than ever," I said with a smile.

"I believe that my husband made the right decision to hire you," Terri said and asked me to follow her husband and children to the dining room where dinner was already waiting on the table. She made a lot of good food, from schnitzel to home fried potatoes, with cucumber salad and chicken soup. It was like as if she knew what my favorite foods were.

"So have you met anyone yet?" Colonel Toldai asked.

"Captain Bartha," I blurted out. "Sort of," I added. I noticed that the Colonel and his wife exchanged looks. "Is there something I should know about him?" I asked. They actually laughed.

"We call him Attila, the Hunter. He goes after every newly hired civilian personnel, the women I mean," Colonel said.

"He was not disciplined because of that?" I asked with curiosity. He shook his head.

"He never really has done anything illegal, and nobody filed a formal complaint yet," he informed me. "You let me know if he gives you a hard time."

"May I ask what did he say to you?" Terri asked.

"He said that he saw me from the window and he thinks that he would like to know me better," I told them.

"What did you say to that?" She wondered.

"I told him that he had to wait for the movie or the book to come out," I replied. I did not expect their reaction, both of them burst into hearty laughs. I personally did not think that it was that funny, but I was pleased that they liked it.

We had a nice evening and I repeatedly thanked both of them for having me over, to have a pleasant memory of my first evening in my new city, in my new life.

WORK, WORK AND MORE WORK

I WAS AT MY new place of work an hour before opening and I began to wonder what I got myself into when I opened the double door to the HR department. First, the door was left unsecured, which was my luck as nobody started to work there so early, it was still only five in the morning. On the other hand it was irresponsible to leave the door unlocked of a place where personal records and information was kept.

I stepped into a very large office and I found myself in a waiting area with four chairs on both sides of the double door, which did not have any sign on the outside or the inside about the hours of operation. I made a mental note of that as well. The front, once entered was separated by a wall to wall chest high counter. I found a flap-top at the very right where our employees made their entrees and exits. It was simple, just lift up the top part of the counter and push the half door in.

Inside the counter were forms lines up for all sort of purposes from health benefit to leave request, and so on. When I glanced at the forms, I quickly realized that the majority of the forms were almost, or the same as were used the Army Garrison where I had my very first job. I wasn't concerned about the rest, I trusted my memory of remembering all of the forms in no time. It was my understanding that the busiest months were June and September when the classes ended and began. In the meantime, our department was responsible for just about everything, including my favorite subject, payroll, luckily we only had to handle the civilian employees payroll, and I mentioned this with great deal of sarcasm.

I slowly walked through the department and surveyed the areas. There were file cabinets everywhere, and when I looked into them, I found nothing less than chaos. Personnel files were in unlocked cabinets and on the top of desks, all in open areas.

I noticed an office where there were no desks or cabinets, only a long table that seated eight, with the right amount of chairs, a small refrigerator and a small file cabinet with a coffee maker on the top. I found the office that had my predecessor's name on the door, which I promptly removed with a screwdriver that I found in the desk. Why that tool was there, I would never know. The top of the desk was cluttered with files and documents that needed to be filed. I opened one of the personal files that should not have been left out in the open, and to my shock, the first thing I noticed that there were some documents filed in there with a different name than what appeared on the label of the file.

At six o'clock the door opened and two of the workers appeared, they were busy chattering and they did not take any notice of me sitting in the side office. I knew that their work schedule was from six o'clock until three o'clock in the afternoon with two fifteen minute breaks and one hour lunch time. The other four employees arrived late, two of them more than half an hour and two of them were more than fifteen minutes late. Despite the fact that they were already late, and even those two women who arrived on time were still having coffee and talking about their babies, their husbands or boyfriends. By six thirty, I had enough. I forced a smile on my face and to their surprise, I walked out of the office.

"Good morning," I said cheerfully. "I am Angelina Aranyi, but you are welcome to call me Angie. Would you kindly tell me your names, please." I asked politely and they did. I motioned toward the office with the coffee maker next door to my office. "Is there a coffee fund?" I asked. The answer to that was of course, yes, as I expected. "Please count me in," I asked. They nodded and mumbled, and began to scatter around towards their desks. "Excuse me," I said and all stopped. "I think that this is a perfect time to sit down with all of you and discuss my expectations."

"We have work to do," said a woman in her forties, she went by the name of Mitzi.

"And you shall do it when we are done," I said with a change in my tone. They began to eye each other but every one of them followed me inside the basically unused place. I looked around and thanked them for joining me. I put down my notepad and my pen. "I would like to say up front that I am the world's easiest person to work for and work with. The magic word here is "work". I would like to have a brief meeting every Thursday afternoon, and once I get an approval, which I have no doubt that I will, we will be closed every Thursday afternoon for training. If we don't train, we will try to use that time to catch up with what we are logging behind. In the future, I expect that when you come for a meeting, you will bring a notepad and pen, and suggestions you may have."

"That would be a waste of time," said a woman whose name was Ruth, I guessed her age in the mid-thirties.

"I am sorry to hear that you feel that way and I sincerely hope that your opinion will change with time," I commented her remark. "Now I would like to address some of the security issues. Who has keys to this department, to the double door and if any, to the side doors."

"We all do. Yours is probably in your desk," said a younger girl whose name was Tess.

"Thank you," I said and smiled at her. "When I came in at five o'clock this morning, the main door was unsecured. I also noticed that the file cabinets with personal files and information were also unlocked. Those two things itself is a major violation of government security codes." I told them as I knew that from my days working at the Army Garrison in Újpest, and at the Defense Ministry.

"We were never told that," said another person in her twenties, her name Flóra.

"Now you know. Additionally, there should be a copy of the security regulation in the common area, where it could be easily accessed." I suggested. "While we are on the subject of file cabinets, I strongly dislike the way they are now and I want them, all of them moved in here."

"Where are going to eat?" Mitzi asked.

"I understand that there is a cafeteria on the next floor, or if you clear the top of your desk and use proper precaution, I would not hold it against you if you consume your food where you work. We will find a place for the coffee maker. Think this way, with all the cabinets out of the way, you would have more floor space," I told them. I personally and professionally did not care if they liked it or not. "Before returning to your desks, I have a very important subject to bring up, and it is tardiness. You get paid from six to three o'clock with two fifteen minute breaks and one hour lunch. I expect everybody be here by six o'clock and not leave before three. If you wish to make a change in your work schedule, I am all open for it."

The double door opened and Colonel Toldai walked in. I got up right away, out of respect, but the others remained seated. He joined us by taking the eighth chair, but before he did that, we shook hands. In five minutes I ran through with all the topics that we discussed so far. He nodded, and he nodded again.

"What I am going to say is not a reflection on you ladies, but Ms. Aranyi here is what this institution needed. Fresh ideas, time saving procedures and security updates. I like it," he said.

"Sir, I would appreciate your opinion on closing this office on every Thursday afternoon for training and/or catching up," I asked him.

"I don't see why not, as a matter of fact, it would be a good time to have meetings too," he said and I smiled, he was most certainly on my team.

"I have two more requests if I may," I asked politely. He nodded. "I would like new locks on the door and to get some manpower to move the files cabinets in here," I pointed around.

"Your wish is my command," he replied still smiling and got up. "Although, I don't take commands because I am the Commandant, however; in your case Ms. Aranyi, I make an exception. And you ladies, I expect your full cooperation with Ms. Aranyi, understood?" He said in a voice of a commanding officer. Every one of the women mumbled, *'yes'*.

As they were leaving the room, I asked Flóra to remain behind. "Did I do something wrong?" She asked with concern. I laughed and pointed at the chair to sit down.

"I don't know you long enough to find anything wrong yet," I said and smiled at her. "I couldn't help but overhearing when you mentioned to your colleagues about your problem with the daycare, would you mind to repeat it to me what the problem is?" I asked her. At first, she was surprised to hear that I wanted to know about her personal problems, but she slowly began to tell me that her children had special needs and because she and her husband started to work at six in the morning, they had to pay extra for the babysitter to take the children to a different kind of kindergarten than all other children were going. Also, she charged them double if they were late picking them up.

"Would it help you if you changed your hours from eight to five, with an hour lunch, or if you only want to take a half an hour lunch, you could leave at four thirty. That way you could drop off your children directly at the specialized kindergarten, and your husband could pick them up after work." She stared at me and all of a sudden tears appeared in her eyes. "I am sorry, did I insult you with my suggestion?" I asked with concern of my own.

"May I hug you?" She asked. I nodded and she did. "Perhaps Colonel Toldai is right, you are a God sent," she said. "That would be a tremendous help financially and for other ways as well."

"Consider it done," I assured her. "I will write up a work schedule and post it on the bulletin board," I told her.

"We don't have a bulletin board," she commented. "I suppose we will have one."

I smiled and nodded, and then I wrote another remark on my notepad, which I was doing already on the discussed subjects. As I was sitting there by myself for a few minutes, out of nowhere I became extremely nauseated. Luckily by then I knew where the restroom was because I had to make a run for it. I hadn't eaten anything out of the ordinary, and while I did not feel particularly nervous about meeting my new employees, I was under a lot of stress and I guess it went all the way to my stomach, not to mention the strong coffee that I drank did not help either.

I washed my face and rinsed my mouth, and as I was leaving the restroom, I found Klára, one of my subordinates standing outside the door, obviously hearing the sound of my vomiting. "Are you alright?" She asked more from curiosity than concern. I nodded. "Are you expecting?" She inquired based on some idiotic idea that if someone throws up in the morning she must be pregnant.

"Hardly," I replied, and then I mistakenly added. "To get pregnant, you actually have to be sexually active." She was smart enough to draw a conclusion and she just grinned.

Returning to my office I reviewed my notes and made a long list what needed to be done and whom I needed to contact. I found a telephone directory for the city and a smaller one for the office numbers at my place of work at the military academy. I also made a huge temporary sign for the outside door that read *"Reorganization in Progress. Emergency Services only"* and put it up.

As I was heading back to the office, the sounds of a hush-hush kind of conversation caught my ears. I quietly walked around the corner where the elevator was and I noticed that Klára was talking with not other than Captain Attila (the Hunter) Bartha. Both of them were laughing after exchanging words, and then they shook hands. Noticing that both of them were leaving, I quickly returned to my office where I left the door open. In my office, one wall was half glass with blinds that cried to be dusted. I pulled up the blinds so I could see the activities in the office, and it also give me a semi clear view of the counter as well, at least I could see the double door and the right side of the counter.

Since it was my first day and my subordinates had an urge to discuss me and what I said during our first meeting, I did not say anything or complain about the quiet chatter, but I knew that I would not stand for an on-going one after my initial day there. Sure, wherever I worked there was always a little bit of talking about personal matters, but not for a whole day, rather, only for a few minutes and then everybody went back focusing what they were working on. I had to do the same thing, so I began the organizational part of my job by calling the supply office and asked them to bring us as many moving boxes as were available.

The entire week turned into a hair raising experience and I hoped that we would survive it without any major setbacks. I told everyone that considering the entire week as a dress down week because of rearranging the furniture and cleaning up the mess. As usual, Mitzi, the oldest of the six woman made a comment that she was not hired to do physical labor. I calmly told her that I did not have any problem about her staying home without pay, if that is what she would prefer. After that, she came to work every day and although she gave me a few "evil" eyes, I just smiled and nodded at her with satisfaction.

The Commandant's office called me on the phone and asked me if and when I needed manpower. I told them that the files were already removed from the cabinets and whenever the men were available, we were ready. In the meantime we folded up the table and chairs, and temporarily moved the coffee maker out of the room where the cabinets were supposed to go. Mitzi, again, complained that if we were to have meeting on Thursdays, where were we going to have it. I replied that I was thinking about having it either by her desk or in her apartment. As the others were laughing, she let herself to give me a cynical smile.

Before the group of cadets arrived to help, I called the Custodial Department and had two people come and sweep and vacuum the floors and make sure that there were no cobwebs on the walls. I didn't want to have a breeding place for spiders in the cabinets. They also gave us some cleaning solutions that we were able to use to clean the cabinets inside and out. By the time, two days later the moving help arrived, we were ready. The cabinets beautifully lined up by both long walls and the third wall, I left the fourth wall, where the door was located free for the bulletin board that I have already ordered.

The next step was for our helpers to move the boxes with the files into the newly designated File Room. I told them to pile them up but not too high, I had to be able to lift it down without difficulty. Prior to their arrival, I let the six woman decide which direction they wanted their desks to face, the only request I had was for at least one of them had to face the door to see when clients arrived. The cadets helped them to move the desks and smaller file cabinets that I let them keep by their desks for files or whatever they were working on, I had one of those myself. The moving part was done in less than three hours and after profusely thanking the cadets for helping, they left.

Next, two of the custodial workers came back and vacuumed and dusted all of the areas, including the blinds on the windows. By Friday afternoon we were done with the moving and rearranging part, and when lunchtime came I invited all six of them to have lunch with me in the cafeteria, I wanted to treat them that day. They were somewhat surprised, but even Mitzi accepted my invitation without any comments.

Their moving job just ended and mine was just beginning. I fully intended to check every single personal and financial folder before they were being filed into the cabinets, which I worked out in my head first and then I wrote it down how I wanted to organize the file system without over complicating it. I created two cabinets for current and active classes, one for potential cadets, one cabinet for dropouts and one cabinet for special cases, court marshals and such, but basically the cabinet system was simple, the folders were filed in alphabetical order.

As my first weekend on Gödöllö approached, it has become clear to me that I would not be able to go home to visit my parents as promised, which left me with no choice, I had to call the Superintendent of the apartment building where my parents lived because she was the only person who had a telephone in the entire house. I asked her to be kind enough to tell my parents that I was going to work through the weekend and I won't be able to come home. She promised to tell them and I ended the call.

The cafeteria was open seven days a week because the cadets remained in their dormitories throughout the academic year and they had to eat somewhere. Before I went to work, I decided to have an early Saturday morning breakfast. All of us who worked for the academy had a card that showed that we were employees, so while we, the civilians had to pay for our food, we were only charged half price versus if a visitor ate there, they would have to pay full price, the cadets and the military teachers' food was free.

I walked into the cafeteria at six o'clock and I found myself in testosterone city. Other than the cooks and the servers behind the counter, I was the only female person present. I could feel my face turning red from the stares as I walked up to the counter and selected some scrambled eggs with bacon and a bagel, and some orange juice to drink. There were comments coming at my way from all directions, but because it was a military academy, there were rules towards females. As soon as one comment was said, someone would try to hush that person off. I paid for my food and looked around in the place, but all of the tables that normally seated two, four or six were taken. I felt dozens and dozens of eyes on me until I noticed an arm in the air, somebody was waiving at me to go to that table.

I made my way to waiving arm just to realize that it belonged to Captain Bartha, also known a Attila, the Hunter, he was the one who was waiving at me. "Please, join me," he offered. I took one more glance around, but there were no other offers, so I sighed, put down my food and sat down.

"Thank you," I mumbled.

"What are you doing up so early on a Saturday?" He asked while he was drinking his coffee, which I promptly forgot to put on my tray, but I didn't make a remark about it.

"I have a lot of work to do," I replied and began to eat. The food was actually very good considering the nature of mass production of it.

"What about the others?" He asked. "You should make them come in to help you." He suggested. I shook my head.

"It is something I want to do all by myself," I told him.

"So you one of those," he said and chuckled.

"One of those who?" I asked because I didn't know what he meant.

His blue eyes tore into mine and I had to look away. His eyes reminded me of Joe's whom I did not think about for a quite long time. The Captain was incredibly handsome and I thought about my first impression about him when for a brief moment, I thought that he was a movie star. He was tall, extremely well built, blonde haired, *hot damn,* I thought. Everything about him reminded me of Joe, even his cockiness, that he knew how good he looked and spread that knowledge around like a peacock spread its feathers.

"The kind of person who doesn't trust very many people," he finally replied.

I finished with my breakfast and looked at him before I got up to place the tray into the collection area. "You obviously correct because you read me like a book." I said sarcastically.

He motioned with his hand for me to lean closer but I did not move. He got up and whispered to me. "I will make a project out of you. I will break you down like a puzzle." I began to laugh loud enough to the people around us to look and listen.

"Captain Bartha, good luck with that," I said fairly loudly and noticed smiles on faces.

"You will see," he said as I was walking away.

"Yeah, right," I said without looking back.

I unlocked the door and locked it back up behind me. I walked to the File Room and my shoulders sank. "Oh, dear me," I mumbled. "Where to start?"

I went to my office which was right next to the File Room and I pushed my desk all the way to the window which was in front of me and moved everything out of the way with the exception of the bookshelf which I emptied the day before. I began to look at every single page of every single file to assure that the documents were filed in chronological order. The major thing I was looking for were misfiled documents. I cut up papers into little pieces and placed a piece on the page that was out of order. Once done with a file, I placed them on the bookshelf in sections, such as files that were correct, which were few, one pile for those who had misfiled documents and the third, that needed processing corrections.

I was finished with two boxes which was pitiful because there were over forty boxes and I began to question my sanity. Maybe Attila, the Hunter was correct, I should have delegated some of the work to my co-workers, but I was too much of a perfectionist to do that. Around twelve thirty in the afternoon, I heard a knock on the door. I got up from the floor where I was sitting and asked through the door who it was. "Its lunch delivery," I heard the Captain's voice. I unlocked the door and opened it.

"What are you doing here?" I asked without inviting him in.

"I got lunch and I got drinks," he showed me a paper bag and on a small tray, two soft drinks and two coffee mugs, he must have borrowed from the cafeteria. He saw my facial expressions. "Angie, please give me a break. I am trying to be nice and neighborly," he said. Well, I was hungry and thirsty, and I made a mental note that I should bring food and drink with me the next time. *Of course, I could just go upstairs and get it,* I thought.

"What do you have in there?" I asked and pointed at the bag.

"Schnitzel sandwich with potato salad," he told me.

"Come on in," I told him and closed the door.

"Aren't you going to lock it?" He asked as he walked inside the large office.

"No, just in case I have to get away," I said and looked at him with a serious face.

"It won't happen," he said and looked around. "Where do you want to eat?" He asked.

"Step into my office," I said and pushed some of the folders waiting to be reviewed to the side. I lowered myself on the floor and sat down.

"Are you kidding me?" He asked. I shook my head. He sighed and joined me. "You are an incredibly strange person," he commented and opened the bags. He pulled out some paper napkins and laid them out before he took out the sandwiches. They were still warm and smelled good. I hesitated before I took a bite.

"Did you put anything into it?" I asked. He had an identical sandwich. He sighed again and took mine out of my hand.

"They are both the same," he said and took a bite out of the sandwich.

"I want that one back," I said to him.

"I already bit into it," he objected but as he looked at me and seeing that I was just staring at him without eating, he shook his head and gave back the sandwich. "I swear that I don't understand you." He commented and began to eat again and so did I. The sandwich hit the spot. I reached for the soft drink and he watched me as I picked up one of them but when I saw that he was watching, I put it back. "Something is very seriously wrong with you," he said and took a sip from both drinks.

"Let's just say, I heard about your reputation," I told him and took a sip from the drink I selected.

He laughed. "I have a reputation?" He asked.

"As if you didn't know," I replied. "They are calling you Attila, the Hunter." He laughed some more.

"I can't help it if the ladies find me irresistible," he said with a grin.

"Not all of them," I replied with a grin of my own.

"I have to work on that one," he answered and reached for the coffee. He looked up at me. "Another taste test?" He asked. I nodded.

We finished eating and he gathered up the napkins, the empty cups and wrappers. "Thank you for lunch," I told him.

"My pleasure," he said. "Are you sure that I couldn't help you?" He asked and noticed that I was about to get up from the floor. He reached his hands out to me and I accepted. He pulled me up and to himself.

"Smooth move," I said as we sort of faced each other, more like I was looking up. He wasn't smiling and it was the first time that I saw his face serious. He leaned down and ever so gently his lips touched mine. I was stunned and did not object.

"That wasn't too bad?" He asked without humor. Every memory I had from the past year's events rushed through me like a tornado. My knees weakened and I felt light headed. He held me tight and safe in his strong arms and it felt good, but not good enough for me have those painful memories brushed aside. I gently pushed myself away from him and he let me go. I looked up at him and tried to control my tears but they had mind of their own and rolled down on my face.

"You are right, Captain Bartha," I said to him softly. "I do like you. Unfortunately there are mountains of obstacles that separate us and prevents us from this happening again, or to happen at all." I told him and sighed.

"Are you going to tell me what they are?" He asked without any sarcasm.

"Basically that I don't date anyone with whom I work with or who works in my work environment," I told him. He shook his head.

"It's got to be more than that," he said, obviously not accepting my explanation.

"I don't talk about my private business to anyone," I replied. He just stood there and I wished that he would leave. "All right," I told him because he didn't move, he was waiting for further explanation. "No, not all right. I don't wish to talk about it." I blurted out.

"I am sorry that I upset you," he apologized.

"I just don't want to date, at least not until I am twenty years old," I said seriously. He looked at me with surprise.

"And when is that going to happen?" He wanted to know.

"A year and few months from now," I answered and I could see how stunned he was.

"You are telling me that you are not even nineteen years old?" He asked. I nodded. "And you are in charge of such an important department as this?"

"I finished college when I was sixteen," I replied.

He just shook his head. "Wow," he said and began to walk towards the door. I followed him and opened it for him. He turned around and said it again. "Wow."

I was fairly certain that I was finished with Captain Bartha, but once again I was wrong about my observation. I worked through dinner and I was about to go upstairs to my apartment when I noticed some major errors in one of the files. I just couldn't leave it, I had to do some research. By then it was midnight and I was so sleepy that I didn't even have the energy to go upstairs. I decided that I was going to sleep a couple hours and continue reviewing the files. I placed folders side by side so I would not have to lay on the floor and made a pillow from five folders and I settled in.

Unintentionally I slept through the night and woke up around five in the morning, my usual wake up time. I was totally shocked when I realized that I was covered with a military issue blanket and that my head was resting on an actual pillow, a small one but a pillow just the same. I must have gone completely unconscious when I slept, because I did not hear a sound or felt motion covering me up and putting the pillow under my head. My joints were stiff from sleeping on the floor, well technically on the top of some folders and I had to do some serious stretching before I was able to move. I went to the rest room and washed my face and rinsed my mouth. My short hair was messy and because I didn't have a comb, I ran my fingers across the top of my head and that was it, I was ready for more work. I concluded that I must have been hungry because I smelled bacon and freshly brewed coffee, and I just assumed that the smell came from the cafeteria which was on the floor above us.

After using the restroom which was located all the way in the back of the large office, I entered my office where I found Attila, the Hunter sitting on the floor with the files moved out of the way. On the top of the paper towels on the floor, there was a bacon and egg croissant and a large cup of steaming coffee. I stopped at the door.

"What are you doing here?" I asked. "And how did you get in? I locked the door."

"I got a set of keys from the custodian's station. Technically speaking, I should have a set of keys as I am the designated fire marshal for the building," he said with a grin on his face. To me it was not funny at all. "Have a sit, the croissant is getting cold," he said and patted the floor.

"No, thank you," I replied. "I need to get going with my work."

"Why are you acting like this?" He asked while he shook his head. "You are sleeping on the cold floor using folders as pillows, I bring you breakfast because you probably did not even have dinner, and instead of thanking me, you are giving me a hard time."

"Thank you, and please leave and take your food with you," I said firmly.

"Why are you like this?" He asked again before he continued. "Someone must have done a terrible thing to you that turned you into such a bitter person," he said and got up from the floor while gathered up the food.

"Captain Bartha, I do not need a therapist, a boyfriend or someone who tries to take care of my domestic needs, such as feed me or keep me hydrated. When I am hungry I eat, when I am thirsty, I drink, and when I need help, I will ask for it. With all that said, thank you very much for your kind gestures and let's just leave it at that." I said, and once those words left my lips, I realized just how cold I must have sounded. He didn't say another word until he got to the door.

"You will come to me someday, but it will be too late." He said.

"Happy hunting," I replied and locked the door again after he slammed it hard.

By noon I was starving and I raided the refrigerator. I found a yoghurt and I ate it after leaving a note in its place that I took it and I will replace it shortly. I wanted to go for lunch at the cafeteria but I felt dirty after hauling boxes and not having a shower for the second day, so after I finished with six more boxes, each had twenty-five folders, I felt satisfied enough to go upstairs, trying to avoid any personal contacts.

I hit the shower first before I revisited the salami, bread and butter again for dinner. Luckily there was some orange soda drink in the refrigerator and I had that along with the sandwich. My body was screaming for some caffeine but while I had a small coffee maker in the kitchen, I didn't have any coffee.

While I ate my sandwich, I made a short shopping list for some essential food items and I was going to ask my co-workers on the following day where would be a close enough market place where I could walk to. I was way beyond tired and after making sure that the door was double locked and had the chain secured, I set up the sofa bed and I welcomed the softness of my pillow that I brought from home along with my comforter. Before I went to sleep, I set the alarm for five, not that I needed an alarm clock. Since I worked, my eyes automatically opened at five in the morning, but feeling as tired as I was, I couldn't be sure that I would wake up on time.

ATTILA, THE HUNTER AND JOE, THE RETURNEE

I LEFT THE APARTMENT at five thirty in the morning and I bumped into several fellow tenants who were in the military. They were just returning from their morning run. Since it was still so early, it made me wonder what time did they start, I found out later that it was four thirty in the morning. Most of them took the steps up to the eighth floor, but some of them took the elevator because I saw them getting out as I was about to get in. Among them was Attila, the Hunter.

"Good morning," he said with a smile. Even being all sweaty from running and exercising, he still looked perfect. "Are you ready for another day of battle?" He asked. I stepped into the elevator and replied.

"Yes, I am. Are you ready for your daily hunt?" As the elevator door was closing, I caught his reply.

"Always!"

I stopped by the cafeteria that opened at five in the morning and I picked up a warm croissant that I missed out on the previous morning and a small package of cream cheese. After paying for it, I went directly to the office. I unlocked the door and entered the large, I mean very large office and turned on the lights. Because my office was such a mess, I decided to occupy the desk where nobody was sitting. At that time I wasn't sure when more personnel would be hired.

The employees began to arrive at exactly at six o'clock as if they were standing outside the door, which I told them to keep open, and waited for the clock to chime six. With the exception of Flóra, she started her new schedule at eight, all five of them showed up and they were surprised to see that I actually managed to set up the coffee maker and that fresh coffee was already in a carafe. Klára, the youngest of my subordinates was responsible for the coffee fund and after she told me my share, I paid her right away for two months in advance.

Mitzi came by my temporary desk and asked me how was my weekend, I turned and motioned to the mess in my office. "You are joking, right?" She asked. I shook my head.

"I can't rest until those folders are not corrected, adjusted and filed according to the filing manual," I replied, but I smiled so she wouldn't think that I was complaining.

"Girl, you are nuts," she said and patted me on the shoulder.

"Well, Mitzi, I will take that as a compliment," I replied instead of telling everyone what a lousy job was done to those files. I always believed that only lazy people misfile documents on regular bases. It happens sometimes, we are human and we make mistakes, but just about every folder I looked at had somebody else's document filed incorrectly in it. Since I had no way of knowing who the guilty employee was, I couldn't really point a finger at anyone. I shut up and gave myself time to do corrections to everything that needed one, and then, when I finished with all of the folders, I will declare war on anyone who file a document in the wrong folder. I was about to create a checklist with all the forms that usually went into the files, and when any of my subordinates filed a document, they would have to initial and date when they filed it. I knew that this procedure was not going to be popular, but they had to follow my lead and not the other way around.

In the early afternoon I was sitting next to Flóra, her desk was pretty far back, she was showing me some of the problem cases that needed to be solved when Klára came to tell me that Captain Bartha was there to see me.

"What does he want?" I asked. She shrugged. "Tell him that I am busy," I told her but then I stopped her. "Wait, tell him that it is the wrong hunting ground."

Mitzi and the other woman turned around and burst out laughing. "He found you very fast," Flóra commented.

"We are neighbors," I told her and pointed at the folder in front of us.

A few minutes later Klára came back and made a face at me. "He says that it is official business."

"Christ," I mumbled and excused myself from Flóra. I walked to the counter at the front where he was standing and waiting. "What can I do for your Captain Bartha?" I asked. He looked me in the eye and opened his lips which made me concentrate on them.

"I am here to do a fire inspection," he said very seriously.

"You have got to be joking," I replied. He showed me an ID and the clipboard in his hand. "Come on in, Fire Chief." I told him and motioned to the flap door.

He walked in front of me, checking on plugs in the wall, and then he stopped at the coffee maker that was already unplugged from the wall. "Make sure that there is always someone around when it is plugged in," he pointed at the machine.

"Yes, sir," I replied sharply. We walked all the way back to the restroom. I stood outside while he went in.

"I need to show you something, please come in Ms. Aranyi," he called me inside. When I stepped into the restroom, he closed the door. I just stood there waiting what he had in mind, and I wondered if my vocal cords were in proper working order so my co-workers could hear me scream if I had too.

"What do you want to show me, sir," I asked, using official salutation. He reached into his pocket and pulled out a pipe. I looked at him not understanding what he was doing.

"Consider this as a peace pipe," he said and wanted to hand it to me.

"There is just one problem with that pipe," I said and smiled. "I don't smoke," I told him. He stepped towards me and I could smell his aftershave that smelled real nice.

"Please, tell me what I need to do to get into your good graces," he wanted to know. I had difficulty breathing having him so close to me.

"I am not sure that you have that in you," I replied in a quiet tone of voice.

"Just tell me," he pleaded with me. I thought about it for a moment and then I looked at him.

"I would never date anyone who had a reputation, I am sure that you would feel the same way about me. Attila, to get to know me better, I need you to be yourself and not being some skirt chaser Casanova who goes after every single new woman at the academy. Like you did to me too." I told him. He shook his head several times.

"You are not like any other woman I have ever met," he whispered to me and then I felt his warm breath on my forehead. I lifted my head and our lips met, quietly and gently. He dropped the clipboard and his arms went around me, but not tightly. I assumed that he didn't want to scare me. His lips parted mine and his tongue found mine that joined his in a slow, pleasurable dance. It has been a long time since I had been kissed, and his kiss showed plenty of experience. "Angie," he whispered. "I promise to become the man you want me to be."

"Attila, you don't understand. I don't want you to change, just be who you really are in here," I touched his chest where his heart was. He smiled and picked up his clip board. What was only about five minutes in there, it seemed like a long time when we left the restroom, lucky for us, there were several customers and my colleagues were busy with them. I escorted Attila to the door, and as I was about return to my office when he stopped me.

"Can I see you after work?" He asked. I thought about it for a moment.

"I have to go to buy some food. If you want to come with me, that would be fine," I suggested. He nodded.

"My last class is at two, I can be back here by three," he said. I nodded.

"I'll see you then," I replied and went back to work.

"How did the fire inspection go?" Mitzi asked with a smile. I handed her the form with Attila's signature. He found everything fine but recommended the replacement of some of the light fixtures in the restroom as well as above the walkway. She acknowledged that it was not so bad and I in turn designated her to be our department's fire marshal.

"What do I have to do?" She asked. I laughed.

"Absolutely nothing," I replied. "When he comes back, you just follow him around, like I did."

"I can do that," she replied and laughed, too.

Flóra and I solved the problem that we were working on and she was on her way to fix it. It was a lesson for me as well for future references to check and double check payroll related issues. Through my working days at the company where Andy worked as well, I never had incident when my office was responsible for any miscalculated income and I intended to continue that tradition. At my new place of work, we had separate issues with the civilian force because the military academy also had over three hundred employees in various capacities from food service workers to custodial, from gardener to gunsmiths.

The first day of my second week at the academy went by quickly, but I still felt the effect of working all day on Saturday and Sunday. Unfortunately, it was not the end of it yet, far from it. Three o'clock came around and Flóra with her new schedule was the last one to remain in the office. Normally it was always myself who locked up the office, but I sort of made a "date" with Attila, so I had to leave. I needed to buy some basic groceries as my refrigerator was just as empty as hungry I was. I mean, it was alright to eat at the cafeteria and that we only had to pay half the price, but I calculated that it could add up eating there three meals a day.

Attila was waiting for me outside the door and I smiled when I saw him. "Are you ready to go?" He asked.

"Where are we going?" I replied as I was under the impression that there was a grocery store nearby.

"I want to take you to a real supermarket, so we are going to drive," he said and took my hand as he guided me to his car, a relatively new red Audi. I was about to make a comment that he must have a rich family, but I changed my mind and I kept that remark to myself. He opened the door for me and I got in.

"This is a very nice comfortable car," I complimented him as he drove.

"Thanks," he replied. "Actually this was a present from my uncle, he lives in Germany." Attila informed me and I was glad that I did not say anything earlier. It took us a brief ten minutes drive before he pulled into the parking lot of a nice big grocery store, or so called Supermarket, the kind I was used to where I grew up. He handed me a basket and he took one for himself.

Having a microwave in the apartment urged me to use it, so I got some frozen dinners, some cheese, ham, some fresh bread, canned and fresh vegetables, a six pack of diet sodas, and just odds and ends. I sort of wandered away from Attila as I approached the canned food section, and it was there where I heard a familiar voice talking to someone.

"You are nothing but a stupid and ignorant bitch. Why don't you put your shit together and make a list next time," said the voice that gave me goose bumps. A young pregnant woman came around the corner of the aisle and while she began to look at the canned vegetable labels, she quickly tried to wipe away her tears. I tried to act that I didn't notice her crying and I asked her if she needed help to reach the top shelf. She thanked me and I gave her the two canned green beans that she wanted.

I walked around to the fresh fruit and vegetable section where I was about to take a couple of bananas, when an arm rudely reached in front of me and grabbed some from the stand. I did not dare to look up or turn around, but when I saw the tattoo on the man's arm, my entire body began to tremble. The tattoo read, "Angelina forever". The man had a body odor that made my stomach turn and then I saw his reflection in the mirror behind the vegetables, he had long and unkempt hair, beard and mustache. He did not recognize me and I was grateful to God for that. Without a doubt it was Joe, but he was not the same young man I used to know. Just minutes earlier I thought that I recognized his voice as the man who was yelling at the young pregnant woman.

I stood there and I didn't dare to move out of the area, I didn't want by any chance to bump into Joe at the cashier's counter. "There you are," Attila said and touched my arm. I turned around so quickly that it startled him. "Are you all right?" He asked with concern. And it happened, Joe thought that I looked somewhat familiar to him and he returned to the produce section where Attila was also getting some fresh fruit for himself.

"Angie," Joe said and his voice became soft a silk. "Oh, God, I can't believe that it's you." He said and opened his arms to hug me. Attila took one look at my face and he was by my side within seconds.

"Excuse me, sir," he said to Joe. "Do you know my wife?" With that said, Attila put his arms around me in a protective fashion.

"Oh, you are married," Joe nodded and brushed his long blonde beard. "What happened to Andrew, your other soldier boy?"

"Friend," Attila addressed Joe as such. "We have dinner to cook, so we have to get going." He turned me around and ushered me to the cash register. I could not utter a word from the shock of seeing Joe in such a bad shape. I paid for my groceries although Attila said that he would, I did not let him. Leaving the supermarket we got into his car, and all of a sudden, I could not breathe. He dumped the peaches he brought in the store from the brown bag, and while held the back of my head, he helped me to get my breathing back to order. The tears came fast and furious and Attila without saying a single word handed me his handkerchief.

"Thank you for being there for me," I mumbled. He reached over and gently touched my face.

"No problem," he replied and started up the car.

I cried in intervals, off and on as he drove without asking any questions. We parked and I got out of the car not waiting for him to open the door for me. He didn't ask if I needed any help or not, he grabbed the shopping bags and we headed toward the building. I almost immediatelly noticed that the Commandant, Colonel Toldai's jeep was parked directly in front of the building's entrance with his driver still sitting in a vehicle waiting for his boss' return.

We just exited the elevator when the Commandant was coming out of Major Sipos' apartment, he was also one of the teachers at the academy. "Well, hello," he said friendly enough, but right away his facial expression changed when he noticed my tear soaked face. "What happened, Captain? What have you done to her?" He went right into attack mode. That is what happens to someone who had a reputation.

"Sir," I mumbled. "He had nothing to do with it." I said in Attila's behalf. The Commandant was staring at him and then he hissed at Attila's direction.

"A word in private, Captain," he told him.

"Yes, sir," Attila replied and handed me my shopping bags. I walked ahead of them and entered my apartment while the two of them went inside Attila's.

I have to say that the walls were not very thick and Colonel Toldai's voice carried, probably all the way to Prague. "Sir, nothing had happened. Angie encountered one of her old acquaintances in the grocery store and he looked so bad that it upset her." He explained.

There was a moment of awkward silence, and then I heard the Colonel's voice. "I want you listen to me and listen to me good. I have put up with all of your crap for over a year now, only because there were no formal complaints about your endeveours, I over looked what I heard about you. I am warning you Captain, if you wish to remain in the Armed Forces, you will not attempt to do anything stupid. I consider Ms. Aranyi as if she was my own daughter, and you know what a father is capable to do if his daughter gets hurt, right?" He asked.

"Yes, sir," Attila replied.

"Good, very good," Colonel Toldai said and I could hear Attila's apartment's door opening and closing. Apparently the Colonel turned around because I heard his voice again. "I just want you to know that I will be keeping my eyes and ears open."

"Thank you, sir," Attila replied.

I stood there and I didn't know if I wanted to laugh or cry. I put the groceries away and laid down on the couch. Joe came to mind right away and the horrible shape he was in. He once was the most beautiful man I had ever seen, someone who drew all the eyes at his presence and made men jealous, and women filled with desire when he looked at them. That poor young pregnant woman, who was she to him? Was she his wife, his girlfriend, or some young fool whom he managed to seduce? Joe looked horrible and I began to wonder if it was my fault or not. He surely did not forget about me if he still remembered Andy's name.

What was wrong with me? Why I had to be in love or love men who either did not want me, or wanted me but not as a wife. I thought about Attila next door and I could not see any probability about him either. His reputation was worse than I first thought, and he surely only considered me a new possible conquest.

I closed my eyes and slowly slipped into a sleep and I didn't wake up until seven o'clock. I felt hungry and stuck a frozen risotto into the microwave. I stood while I ate and once again my thoughts returned to Joe. His presence in the city of Gödöllö upset me to the core. I was sincerely hoping that perhaps they were just passing through, but getting canned green beans was an indication that she did some cooking, the question was, where. I hoped and prayed that they just stopped by at the grocery store because it had selection and not because they actually lived nearby.

Finished with my meager dinner, I grabbed a can of orange soda and headed downstairs to continue my work on the folders. I locked the door behind me and went back where I left it during the day. I did work on them during regular operating hours as well, although the concentration was a lot harder because there was a constant "buzz" around me and customers came all day long.

I took a pillow from my apartment to downstairs so I didn't have to sit directly on the floor and I began to work. I am certain that it is probably a common observation that when you are concentrating on a project, the time just simply goes into a fast forward. I finished my eleventh box and the space on the book shelf was getting less and less. I had to make plans where I was going to put the next batch of folders. Unfortunately for all concerned, there were more folders in the "be corrected" and "had misfiled documents" piles than in the correct ones. I thought about perhaps I should select one of the employees just to make corrections and remove misfiled documents to file in the correct folder, but I put that thought aside as all of them had their own workloads to do, and the office was missing the seventh employee, other than myself, whose work load had to be shared by the other six employee.

I looked at my watch and I could not believe that it was already two o'clock in the morning. I gathered myself off the floor and used the bathroom because I was sure that I could not make it upstairs. The building was very quiet and I could only hear the cables of the elevator as they pulled the cabin up to the eight floor. I yawned as I stumbled toward my apartment which was to the left of the long hallway. I reached for my keys in my pocket when I noticed a shadow by the door. I was so glad that I used the bathroom, otherwise I would have lost the content of my bladder.

"Angie, it's me," Attila said. I stepped up to him and slapped his face. He was genuinely surprised. "What was that for?"

I was so angry that I didn't even want to look at him. "You almost scared me to death."

"I was worried about you and I was heading downstairs. When I knocked and you didn't open the door, I just assumed that you went back to do some more work," he explained while he pressed his hand on the right side of his face.

My heart was still beating so fast like a jazz drummer's sticks on a fast speed solo number. "What are you trying to do to me, shorten my life?" I asked while I unlocked the door. Before I was able to close it behind me, he followed me inside. "What do you think you doing?" I asked him. "I am too tired for a conversation, I am ready for bed. I only have three hours left to sleep."

"Fine," he said. I left him alone in the room and went to brush my teeth. I thought about taking a shower but I decided that I would take one before I went to work. I returned to the room and I made a face because Attila already opened up the sofa bed and arranged the pillows and the comforter. Luckily he was gone, and I didn't have to face a lengthy explanation and conversation with him about anything. I liked him, but I also liked good books, movies, and at that early in the morning, I liked a good night sleep much better.

My eyes popped wide open as usual exactly at five o'clock. Half-awake I heard commotion on the hallway, I assumed, correctly, that the military personnel were leaving or coming about their morning routines. I took a shower and I was out of the apartment by five thirty, with plenty of time left to stop by the cafeteria to get some breakfast. I did not know the early morning eating habits of my subordinates, but I bought seven ham and cheese croissants and a banana for each of them, including myself. A young cadet who stood behind me in line for the cash register, even they had to show an ID but they did not have to pay, he leaned to me.

"Are we hungry this morning?" He asked. I turned to him and replied with a smile.

"Yes, very. Me and my six children are starving this morning," I replied and blinked at the older woman who was working behind the cash register. She must of had the humor of a guinea pig because she looked at me as if I was the eighth wonder of the world.

"Six?" Repeated the soldier and just stared at me as I took the entire tray with me.

I opened up the table that was previously located in the File Room and set it up, not to mention that I also made fresh coffee. Their surprise was genuine when they arrived, and it pleased me immensely to see their smiling faces. We put Flóra's portion into the refrigerator and began to work. Mitzi walked by my room and noticed more empty boxes. "When did you work on those?" She pointed at the empty boxes.

I shrugged. "Late afternoon until two in the morning," I confessed. She did not make a comment just shook her head and went about her business.

The academy let out its students for lunch break between eleven thirty until one, but we only closed our doors from twelve until one o'clock. Five minutes 'til noon I looked up and I noticed that Attila was standing by the counter.

"Can we get some service here?" He asked jokingly. I turned around, I noticed that Ruth rose up to go to the counter, I motioned to her to stay put. I got up and walked up to the divider.

"How may I help you Captain Bartha?" I asked without smiling.

He leaned over the counter and turned his head so his left face was towards me. "Please, sir, may I have another?" He said the line from the movie *Oliver Twist* in a little boy's voice.

"Get off my counter," I told him and playfully pushed on his shoulder. He straightened up.

"I would like you to join me for lunch," he offered.

"What's the occasion?" I asked and considered his offer.

"Because it's Tuesday," he said seriously.

I took a deep breath. "Fine, in that case, I go with you." I finally agreed.

"Another sacrifice in a young life," he remarked jokingly. I turned around.

"There is still time to change my mind," I commented and grabbed my purse. I told the women that I'll be back in a little while. Ruth and Klára whistled but I ignored them.

We took the stairs up as the cafeteria was only on the second floor and by the time we got in, almost all tables were taken. "Why don't you try to get a table," he suggested. "I'll get your food."

"You don't know what I want," I objected.

"Yes, I do," he replied with a sheepish smile.

The place was almost completely full, although I saw that some of the cadets and employees were just sitting around. I noticed a four chair table where only two cadets were sitting, so I walked up to them. "Gentleman, are these seats are taken?" I asked politely. Right away smiles appeared on their faces.

"We were holding them just for you," one of them said. I sat down.

"Both of them?" I asked smiling.

"One for you and one for your girlfriend," the other cadet replied. "Two boys, two girls." I noticed that Attila was heading towards the table.

"I need to make some correction in your math, three boys and one girl," I replied and looked up when Attila placed the tray on the table. The cadets immediately got up and saluted him as he was one of their teachers.

"At ease," he replied and sat down. The cadets, already finished with their lunches anyway, picked up their trays and left in a hurry.

"Poor guys, you terrified them," I scolded him playfully and looked down on my tray. It was a chicken schnitzel with dumplings and gravy, and indeed it was tasty. "I owe you," I mentioned, but he just shook his head. "No, I owe you," I insisted.

"A girlfriend doesn't have to pay when the boyfriend is treating her," he replied and began to eat. I put down my fork and knife and looked at him with questions in my eyes.

"That is what we are Attila, girlfriend and boyfriend?" I asked him with a lowered voice. He put down his silverware too.

"I am only hoping," he whispered. He noticed the hesitation on my face, the hesitation of saying something that he probably did not want to hear. "Can we just have a decent lunch without bickering?" He asked. I thought that he had a good point and I began to eat again. He did not say two words to me until almost at the end of the lunch. "Would you like a refill of your soda?" He asked. I nodded. He got up and went to the soda machine. I looked after him and just then I realized that people were actually watching us, and there were some whispering at the next table that I was unable to hear.

I began to wonder what sort of reputation that he really had to receive so much attention from the cadets. After hearing what Colonel Toldai told him, I assumed that the Commandant's threat meant something to him, and that his intentions had been modified, whatever they may be. Since we finished with our lunch, I got up when he arrived back to the table and placed the plates and silverware on the combined two trays. After he handed me my soda, he picked up the trays to put them on the top of the proper collection place.

We silently took the stairs down to the first floor, but before we opened the door to the hallway, he pulled me to him. It was not a safe thing to do because the cadets had the tendency to use the staircase versus the elevator, but at that particular time, we were the only ones in the stairway. I had my hands on his shoulder and his arms around me waist.

"What are you plans for tonight?" He asked, I shrugged my shoulders. "Working?"

"I am afraid so," I replied.

"Will you ever have time just for me?" He inquired. I pushed him away.

"Look, if you have other plans, go about them," I told him and opened the door.

When I walked into the office, Klára whistled and Mitzi made some comments about good times, which stopped immediately when I turned towards them with a face that reflected my darkening mood. I grabbed a box of folders and let them drop next to my temporary desk. I must have stared at the same page for a while because the next thing I knew I saw a tear drop falling on the desk in front of me.

There I was, surrounded by people and yet, I felt alone. I was just turning nineteen years old with a six yearlong unfulfilled love for Joe, and an over two yearlong engagement and betrayal behind me by Andy. Am I ever going meet someone who is going to be honest with me and treat me well? Treat me with passion and true love? Was I a magnet for men who just tried to have me, to have fun with me and then toss me aside? Why was it that when I loved someone, that person had to turn out to be a would be rapist, or a cheater, or someone like Attila whom I really liked but could not trust because of his skirt chasing reputation. I concluded that there had to be truth about his reputation if the Commandant himself threatened him with bodily harm if the Captain hurt me one way or another. By the way, I always thought of Colonel Toldai with great fondness for the rest of my life, because he and his family made me feel very special, as if I was a member of their family.

I stayed in the office an hour longer after Flóra left, and then I locked up and went upstairs to my apartment to rest and to change into clothes something less formal than I was wearing during working hours. I decided that I would rather nap than eat, so I laid down on the sofa bed and I was out as if I was hit on the head. I woke up to the smell of pizza and I wasn't sure if it was a dream or not, but then I heard movements in the kitchen and I glanced at the door. I cursed myself because I forgot to put on the security chain.

"Good, you are up," Attila said and motioned to the chair by the kitchen table. I sleepily looked at him and went to the bathroom to freshen up. Returning to the kitchen, I sat down at the table and just stared at the pizza which looked good and smelled heavenly, and it was not the food that bothered me. "What's wrong?" He asked the inevitable question.

"Attila," I looked at him across the small kitchen table. "I am far from not appreciating your efforts, especially trying to take care of me. If you really, I mean really want to be my boyfriend, and with that I would break a major rule in my work related rules, we need to lay down some ground rules." He put his pizza down and wiped his lips with a paper napkin.

"Alright, let's hear it," he said and looked at me with a challenge on his face.

"This is not a railroad station and there is no revolving door for the apartment. I like being in your company, but this is apartment albeit only temporarily, is my home for now. I would appreciate if you let me know when you are coming over. It goes for work too, after working hours I mean," I told him. His blue eyes did not look happy and he acted accordingly. He folded the pizza box with the delicious looking pizza in it and left the apartment, slamming the door behind him without replying with a single word. "Well, that went well," I thought and wiped the tears off my face.

I stood in the kitchen and it dawned on me that it was not easy living alone. It was the very first time that I was complitely on my own. No, I did not need guidance. I knew my place in the world, I knew life's dos and don'ts, yet I felt the need of companionship. Despite Terri's, Colonel Toldai's wife's invitation for any day or for any time, I would not and could not do that.

I took a deep breath and took out a frozen chicken fillet from the freezer and put it in the microwave. The six minute cooking time went fast because I cried during the waiting, I was way to busy feeling sorry for myself.

I barely swallowed couple of bites when there was a knock on the door. I wiped my tears again and looked through the peep hole, it was Attila. I opened the door and I just stood there with tears on my face. He stepped forward and I took a step back. After closing the door, he reached for me and pulled me close to himself so tightly that I could feel his heartbeat. He lifted my face with his finger and kissed me softly, and then he began to kiss the tears off from my face. For a few brief moments it also dawned on me that perhaps he thought that I was crying because he left, perhaps just a little bit, but I was crying because, yes, I admitted, I actually missed my parents.

He picked me up and then gently laid me down of the sofa, it was not opened yet into a bed and he sort of laid down on the top of me. The sofa was big enough for two people who were not too heavy. He smiled as he looked at me.

"You are so beautiful," he told me. "I am sure that you heard that before."

"Just once or twice," I replied and focused on his lips. I closed my eyes because they reached their destination and they devoured mine. My arms were around his neck and I didn't want to let him go, but he had other areas of my body in mind. I knew for certain that I could never again go as far with any other man like I did with Andy.

Attila pushed up my blouse and kissed me stomach, and then he discovered my breasts. He tried to reach behind my back to unhook my bra but I shook my head and he stopped, he refocused on kissing me with passion, actually with so much passion that even my toes were tingling. I felt his left hand touching my breasts and the right one reached into my pants and touched me through my panties. That was when the music stopped.

"Please, don't," I whispered to him first, and as if he didn't hear me, he tried to push his hand inside my panties. I reached down and tried to pull his hands out of my pants. Needless to say, he was much stronger than I was, but I was angrier than he was and nothing was worse than when somebody made me angry. It was Joe's case all over. "NO," I yelled at him and rolled off the sofa to the floor, banging my head on the small but heavy coffee table. I could feel blood rolling down on my face where the wood broke the skin on the ride side of my face, not far from my ear.

"Don't tell me that you are still a virgin," he said, breathing heavily.

"Get out of here," I hissed to him and pulled up my blouse to press it on the wound.

"Oh, my God, you are hurt, I am so sorry," he said and I could see that he was genuinely concerned. He went to the kitchen and brought back two sheets of wet paper towels and tried to touch the wound with it. I stepped back.

"I am going to say this once, and only once. Attila, get out my apartment and get out of my life," I told him and turned away. I could see hesitation on his face and then he slowly walked to the door and left.

I went to the bathroom where I had a small first aid kit that I brought from home, and after washing the wound, which was not very big but surely was going to leave a scar, I pressed some antiseptic cream into the cut, and then covered it up with a band aid. While I changed my blouse I also warmed up my food, I ate, made some more coffee and went downstairs to do some more work.

THE VISITOR AND MRS. TOLDAI

AFTER THAT NIGHT, Attila stayed out of my way as much he possibly could. The class that he taught was on the fourth floor and also in Section C of the humongous L-shaped military academy building. We were in Section A, the main complex. As I mentioned, the main cafeteria was located on the second floor, but there was another cafeteria in Section E, which was in the middle section. My second week at the academy, I learned that Section E also had a small but well stocked commissary, which I could visit as well if I did not want to leave the premises.

During the middle of my fourth week on the job, I attended my first "General Meeting" that all teachers, twenty-five in number also attended. Twenty-two out of the twenty-five were active military officers, the rest of them were retired from active service officers with teaching degrees. The twenty-five personnel present, well, twenty-six including me were representatives of their own department.

When I walked in, I had to take a deep breath because other than me, there was only one other female, a woman in her fifties who held a doctorate and was a professor of languages. The person in charge of the cafeterias and the commissary was a man who always looked grumpy, but I talked to him on a few occasions and he turned out to be very nice. Why shouldn't he be nice to me? When he needed more employees, I was the one who could get them for him.

The set up in the conference room was very interesting. There was a huge U-shape table and it had chairs all around, there were also chairs along the wall in case additional seating was needed. I looked around and my eyes met curious looks, but everybody politely said *'good morning'* as I walked in, including Attila who was talking with another Captain. I saw the Commandant, Colonel Toldai standing by the head of the table as he obviously chaired the meeting. He noticed me as well and waived at me to join him. "Good morning, sir," I said stepping up to him. He reached out his hand and we shook hands.

The Commandant, who also held the title of "Dean" of the academy, checked his watch. The door opened and possibly the last person arrived; I couldn't see who it was from all the tall men around me. "I want you to sit to my left," he told me. I was not sure if it was appropriate or not, but I was not in the position to argue. Another Colonel, his name was Kertész, nodded at me in acknowledgement. I smiled back at him as he took the seat on Colonel Toldai's right. The Commandant nodded to Colonel Kertész who commanded to the small crowd.

"Attention!" With that one word said, the personnel present stood behind their selected chairs and waited for further commands. I heard footsteps but I didn't dare to turn around and with some surprise I realized that almost all eyes were staring at me.

"Ladies and Gentlemen," Colonel Toldai began. "We have the honor to have a very special guest today at our meeting." As soon as he said that, I felt hands on my shoulders and they turned me around.

"Oh, my God," I whispered and I grinned from ear to ear. It was Major General Toldai who was supposed to be in Washington, DC, being the military attaché at our country's embassy. I was so nervous, I didn't know what I could and could not do, but he knew me well and he opened his arms for brief hug, and touched a light kiss on my forehead. I turned tomato red and I heard quiet laughter in the room. He leaned to me.

"Dinner tonight, we need to catch up," he whispered. I nodded.

He apologized for the interruption and took a seat next to his brother who kept a chair vacant for him. My eyes kept going back to him. We smiled at each other like old friends, and then all became strictly business. First, Colonel Toldai introduced me to those who did not have a chance to meet me yet, and then the "question and answer" session began. Each of the department heads reported anything new, or the lack of it. We went around the table and I looked down on my notes to brush up on my memories about what I was going to say.

I stood up just like the others, but the Colonel told me that I could sit if I wanted to, so I did. "First, I am pleased to report that the basic renovation to our office was completed and the final phases of reviewing the folders should be completed in a week, week and a half. The HR department as you know is basically the heart and soul of the institution; we keep the heartbeat going on paydays and souls filled with the timely processing of documents. At the present time, the academy has eleven hundred students, not counting the corresponding students, which is not our department's responsibility. We presently have seven employees and that also includes myself as well. One may don't think, but the size of this institution requires at least ten employees to provide the type of care that all cadets, students, trainers, and civil employees deserve. It is my understanding that before I began to work here, the department had a total of eight employees, which placed extreme pressure on everyone. I have a full understanding of budget cuts and such, but in my opinion, an overworked employee is a subject of making mistakes, and when the mistake is discovered, more time is spent on corrections. With all respect, I would like to request four more employees, one position is still open, and three more to be created."

A cadet who was actually seated at the table across from me was taking down the minutes. "We will take your request under advisement," Colonel Toldai told me.

"Thank you, sir," I replied.

"Is there anything else?" He asked around. "Any recommendation, suggestion?" I raised my pen. "Yes, Ms. Aranyi."

"There are a couple of things I would like to mention, one of them is that once our office gets back on its feet, I would like to provide some statistics about various costs and trends to the participants during any future general meetings," I said and looked around, there were nods all around. "The second one is a suggestion, sir."

"Go ahead," he encouraged me. His brother, MG Toldai looked at me and tried to hide his smile.

"I learned from my subordinates that around September our office had a tendency to be chaotic when the new students arrive and cadets returning back for their new school year. As all of you are well aware, the in-processing is very time consuming because of the number of forms need to be completed. Students and cadets either fill out the forms when they receive the package from our office, or bring it back, another waste of valuable time for all concerned. It means that our employees must deal with the in-processing person twice, sometimes three times. It is also my understanding that there is a completed acceptance list of new cadets in your office by early August. If my office is able to get a copy of that list in the first week of August, we could mail out the packages to already accepted students for completion prior to their arrival. I am fully aware that there will be more questions about some of the items on the forms, but the majority of the forms would be ready for review when they are turned in." I stopped talking and when I looked at my former boss, he was openly smiling and shaking his head. I could feel that my face was turning red again.

"There is a reason why Ms. Aranyi came highly recommended," Colonel Toldai remarked. "It is an excellent idea and all you have to do is submit your proposal in writing. I will approve it as soon as I received it." I bit my lips and with a sly smile on the corner of my mouth, I pulled out two copies of the request form letter and pushed them in front of him. Well, let's just say, there was a sound of unusual laughter in the conference room. The Colonel without blinking of an eye, took a pen in front of him and signed both forms, one was for him, and one was for my record.

There were some military training issues discussed and then most of them were dismissed, most of them but not Captain Bartha and me. We were told to go directly to the Commandant's office. As I was walking toward the large office, Attila walked right behind me. I heard my name called although I was certain that it was not him.

"Angie," I heard MG Toldai's voice. I stopped and he caught up with me. "I'll pick you up at six, is that alright with you?" He asked.

"Yes, that would be perfect," I replied.

"Looking forward talking to you," he said and then he turned around and headed into the other direction. I looked up at Attila and the look in my eyes said, *"I dare you to make a comment"*, but he did not.

The Commandant's on-duty aid told us to go ahead inside, the Colonel was waiting. As we walked in, he offered me a chair but he had Attila stand by the side of his desk.

"Ms. Aranyi, it came into my attention that your have been working after duty hours, way into the night and even through entire weekends. Is that information correct?" He asked. I bit my tongue but deep down inside I was fuming.

"It is, sir," I replied curtly and at the same time I glanced at Attila who was staring at some pictures on the opposite wall of the office. "Sir, I had the time, knowledge and patience, nobody was forcing me, and therefore I am not even certain why is this become a subject. If I may ask, is the person who reported my after duty hours activities, did that person report anything else?" I asked and without hiding my controlled anger, I looked directly at Attila. It got the Colonel's attention. He leaned forward, towards me.

"It is a good time to determine if there was anything else to report," he said and stared right into my eyes. I didn't blink, but I glanced toward Attila, he did.

"No, sir, there is nothing else to report. However; I would like to take this opportunity to explain those hours I have spent reviewing the folders," I requested.

"Go ahead," he told me.

"Sir, I found an extensive number of errors and misfiled documents virtually in all folders. I do not wish to point a finger at anyone, nor do I wish to reprimand anyone. Unfortunately, to correcting the filing and the processing errors we would not have enough personnel to run a problem free department with the ever-increasing student body. That was one of the reasons of my request to increase the number of employees," I explained. He thought about it.

"Would you have enough space to put three more desk and smaller cabinets in there?" He asked. I nodded.

"It is a very large office and there is plenty of space that is not put into use," I replied.

"Very well, you convinced me. I'll just have you forward the recruitment requests or, let me guess, you have that already typed up as well," he said with a smile.

"Yes, Colonel Toldai, I did," I said and handed him the recruitment forms. "I would like to wait with the recruitment until I am finished with the corrections and such," I commented. He nodded that he understood.

"Don't overdo what you are involved with, someday you will need to trust others," Colonel Toldai said as I stood up.

"Someday, sir," I replied. "But not yet." I thanked him again for his support and I left the office, leaving Attila behind with the Commandant.

Instead of walking through the labyrinth of hallways, I opted to walk through the huge courtyard. The moment I stepped outside, I wanted to go back inside. There was a formation going on and if you have ever walked in front of over one thousand, perhaps even more young men, well, then you would know what I mean. It was a stroke of luck that there were officers and enlisted non-commissioned officers around, still, there were remarks, although pleasant ones among the unwanted ones as I walked alongside of the building. By the time I made it back to my office, my face was red from trying to walk real fast.

When I walked in, the women looked up and Mitzi stared at me curiously. "Tell me honey, did you just bump into a formation?"

"Aha," I replied. "And now, ladies, I am ready for a cold shower," I said and they all laughed. I put down my leather folder and looked at every one of them while I debated should I tell them the news or wait until our Thursday meeting.

"How was the meeting?" Flóra asked. They all looked up again.

"It went well being my very first one," I answered, and then I made a decision. "What would you think about getting more manpower?" I asked.

Mitzi did the sign of the cross on herself, but I wasn't certain if she did that from getting relief or was a heaven forbid sign.

"We would bless you for it," Ruth said, and then she added. "And I am speaking for everyone." I pulled out the authorization form.

"We got it," I informed them, and then I told them that I want to finish with the folders first before I begin interviewing people. In the meantime we could get the furniture rearranged in the office to be even more efficient.

The afternoon went by real fast and I was excited to have dinner with my former boss. I must admit, I have thought about him often, he was a man that I admired on all levels. He was a super boss, firm yet just, he always listened to my suggestions, he criticized when he had too, yes, it did happen sometimes, but most of all, I found security with him. I knew that he would protect me from any outside force. On the other hand, outside the professional level, I never quite thought about him as a man, other than my boss as he appeared to be happily married with a child.

MG Toldai never talked about his wife, and after we moved onto the Defense Ministry, he talked about his daughter less and less as well, but sometimes men were like that. He was a very handsome man; he had short dark hair, cut in military style and green eyes, with nice lips to go with his handsome face. I smiled as I thought about him and looked forward hearing about his life in America.

I stayed behind until five o'clock and then I went upstairs to take a quick shower. It was always easy to get ready as I never wore makeup, nothing other than just some lip gloss. Ten minutes to six, I grabbed my purse and headed downstairs. As I turned around, I heard the sound of a door opening and I didn't have to turn around to see who it was, I knew that it was Attila. The elevator came, I stepped inside and then I turned around. He stood there without moving, not even waiving. *Whatever,* I thought.

My former boss was on time and his car pulled up to the entrance door exactly at six o'clock. He got out and being a true gentleman that he was, he opened the door for me. For the record, it was the very first time that I saw him in civilian clothes and he looked great. He wore a suit with a pale blue polo shirt, and if somebody looked just a touch closer, he or she would have been able to see his abs through the clothing. He had to work out even if he was a senior ranked officer, and besides, I knew that he always worked out before he came to work. "You look very nice," he complimented me. I was wearing a red dress; red was my signature color, with a white evening wrap around my shoulders. I thanked him and off we were.

"Where would you like to go?" He asked. I shrugged, although I knew that it was not ladylike.

"I have never been out in a restaurant in this city," I commented.

"Hmm," he said. "The only restaurant I know is at the hotel where I am staying. I suppose you don't want to go there, given the fact that I am also staying there," he commented.

"If the food is tasty and the service is good, why not," I replied.

"I guess that is settled," he said and turned around the corner.

He parked the car and it took a few minutes to walk inside the hotel. Since it was still relatively early in the evening, the place was not overly busy and we didn't have any problem getting a table by the window that overlooked the garden of the hotel. The waiter arrived a few minutes later and asked about our choice of drinks for the evening.

"You still don't drink?" He asked. I nodded. "Sorry," he told the waiter. "I can't drink either, so can we have two lemonades, please." The waiter smiled, nodded and left to get our drinks. We selected our food and when he returned we were ready to order. I ordered chicken soup with liver dumpling, beefsteak ala gypsy, which had a little bit spicy sauce and potato dumplings. He declared that it sounded good to him too and he ordered the same food as I did. We kind of looked at each other awkwardly for a while, and then he broke the silence.

"I missed you," he said quietly. Those three little words had a big surprise effect on me.

"I missed you too," I replied. "Tell me about your life in America, I am genuinely curious." I told him.

"Well," he began. "Life is good there, nobody can't deny that, and for some people, life is way too good." He said and stared down at his still empty plate. It did not sound right or good to me.

"Did something happen?" I asked in a quiet tone of voice, although the tables directly around were still unoccupied. He shook his head.

"You always had this in you, to feel if something was going on," he commented.

"Sir, are you going to tell me?" I asked and noticed that his fingers were tapping on the table. He looked at me.

"Please, Angie, don't call me, sir, I am not your boss anymore. Please call me Viktor," he asked. I agreed and waited for his response. "My wife left me for an American military officer whom she met at one of our social functions, she took my daughter with her." He told me. I did not reply right away, I put my right hand on his. His fingers intertwined with mine.

"That is why you are back home?" I asked.

"Yes," he replied. "I am finalizing the divorce so they could get married." I was surprised to hear what he was saying.

"You are way too kind of a man," I said and squeezed his hand. He had a sad smile on his face.

"I really think that it was inevitable. There were some serious issues in our marriage, and I knew for a long time that she was not happy. We got married when she got pregnant and it was an honorable thing to do," he said and let out a soft sigh.

"You two seemed to be getting along so well," I commented, although I only met his soon to be ex-wife twice and even then, only briefly.

"Well, she liked the prestige that came with my promotions," he remarked just as our food arrived. It was delicious and if I wouldn't have been embarrassed, I would have asked for some more, it was that good. While we ate, he talked about the American capital city and all the places a person could visit there. He mentioned that on a brief vacation he made it down to Florida with his daughter to go Disneyworld. Viktor emphasized that only he and his daughter went there. He talked about huge department stores and supermarkets for groceries, and about great restaurants that were somewhat expensive for their budget. He didn't talk about his work and I wouldn't even think about asking him.

The restaurant where we had dinner was very nicely decorated and it had an old time charm. It was named for Queen Elizabeth, or so called Sissi, a much-loved person by the Hungarian people. We finished with dinner and we just hung around for a few minutes, talking about my job that I left before I took the one offered by his brother. "I have something for you and I could bring it to your office tomorrow," he told me.

"Something from America?" I asked. He confirmed it with a nod.

"Actually I can go upstairs to get it, you can wait right here," he suggested.

"Why don't I go with you," I suggested in return. He was somewhat surprised.

"I wouldn't have dared to ask you," he admitted. I shrugged. We walked up the stairs to his second floor room and I was very impressed with the decoration. It was very specious with two large beds, with a small desk and a television on the dresser. I sat down on one of the beds and he handed me a beautiful large and colorful picture book, simply titled, *"America"*. I flipped through the pages and I knew that I would be looking at that for a long time to come.

Viktor pulled the chair from the small desk and turned it around to face me. "I didn't want to ask you in the restaurant, what happened to Andrew?" Hearing that name I slipped into a darker mood and I could not help it, my smile disappeared. He motioned with his hand. "If you don't want to talk about it, it's fine." He assured me. I looked at him and bit my lips. I have never talked about this to anyone other than my parents.

"He did not want me," I said, and despite all of my efforts not to do it, tears rushed into my eyes. "After knowing him for over two years, after being engaged to him for two years, and after him telling me every day that he loved me and I meant everything to him, he got one of their tenants' daughter pregnant." I sighed. He reached out and with his fingers and wiped the tears off from my face. "The whole thing is really comical," I said. "She got an abortion while he was recalled for active duty. When he was discharged he got a divorce and wanted to come back to me as if nothing happened."

I just couldn't help it. I thought that I was already over that painful period of my life, but who knew that it still hurt so much to talk about. It also dawned on me that the whole thing might have sounded childish to Viktor. He pushed the chair away and knelt down in front of me, and then he softly touched both sides of my face with his warm hands.

"I am so sorry that you hurt so much," he whispered. I leaned forward and he hugged me. I felt so comfortable in his arms that I put my head on his shoulder and we remained like that for a minute or so.

He gently pushed me away and I noticed that his green eyes were shining, but I knew that not from tears. After an ever so brief moment of hesitation, he slowly and very gently kissed me and then almost immediately he pulled away.

"This is very wrong," he said, but his arms were still holding me. He kissed me again and I hugged him back. "I can't do this," he declared and sat down on the other bed. "Angie, I am sorry," he told me. I nodded and took some tissues from the nightstand to wipe off my tears.

"I understand," I said and got up to leave. "That is what Andy said too," I remarked and headed for the door. Before I reached it, he was right behind me and turned me back towards him.

"You have no idea how desirable you are," he told me. "But I am over two decades older than you." I dropped my purse to the floor and because he was taller than me, I stood on my toes and wrapped my arms around his neck. I kissed him with the passion that I must have harbored deep inside my heart and soul for him. His tongue began to work on mine and soon, my dress was on the floor and I kicked off my semi-high heel shoes.

Off came his polo shirt and his pants, he took off his jacket earlier. We kissed all the way to the bed. He tossed the comforter aside and I laid down on the bed with Viktor right beside me.

"Have I ever told you that I always thought that you were just about the most beautiful woman I have ever met?" He asked between kisses.

"No," I whispered breathing hard. "You did tell me that I was an efficient typist," I replied. He laughed and stroked my hair.

"What happened to your incredibly beautiful hair?" He asked and I felt his hand unhooking my bra.

"I got mad one day and just cut if off," I told him and felt his lips as they discovered my breasts. "Oh," I moaned softly. He looked up and had a grin on his face.

"I guess I better not get you upset, I wouldn't want anything to be cut off," he said and his lips returned kissing other parts of my body. I wanted to laugh but I could not because I was too busy enjoying what his lips, his mouth and his hands were doing to me. For some reason I did not feel embarrassed, and the way he looked at me, I actually felt good because his eyes were smiling along with his lips.

I was on fire, something I had not experienced in years. When Viktor reached my private area, he refocused and kissed me long and hard. I wished in those moments that his lips would never leave mine. I wrapped my arms around his neck and kissed him back with all the desire that rushed through my entire body.

While his left hand caressed my breast, his lips once again found the route down to my thighs, but he did not stop there, he kissed my legs down to my toes and back. He leaned forward to kiss my lips again as a reminder that he didn't forget that his kisses were equally important on them too. He gently parted my legs and with his hand and lips he discovered areas that were barely visited but not yet occupied by any man before.

"Viktor," I whispered his name. Leaving his hand between my thighs, he kissed my breasts and with passion that I have experienced with him a few minutes earlier, he kissed me so deep that I thought that I was going to suffocate. At that very moment, I felt that magical feeling that I have known but almost forgot. I locked his hand in the place where pleasure was lurking and moaned when I could not stand it any longer.

"Angie, my sweet Angie," he whispered into my ear. I just couldn't get enough of his lips and my lips sought out his, whenever he was not busy showering my entire body with kisses. His tongue-touched areas that I didn't know could give so much pleasure, but they were secret no more. I thought that if something was not going to happen shortly, I would just burst into a ball of fire and taking with me whoever did not fulfill my desire. I knew that such desire existed but I had never experienced it before. I pulled Viktor on the top of me and I opened up for him so he could finally take me to the place that was not only forbidden, but possibly was also filled with pleasure. I held my breath when he entered me, and then he stopped and looked at me.

"Are you sure?" He asked me quietly, somewhat urgently.

"Please, be gentle," I asked him and I felt his hardness entering me slowly, and then thrust himself deeper inside me. There was a sudden but short pain from which my body froze for a moment.

"Angie, I didn't know," he said with surprise.

"Don't stop, please," I begged him and I hugged his back as tightly as I could while he moved inside me. The pleasure was more fulfilling than I ever imagined it would be and more than I ever hoped for. *So this was making love*, I thought. *Damn you Andy, damn you another thousand times.* I lost track how long we made love but it felt wonderful and then I felt as he quickened his movements, a sure sign that his pleasure was near. He reached down and touched me with his fingers, and as if I was a volcano, I erupted in a joyful climax at the same time as he did.

Breathing hard and trying to catch my breath was an indication that it really happened; I was no longer a virgin who was once wanted by someone and who did not do anything about it. But Viktor did, and he gave me pleasure more than once. He was not only a passionate, but he was also a considerate lover. I was grateful that he took his time for me to have my own pleasure as much as he had his. He showered me gentle kisses and his arms never left me, I nestled down next to his chest.

"Are you all right?" He asked. "Did I hurt you?"

"No," I whispered and kissed his chest.

"I think it would be a perfect time to be honest with you," he said in a quiet tone of voice. I held my breath. "I have been in love with you since you caused that scene in the visitor's center." He confessed and then he added as he kissed my shoulder. "I just never realized how much until now."

I pulled myself up and looked at him with the love that I felt at that very moment. "You have always been a perfect man in my eyes." I said to him and kissed him. It felt incredible being in his arms and I thought that I could easily get used to sleeping next to him, securely wrapped in those toned arms. We fell asleep and I have never slept as well as I did then, next to him, next to a real man, my very first lover.

I woke up around four thirty and I decided to take a shower as I had to get back to the academy to change clothes, in other words, to get ready for work. I carefully and quietly as I could slipped off from the bed and went to the spacious bathroom. I started the shower water and tried to get the right temperature for the water when I noticed that the bathroom door opened and Viktor walked in.

"May I join you?" He asked. I nodded and he stepped inside the shower too. He grabbed the sponge and poured some body wash liquid on it. "Turn around," he asked me and I did. He washed my back and neck and then I faced him again and he washed my front as well and he washed away the small amount of blood, the last proof of my lost innocence. He did not make any comments, he was very gentle and when he finished, he handed me the sponge to do the same to him.

It's not that I hadn't seen naked man before, but it was still very new to me to be in a shower with one, with my lover actually. Oh, that word kept coming back into my mind. When I washed the lower part of his body, he became erect in no time and immediately I felt his arms around me. He lifted my right leg up and within seconds, he was inside me. I gasped feeling his hardness and having the warm water running down our bodies while we became one and with the pleasure that we gave to each other, I almost felt faint from the sensation.

"Oh, Viktor," I moaned his name and in those moments, when he moved inside me, he urged me to join him in a rhythm that turned into pleasure. I let my reappearing thoughts about what future we may have in the horizon wash down with the shower water into the drain. I concentrated on that pleasant moment when I felt his body tremble as he climaxed inside me. We clung to each other as if there was no tomorrow and I was glad that the water was running because I just couldn't stop crying for reasons I could not explain or analyze right then and there.

He helped me to step out of the bathtub and with a large, soft towel he began to dry me from my head down to my toes. After drying himself as well, we went back to the room to get dressed. It was slightly after five in the morning and he drove me all the way to the entrance of the building. Not a single word was spoken since we left the hotel and when he stopped the car, he got out and opened the passenger door for me. We hugged tightly, and then he kissed me, and after that he kissed me again and again. I smiled and gently pushed him away. "I'll call you." He said and I nodded that I heard him.

"Bye," I said and rushed into the building. The elevator couldn't come fast enough and I prayed real hard that Attila, the Hunter would not be around. I was lucky, he was probably just finishing his morning physical training. I quickly changed clothes and as I looked into the bathroom mirror, I checked my face left and right, but I didn't see any changes, I was still me and yet, as far as I was concerned, I officially became woman.

The day was excruciatingly long and each time my phone rang I grabbed it as if I was expecting a phone call about a life and death situation. Despite the excruciatingly long wait for Viktor's call, I just couldn't help it I smiled all morning. Needless to say, it was noticed by all of the women in the office and I was teased about it pretty much all day. My thoughts kept on returning to that moment when Viktor and I had become one, and the sweet words that he whispered to me. I actually had to go to the restroom to wash my face as I was experiencing hot flashes, although I was not even close to a change of life hormonal situation.

I didn't leave for lunch and I asked Ruth to grab me something in the cafeteria. Instead of staying in the general area of the office, I went back into my office, which by that time was finally getting in order. I worked almost all weekends, with the exception of one, when I had no choice but to go visit my parents. I got a threatening letter from my mother that she would report me as a "missing person" if I don't go visit them. I also worked after office hours way into the late night hours to finish sorting the folders by problems. By the time of the general meeting I was almost finished, so I had a chance to rearrange my office, push the desk where I wanted it, which was facing the door and the window with my back to the wall. The file cabinet and the front of it were still full with folders and there were reviewed folders in boxes stacked up by the wall as well. At least I had access to my office where I could sit by my own desk and addition to my daily work, I also start working on removing incorrectly filed documents and making notes on found processing errors for correction.

If anyone knew me well, they could easily draw a conclusion that I always thought that things could have been done better and more efficiently, and that I would never be pleased, which of course was only partially true. I was not happy with myself regarding the folders as I pushed myself to finish the huge project without any help, simply because my trust level was very low. The sad fact was that the majority of those people who misfiled and processed data incorrectly were still working there. They had to earn my trust, but until then, I had to keep my eyes open about everything, which meant that there was no rest for the wicked. Of course, I still had my regular duties to perform which included reviewing all newly processed documents and payroll forms, attendance records and such. However: unlike my previous place, we didn't have to be involved on actual paydays because we telexed the timesheets with my signature on the bottom to the Defense Ministry, who sent the money with special couriers.

Back to the phone call, I was in my office during lunch when I heard voices at the front, by the counter; I recognized Klára's voice talking to someone. I got up and hid behind the wall of boxes in the corner. The blinds were down but she stopped by my office without entering.

"There is no one here," she said.

"How is she doing?" I heard Attila's voice. It was not a mocking voice, rather, it sounded serious and concerned.

"She is fine. Actually she seemed rather happy today, obviously not because of you." Klára told him.

"Angie is a good person," Attila said and I made a face when I heard it. "Endlessly stubborn and yet, vivacious," he added. "I miss talking to her."

"I think that you blew your opportunity," she remarked.

"You are right about that," he replied. "I actually thought that she was the one I am looking for." Klára laughed hearing that.

"You and one woman?" She was still laughing. "Well, like her or not, you failed our bet so you need to pay off your debt." If I was smiling, the smile was gone from my face. "I knew that it was a safe bet and that she won't give in to your charms, not like some of us did." She remarked, and it made my stomach turn.

I carefully pushed up two blinds so I could see. Attila took money out from his wallet and while he made a face he handed the money to Klára. "Thank you, sir," she said. "Until next time?" He shook his head.

"There won't be a next time," he replied with a serious tone of voice and just then my phone rang. There was no way that I was not going to answer that, but the problem was, the phone rang at my temporary desk. I had no choice but to leave my office and rush to the phone to the desk across my office. I quickly glanced toward their direction and the stunned look on their faces remained with me for a long time to come.

"This is the HR department, Ms. Aranyi speaking," I replied.

"Ms. Aranyi, it's me, Viktor," he said and I could almost see him smiling.

"I was hoping that you would call," I mumbled into the receiver and watched as Attila exited the office and Klára just stood there by the counter. "Please give me a moment, I'll transfer the call to my office."

I rushed into my office pulling the door almost closed behind me and then I picked up the ringing phone. "I am here," I told the man in my life.

"Listen Angie, I wanted to call you earlier but I got stuck in back to back meetings," he told me. "Luckily I had a chance to get my final divorce papers before the first meeting, so I am a free man."

"I am not sure if I'm supposed to say congratulations, or happy for you," I told him.

"Well, for one, I am a free man and I can do what I want," he said and laughed.

"And what do you want?" I whispered in the phone. There was a moment of silence and I heard his voice firm and serious.

"I want you," he told me. It was my turn to remain quiet for a brief second.

"It goes both ways," I replied.

"Angie, I have to go. I don't know what time, but I will see you later," he said.

"I'll be waiting," I replied and ended the call. *He wants me,* I thought happily and then I did what I have always done since my break up with Andy, my thoughts turned dark. The words "*for now*", came to mind. And then, I saw Klára hurrying by my door.

"Klára, please come in," I yelled after her. Lunch hour was almost over and the others were also returning. She backed up to my door and looked in. "All the way in here." I told her. Once she was inside, I asked her to close the door.

"The door?" She repeated. I had seldom ever had the door closed before. I nodded. After she closed the door and I motioned to a chair in front of the desk. It had folders on it too; she put them on the top of my desk.

"Klára," I began. "I need you to look at me and tell me what you see." I told her. She immediately became confused what I was asking her to do. "Just look at me and tell me if you see a clown, a devil with horns or a halo above my head? What do you see?" Tears rushed into her eyes. "Look, I am almost nineteen years old and I am sitting in this chair and I am your boss. I am the one who makes the decision who will remain in this office, who gets promoted and who is getting hired. You understand what I am saying?" She nodded. "You are what, twenty-three years old?"

"Yes," she mumbled.

"So if am not yet nineteen and I am a boss of the HR section, and you at twenty-three making bets on people, who do you think is the adult?" I asked. She began to cry. "Did anyone die? Did anyone beat you up?" I asked.

"No," she mumbled again.

"So why are you crying? Have I done anything to you, did I threaten you in any ways? Did I say to you that you are incompetent in your job, did I hurt your feelings? Or did I bet on you with Captain Bartha? Did I?" I asked. She shook her head. "So please tell me what was that bet all about?"

She was crying and I gave her a couple of minutes to calm down. "I went on a couple of dates with him but he didn't asked me out again. When you started here, he asked me what I knew about you, especially if you have any boyfriends," she said and finally lifted her head to look at me. "I told him that you are actually a very nice person and I didn't think that you had a boyfriend and that you . . ." she stopped and tried to find some words but she could not. "That you are probably still a virgin."

I did not say anything, I overheard them talking about their bet, but I wanted to hear it out loud coming from her. "He said that he would bet five hundred forint that you wouldn't be a virgin after three weeks. I told him that from what I learned about you so far was that you have strong principles, and that you won't fall for his charms," she made a face. She pulled the money out of her pocket and put it on my desk. I looked at the money and then I looked at her. "I am very sorry," she said the words I wanted to hear and I didn't care if she meant it or not.

"All right, Klára," I said calmly and collectively. "I want you to know that I am not mad at you. The truth is that it is rather easy to fall for Captain Bartha's charms, which one may find charming; someone else may find it as a turnoff. I have good news and a bad news to tell you."

"Please, don't fire me," she said quietly. I shook my head.

"I won't do that, not yet at least. The good news is that once you leave this office, this whole incident won't be mentioned again, unless it reoccurs. The bad news is that this incident put you way down to the bottom of my trust list. It is a workable list which only improves with time and with your attitude."

"It won't happen again," she promised, unfortunately for her, I no longer believed in promises.

"Yes, I know it won't," I told her. I pointed at the money. "I don't want your money."

"I don't want that money either. Should I give it back to him?" She asked.

"Heck no, you won the bet," I replied. I remembered seeing a small box in the bottom drawer of my desk. I pulled it out and put the money in it. "Now we have petty cash, do you agree?" I asked. She smiled and I nodded. "You will be the keeper of the box."

"Thank you for your time," she mumbled.

"Thank you for telling me the truth," I responded and picked up the phone as a sign of dismissal. She left my office leaving the door open. I heard Mitzi asking her what happened, to which Klára replied that we talked about petty cash and that now we have five hundred forint in the box.

Five o'clock couldn't arrive fast enough, it was the time that I was finally alone in the office and I could concentrate on the folders, at least for another hour. I didn't want to remain in the office too late in case Viktor arrived. At six o'clock I went upstairs and not wanting to eat frozen food, I made a large sandwich and I ate it while I watched television. I took a quick shower and at seven I opened up the sofa bed just to settle down on it wearing only my soft bathrobe. I watched a movie I could barely recall later because I focused on any noise in the hallway, but most of all, I waited for a knock on the door.

I must have dozed off because I woke up around eleven o'clock and disappointment began to linger all around me. Eleven thirty I heard a knock on the door and I must have flown to the door because I was there before the second set of knocks were heard. I unhooked the chain and when I opened the door I saw Viktor standing in the door, holding a huge bouquet of red and white roses. I did not say anything, no hello, nothing at all; I took the bouquet of roses and dropped them on the floor. I pulled him inside, locked the door and put the chain back on. I reached for his tie and pulled it off, and next I removed his uniform jacket. He pushed down his trousers and he kicked off his shoes. I wasn't sure if I ripped off any buttons from his shirt but within seconds that came off too, and then the undershirt and his underwear.

He picked me up and when he did that, my bathrobe opened revealing that I was not wearing anything. When he put me down, he rolled me to the left and right to remove my robe and I grabbed his neck as if I was a hungry child. I pasted my lips on his and my tongue was in his mouth in no time. I wrapped my legs around him and he was quickly inside me, but even then, he tried to be gentle as he could but I wouldn't even mind the temporary discomfort just to feel him, all of him. He kissed me feverishly and I touched his buttocks urging him to do more and boy, did he ever. He put his hand on my mouth when my pleasure exploded because I was moaning so loud that no doubt the Captain next door would have his own orgasm, although he was all by himself just hearing me.

Viktor rolled on his back and I was on the top of him, it was all new to me but with a little guidance from his part, I was on my way to have a second explosion simultaneous with his. I bent down to kiss him although our breathing was labored, but I just couldn't get enough of his kisses. Eventually I rolled to my side and his arms automatically took me in and my head was resting on chest. He kissed the top of my head.

"What have I done?" He whispered. I looked at his handsome face.

"What do you mean?" I asked him with a question of my own.

"I think I unleashed a hungry tigress in you," he said with a smile.

"That may be true, but this tigress only feels hunger for you," I replied. He chuckled.

"So there I was, sitting in this huge conference room in the Defense Ministry's building, and there was a presentation about the NATO Alliance. All I could think of is that you were waiting for me and how much I wanted you, to be with you and to be inside of you," he said and just then, right then at that moment I realized that I was deeply in love with him.

Perhaps it was not a new feeling that I felt about him. Maybe once or twice before I thought about him as a man, but because he was my boss and because he was married when I worked for him, I never dared to pass the "*I am his employee*" stage. Somewhere deep down inside I must have been in love with him for a long time, because when he was talking to me, the way he was talking to me, the feeling of love for Viktor was so strong that it spread through my entire body. It simply could not have been a new love. I began to tremble from that feeling and from the sensation that I was lying next to him and I could feel his strong body so close, so erect.

He turned me on my back and he lowered himself on the top of me while he was kissing me. I put my arms around his neck and raised my head for another kiss, and then another. His eyes were smiling and his lips were smiling and I was smiling right back at him. "I love you," he said softly, yet meaningfully. I kissed him again and as I laid back on my pillow, his lips less than an inch from mine, I replied.

"I love you right back." He kissed me yet again as a confirmation and a second later; he buried his head in my thighs.

I woke up to the sound of the alarm clock, and although my eyes under normal circumstances would automatically open at five, as they always did, but not on that morning. Being time conscious, despite that I could wake up without an alarm clock, I never failed to set one anyway. I reached out to the other side of my sofa bed and it was empty. I tried to calculate just how many hours I had slept, but I was unable to figure it out. Most of my body parts were aching, the kind of ache that make you smile just thinking about how you got them. I pushed myself off the sofa bed and after placing a fresh set of bed sheets, along with the comforter inside the frame; I closed it up as it always gave more space to the room.

I saw Viktor's uniform neatly folded and his jacket placed on the back of the armchair. I remembered the roses that I dropped to the floor because something else was more important to me; I found those pretty flowers in a vase decorating the kitchen table. For the first time I also noticed that there was a military duffel bag in the corner of the kitchen, behind the second chair.

I let the warm water soak and wake up my somewhat tired body. I washed my hair too as it dried very quickly, which is why I began to like to keep it short. I got dressed in a grey dress suit with a crispy white blouse and a red ribbon tie, and as I was about to leave a note behind that I left for work, when I heard voices in the hallway. I opened the door and saw Attila and Viktor walking towards the door.

"Good morning," Attila said.

"Good morning," I replied and did not even look at him. Viktor, somewhat sweaty from running and physical activities, was carrying a tray with scrambled eggs and bacon, with orange juice and a coffee in a paper cup.

"Hi, sweetheart," he said and kissed me.

"Darling, what have you got there?" I asked smiling.

"It's your breakfast," he said and pushed me backwards with a tray. I looked up and I noticed that Attila was watching us. When our eyes met, I smiled and turned my attention back to Viktor and the food. I closed the door behind him not bothering to look at Attila again; he apparently was having a "problem" opening his apartment's door.

I looked at my watch and at the food and I decided that I still had some time to eat. I was about to sit down when Viktor pulled me to him to sit on his lap. I shook my head when I felt that he was aroused. "I have to get to work," I whispered to him.

"You don't have too far to drive," he whispered back and pulled off my panties. I sat back across his lap and he was inside of me within seconds. I bent backwards and I took him, all of him in as he buried his face in my once crispy white blouse, which he unbuttoned with one hand. My breathing became labored as his movements quickened when he reached down and touched me.

I could not help it, I cried out from the pleasure and to quiet me down, his lips pasted themselves to mine as I clung to him like as if he was a life vest.

"Oh, God, Angie," he exclaimed while my head was resting on his shoulder. Once my breathing became somewhat normal, I put my hands on both sides of his face and kissed him.

"I love you so much," I told him with tears in my eyes.

"I love you, Angie, I love you terribly," he replied. It took another few minutes to regain our full composures and I carefully stood up from his lap. I had no choice but to use the bathroom again and change clothes, not that it had anything on it, but I knew that I would have difficulty being in that outfit and not keep thinking about what just happened.

"I really have to go," I told him and kissed him goodbye. "Oh, by the way," I turned around from the door. "What are your plans for today?"

"I have some business to attend and some favors to cash in, but I'll be here later tonight," he promised. I threw him a kiss and went to work. The elevator door almost closed when a hand appeared to stop it from closing. Attila got in; I supposed that he was going for breakfast and then to teach a class as he was in full military uniform. I pushed the number one button on the elevator and the door closed again. He reached out and pressed two. The elevator was slow as always, but I was simply glad that it worked at all. Attila kept looking at me, I could feel his glare, but I just stood there without showing any emotions on my face, although I was bursting with happiness inside. When the elevator reached his floor and the door opened, he held it back from closing after he stepped out of it. He turned around to face me.

"Just tell me one thing Angie, what does he have that I don't?" He asked. I looked straight into his blue eyes that always reminded me of Joe.

"Decency," I replied and pushed the close the door button. He let it go and I was on the first floor a few seconds later.

I was surprised to learn that Klára was already there; actually she was making coffee as it was a tradition that whoever arrived first had the chore to make the first carafe. "Good morning, Klára," I said cheerfully and with my coffee in hand walked into my office.

"Oh, good morning, Angie," I heard her response.

A few minutes later all others with the exception of Flóra arrived, she is the one who started two hours later, and then I heard the door open yet again. Although we started our shift from six o'clock until three o'clock in the afternoon, our hours of operation was from seven o'clock until two thirty. Mitzi who was getting her first cup of coffee put down her mug and headed toward the counter. I pulled up the blinds and noticed Viktor was standing there with a plate wrapped in aluminum foil. I quickly made my way to the counter and used the flap door to go to the front of it.

"Sweetheart, you forgot your breakfast, I warmed it up for you," said and handed me the food.

"Thank you, darling," I told him. He pulled my head closer to him and kissed me. It was a light kiss, yet I could feel a wave of tingling in my body. He leaned towards me and whispered.

"Try not to drive anybody crazy until I'll get back." I couldn't help it, I laughed out loud and shook my head. "Ladies," he waived at the others and left. I turned around and six pairs of eyes were on me.

"Darling, sweetheart, and a General?" Mitzi teased me.

"Alright, alright, so he is a nice guy," I told them but I was grinning ear to ear. *What has that man done to me?* I thought. I could not control my smiling face.

"A nice guy?" Mitzi mocked me. "Honey, he is soooo handsome." She stretched out the word.

"Back to work you peep hole addicts," I said jokingly and I have never heard a group of people laugh all at once like they did, as if it was a cabaret show.

I could hardly wait for the evening to come, but to my disappointment, Viktor called in the early afternoon to tell me that he wouldn't be back that night.

"Sweetheart, I just could not finish everything I planned to do and I also have to wait on a couple of things. I will have one more meeting at the Defense Ministry with someone and I am hoping to hear good news. I can tell you this much, it's worth waiting for." He said and from my immediate silence he knew that I felt sad. "Oh, darling, don't do this to me." He pleaded with me. "Don't you think that I would rather be with you? What I am doing must be done and you know the military, it's a hurry up and wait business." He said trying to make me understand the situation. I knew all that, I had been around military before, actually twice.

"I know," I assured him. "I hope to see you tomorrow night," I remarked.

"I'll try my best, but if I can not make it, I will most definitely call you, alright?" He asked me.

"Where are you staying?" I asked him.

"I am staying at my old friend, Colonel Magyari's house, he used to work on the second floor when you worked there." He explained and gave me his friend's home phone number in case I needed to call him. I murmured a sad goodbye and ended the call.

The next day was Friday and he called again and apologized for not being able to come back again until the following day, Saturday. He repeatedly assured me that it was for certain. I tried to act that it was all right with me since I couldn't do anything about it, when in reality hundreds of questions were piling up in my mind as what he was doing and what favors he wanted to cash in.

Friday was a milestone in the office; I had finally filed the first folders in the file cabinets, the ones that were correct, only unfortunately from out of the last couple of thousand I reviewed, less than a hundred were correct without any errors or without any misfiled documents. Nevertheless, at least I could see the light at the end of the tunnel, because before that I could not even see the tunnel. Since Viktor was not coming back on Friday, I went upstairs and changed clothes, and then I went back to the office with a couple of sandwiches and orange sodas to do some more work.

It was a big job but I made it easier when I was reviewing the folders. When I found a misfiled document I placed a small piece of paper there so I knew where the page was. My new task was to remove all of those pages and file the folders away. The plan ahead was that once I had the pile of misfiled documents, to pull the correct file and place the documents in its proper place, as I mentioned earlier, the documents were filed in chronological order.

Actually I was moving along really well until my eyes began to hurt and I had to end my crusade on the folders and get some rest. I cleaned my area of food as I didn't want any ants or bugs around and went upstairs. I took a shower, and when I glanced into the mirror, I could not believe how bloodshot my eyes looked. Since I was by myself, a good night's rest was in order. Sure enough, when I put my head down on the pillow I was out of this world and travelled to Dreamland.

I slept through the night and for the first time in years; my eyes did not pop open at five o'clock and my alarm that I did not sat also remained silent. It was a clear sign that I was overworked. I looked at the clock; it was almost nine o'clock in the morning. I made the bed by turning it back into a sofa and then went to get some orange juice before getting dressed. The moment I sat down at the kitchen table, I heard a knock on the door. I looked through the peephole and I pulled back, and then opened the door.

"Good morning, Angie," said Terri, Colonel Toldai's wife. She clearly saw the surprise on my face. "I am sorry to trouble you this early in the morning, but I need to see your wardrobe."

"My what?" I asked because I thought that I heard her wrong, but she repeated it. "May I ask why?" I inquired again. She stopped and looked at me.

"Ask me no questions, I'll tell you no lies," she said seriously, and as a matter of fact so seriously, that without saying another word, I pointed at the shrunk on left side of the room. I put my orange juice down and followed her in the room. Without hesitation she opened the shrunk's door and reviewed my outfits. She removed an off white dress which had a wide red belt made out of silk and then she reached down and took out a pair of red sandals. "Would you please get dressed, my husband is in the car waiting."

I raised my hand. "Terri, what is this about?" I wanted to know.

"Angie, please get dressed," she said and smiled, and then she winked. "Just be a good girl and get dressed."

She went to the kitchen to give me privacy while I got ready. I didn't have time to shower so I quickly washed up, brushed my teeth and got dressed. I was down in ten minutes and then she asked me turn around. When I turned, she declared that I looked very pretty and guided me to the door. "Don't forget your purse," she instructed me, but I already had it with me because I always carried what all citizens were required to carry. The burgundy colored pictured identification booklet included all my personal data, my parents' name, where I lived and worked, if was married my spouse's name, and if I had children their names would be also listed as well. This was way before computers.

Colonel Toldai was all smiles when I got into his car, and he too complimented me that I looked very nice. I inquired where their children were, to which Terri replied that they had a babysitter.

"May I ask where we are going?" I asked from the Colonel.

"No, not really," he replied and laughed. Well for one, I did not like to be kept in the dark, but since his wife was there too, whatever was happening couldn't be so bad. The drive was short and when we stopped, he parked the car in the Queen Elizabeth Hotel's parking lot. "Let's go," he declared and Terri put her arm in mine as we walked. *She doesn't want me to run away*, I thought, but both of them were smiling and giving each other looks that gave me the impression that obviously they knew something that I did not.

We crossed the road to Freedom Square and I noticed a small gazebo that I have never seen before. From the distance I could see people sitting on benches in front of the gazebo, which was decorated with our national colors, red, white and green ribbons. I stopped and took a second look; the people whom I saw sitting on one of the benches were my parents. They got up when they noticed that I was getting closer to them. A strange tall man was standing in the gazebo, next Viktor. Colonel Toldai and Terri's three children immediately rushed to welcome me.

I kissed my parents and asked them what in the world was going on, but my mother, who by the way was all smiles and teary eyed at the same time, pointed at Viktor. "He knows," she said and wiped off her tears.

"Did he upset you?" I asked. She shook her head and hugged me.

Viktor was in his Army dress uniform and the smile on his face was priceless, while my face probably expressed questions that I had about not knowing what was going on. They are all gathered around us when Viktor walked up to me and gave me traditional kisses on my cheeks. Before I could say *"what"*, he got down on one knee.

"Angie," he began and I could see that his hands were trembling. "I am so full of emotions and great love for you at this moment that I could barely speak, or even think, but I must." I smiled down at him with all the love that I felt in my heart toward the man who lifted me out of emotional darkness and carried me away toward a hopeful future. "You reentered my life when I felt lost in my private world, and you showed me that there is so much beauty, love and passion that I still have not known. All of them which you possess and already shown me. I don't want to waste a moment in this life without you. Would you do me the honor to be my wife, my guiding light for the rest of our years to come?"

I was totally and utterly speechless. This man that most women could only dream about was asking me to be his wife? I bent down and touched his face. "You made me so happy that I could not even start explaining how it happened, but you did. There is nothing in this world that I would rather do, so yes, Viktor, I would be your wife for the rest of our lives." He got up and kissed me.

"I suppose that there is only one thing left for us to do," he commented and led me up in the gazebo where he introduced me to the tall man who turned out to be a Justice-of-the-Peace. I looked at Viktor, was he joking, getting married right then? He took me into his arms. "I know that it is all too rushed, but I don't want to wait and to be engaged for a long time. I love you and I want to marry you, right now. So what do you say?" He asked with some concern seeing my face.

"What are we waiting for?" I asked. He sighed and looked upward to the sky, as if he was giving God a *thank you* for my response.

The Justice-of-the Peace collected our Personal ID books, checked our marital status, and then he made a short speech about the meaning of a marriage and he asked for the rings. Colonel Toldai, my very soon to be brother-in-law handed Viktor a jewelry box. It had two wide identical wedding bands and a diamond ring as an engagement ring for me inside. He pushed the ring on my right hand ring finger, which represented that I was married and he put the engagement ring on my right hand ring finger. I did the same thing with his wedding band while I could still not believe what was taking place. Within a minute later we were announced husband and wife.

My parents seemed very happy and so were Viktor's brother and his family as well, but nobody was happier than Viktor and me. We kept hugging and kissing each other, and frankly, it took me several hours to fully comprehend what just happened. I got up that morning worrying if I would ever see him again, and unknown to me; he spent two days organizing everything.

Terry and Nicholas arranged the reservations at the Queen Elizabeth Hotel's restaurant, which was ironic as Viktor and I had our first dinner there together.

I found out that he actually went to see my parents on Friday and he told them about his intentions. My mother was overwhelmed by emotions and to my surprise; she never once brought up the being Jewish issue. Viktor knew about my religious background but he also knew, because we talked about it way back when, that I was determined to marry whomever I loved and not by someone specifically because of his religion. He told me that he respected that I believed in God, and that was all of our conversation about religion. I suppose my parents were amazed that a real life General fell in love with their young daughter, and they were impressed because Viktor had that talent to easily impress the non-believers.

My parents left in mid-afternoon after making Viktor promise that he will always look after me and that he will take good care of me. He told them that he made that a purpose of his life. We stayed at the hotel overnight as we could not go on a honeymoon yet, and we didn't get out of bed until late Sunday afternoon when hunger became too overwhelming.

LOVE AND MARRIAGE

I SLEPT, WHEN I finally slept that is, very deeply and without dreams. Why would I dream when I was living one? After we leisurely made love what seemed like a very long time, before I fell asleep I thought about all the things he, my husband, who was also sleeping peacefully next to me with his arms around me, protecting me from the evils of the world, had done. Things like; getting documents that permitted us to marry, to asking my parents' permission, although he later told me that he would have married me anyway, and to pay off the Justice-of-the-Peace to marry us at the gazebo instead of at the city hall.

On the crude and rude Monday morning warm hands and even warmer kisses awakened me. "Good morning, Mrs. Toldai," he said with a smile and pulled me on the top of him.

"Good morning, sir," I said with a grin. He laughed and held me tight even though I was by no means a featherweight person.

"When we worked at the garrison and later in the ministry, when you came into my office for whatever reason and left, I would stare after you even when the door was already closed. I would have never in a million years dare to approach you, not just because I was married, but mainly because you were engaged," he told me. I kissed him.

"I know," I assured him. I knew because I always believed that he was a decent man.

I had no way out, I had to go work, so I climbed off from the bed and went to take a shower. Viktor was already in the kitchen when I got dressed. "So what are your plans for today?" I asked.

"Do you want another surprise or do you really want me to tell you?" He asked.

"You are getting a divorce from me already?" I asked jokingly. His face turned very serious.

"I would rather die first," he replied and handed me a cup of steaming coffee. "I have appointments to see two houses. Now that we are married, we cannot stay here."

"You are buying a house?" I asked with surprise. He shook his head.

"No, my love, we are buying a house," he corrected me.

"But I hardly have any money. I did save some by living here, but hardly enough to pitch in," I told him honestly. He reached out and gently touched my face.

"Let me take care of it," he said softly. I glanced at my watch; I had ten minutes to make it downstairs. "I'll see you later," he said and kissed me goodbye.

He was on two weeks leave and it was his second week to take care of some things, apparently getting married, get a house and move into it. Viktor accomplished as much that he did not have to return to the United States, and he applied for a teaching job at the same academy where his brother was a Commandant. When he attended a military academy himself, he specialized in strategic maneuvering tactics and he earned a teaching degree. Unfortunately because of his high rank, it was still very questionable if he was allowed to teach where the highest ranked teacher was a Colonel. A week after our wedding, we found out that one of the favors he "cashed" in came through, he got a one-year contract to remain at the Military Academy in a teaching position, but he did not know what his next real assignment was going to be. I thought at that time that at least that one-year would be nothing less than one long honeymoon.

I arrived only five minutes 'til six at work and made some coffee. The employees arrived a few minutes later and I didn't say anything when Ruth walked in ten minutes late. I just stood there by the coffee maker and refreshed my coffee that was made by Viktor.

They were talking about how they spent their seemingly short weekend, and I was just smiling and daydreaming, listening to them as they exchanged their weekend stories in ten minutes. "So, Angie how was your weekend?" Mitzi asked curiously.

"Well, I slept in, got married and that was pretty much it," I said in a normal tone of voice. They looked at each other.

"Can you back up a little bit," Mitzi said. "What was after you slept in?"

"Got married," I said and they surrounded me with great curiosity. They admired my rings.

"So what happened, how did it happen?" Ruth asked.

I gave them a brief recap how Terri got me dressed and drove me to Freedom Square, how my parents were there too. Viktor drove them from Budapest and how he proposed and how we got married five minutes later. I got hugged by all of them, even by Klára. Mitzi confirmed that I got married to the same person who brought my breakfast and expressed playful envy. Then it was time to work.

Around ten o'clock I heard a wave of whispers, I got up and went outside my office to check out the reason for it. I saw my smiling husband talking to Flóra. I forgot all about that he also had to in-process and he waived when he saw me. "Hi," I said cheerfully, the way I felt when I walked up to the counter. Flóra turned to me and whispered.

"I never in-processed a General, what should I do?" She asked.

"I'll show you," I smiled at her and patted her hand. "Sir," I turned to Viktor.

"Yes, ma'am," he immediately realized that I was being formal because I am treating him like a customer.

"General Toldai, would you please follow me," I said and opened up the flap door. He walked through it. "This way please," I motioned to my office.

"Thank you, ma'am," he replied. When he followed me into the office, I turned around and motioned to Flóra to come too. I offered him a chair which he accepted and placed his in-processing package on my desk.

"Sir, this is Ms. Flóra Kalmár, she will be assisting you with the in-processing. Should you have any questions, please feel free to ask her." I said and left the office. I turned around from the door and gave thumbs up to Flóra. I walked up to Mitzi's desk and sat down on the chair by her desk.

"That was classy," she said and nodded.

"Well, classy or not, privacy should be applied in all cases for officers from the rank of Colonel and above," I told her. Marianne, who was so quiet most of the time that I often almost forgot that she worked there, had a question for me.

"Angie, may I ask you something?" She asked and I agreed. "You are not even nineteen years old, already graduated from college and you seem to know a lot about everything in this office. How do you know so much?" I smiled.

"Well, I began to work right after my graduation at age sixteen, and I worked at an Army Garrison in Budapest, in the fourth district. It is important to mention that I had a good teacher. That is why I believe in mentoring, so I am here for anyone who has questions." I replied. She smiled too that she understood and went back to work. Technically she was an ideal employee, came in, did her job and went home. She listened when others talked, but she never got involved with telling stories about herself. Once, gently as I could, asked about her private life, she immediately became withdrawn so I dropped my inquiry.

Mitzi knew pretty much everything about everybody in the office, perhaps with the exception of me. She told me one time that Marianne was an abused child and her father killed her mother, and then himself, sparing their daughter's life. She grew up in an orphanage in good hands, but by then she was scarred for life. Twenty minutes later I rejoined Viktor and Flóra in my office as they were about to finish with the in-processing.

"Is everything completed?" I asked from Flóra.

"I believe so," she replied nervously.

"Did you get a set of transfer orders?" I asked and that moment I knew that she did not. Viktor opened his briefcase and handed her a set of his orders.

"Thank you, sir," Flóra said.

"It's my fault, she asked for it and I failed to give it to her," Viktor said and I knew that he was lying. He was one of those decent men whose sheer nature was to protect everyone who needed protection. Flóra gratefully looked up at him and left us standing there.

"Thank you for your assistance Flóra," I said to her when she about to walk away. She nodded a couple of times as a response.

I escorted Viktor out to the hallway. "I'll pick you up at four o'clock," he told me. "I think that one of the two houses I looked at earlier this morning is for your liking." Because there were people walking about in the hallway, I leaned to him.

"I would live with you in a shack if I you want me too," I whispered to him.

"Thank you for being you," he said, bent down and gave me a goodbye kiss. Some heads turned but it was a light kiss, something that was permitted by military regulations when a soldier wearing a uniform greeted family members.

I returned to my office and looked at the women in the office. All of them watched me enter and they were all smiling, even the always serious looking Marianne did as well. Flóra motioned me over.

"Angie," she said after taking a deep breath. "I have met a lot of senior ranked officers since I began working here, never a General. He was just about the nicest person I have ever encountered. He spoke softly and with respect, and not for a moment did he remind me who he was."

"That is the way he has always been," I agreed and walked back to my office. I was making good progress and I was down to the last box that needed to have misfiled documents corrected. I had four boxes, approximately two hundred folders that had some sort of errors to correct, I saved that time consuming task for last.

Although I fully concentrated on what I was doing, between going from one folder to another, I thought about how strange life was and how unexpectedly real and true love came into my life. I haven't thought about many things until Flóra brought me Viktor's in-processing packet along with his service folder for review. I never thought about the fact that Viktor's daughter was only about six years younger than me; in fact the subject never came up, perhaps because it did not matter to me at all.

I also discovered that Viktor made a substantially large amount of money that in comparison would put my income to shame, although I was one of the better-paid civilian employees at the academy. He also had a power-of-attorney completed by our legal department and he had that placed in his official personnel folder. I made a copy of that for my record as it was completed with my name on it. The file regulation required that all general officers, above the rank of Colonel official folders to be forwarded to the Ministry of the Defense and Viktor's folder was mailed there as well.

Military personnel's life insurance benefit forms were mandatory to be filled out due to the nature of their profession. Although Hungary was at peace, and its soldiers as far as I knew were not present in any other country in the world during those years, one could never know what may happen on a moment's notice. I looked at his beneficiary forms, including his retirement beneficiary forms both in a professional and personal capacity, and it showed that he left me eighty percent of everything and twenty percent for his daughter. I personally would not have taken offense if he left everything to her, but I appreciated the fact that by leaving the majority of the benefits to me, Viktor confirmed that he thought of me on long-term basis and he wanted to make sure that I was taken care of if something unexpected should happen to him.

After work he was waiting for me at the entrance/exit and we drove to a house, actually a walking distance away from his brother's house. It was a three-bedroom house, very spacious, and it came with some old fashion furniture, which I could have lived without, but I did not have any problems living with them temporarily. The previous owner was an elderly couple who were unable to keep up with everything, including the nice size backyard and they moved into an assisted living place when their number came up on the waiting list.

The second house was at the end of town, surrounded by two parks. I instantly noticed the heavy traffic in the area as the Grassalkovich Palace was nearby, so there would be a lot of tour buses, vehicle and pedestrian traffic. We decided to take the first house and Viktor promised me that if I didn't mind to stay in the apartment at the academy for another few days, he would get rid of the old furniture and we get new ones. I gave some thoughts to his offer and I agreed to a few more days, so at least he could change the master bedroom furniture, as I did not want to sleep in the same bed as those old folks did.

The furniture store did not have an overwhelming selection, but we compromised on modern furniture and it was a plus that they were also able to deliver the following day. It took another three days before we actually moved in, even before we signed the final real estate papers. To my big surprise, Viktor paid cash for the house; it was something I could never imagine that anyone was able to do. Viktor explained that he was never a big spender and that he and his brother inherited some money from their late parents, which is how Nicholas bought their home too.

We started a new tradition when we began visiting his brother and his family on Saturday nights for dinner and eventually, when I got into the groove of cooking, yes, I could cook some things, not everything, they came over as well.

I loved being married, not just because of the fact that I never really liked dating, but I was married to a great, loving and passionate person who cherished me no matter what I had done. I heard women talking about what a "great night" they had; I did not share that feeling because with Viktor, I had a great night every night. My mother told me once that the first few months are like honeymoon, making love every night, but that it would eventually wear off as the marriage was moving along, and if a woman was lucky, her husband would make love to her every so often, sometimes only once a week.

I had no idea if my mother was speaking from experience, or if she just heard others talking about it, my life was nothing like that. I could be just cooking dinner when Viktor came home and when we kissed hello, he would pick me and carry me off to bed or, just brushing off everything from the kitchen table, we made love then and there. We often exchanged sheepish looks when people were over for dinner. As far as I could tell, Viktor never had enough of me and I was more than willing to embrace that challenge.

I loved Viktor with every fiber of my body. Yes, I used to love Andy too. Viktor and I talked about that after a long and passionate lovemaking, which always left us exhausted but completely satisfied. He told me that he liked Andy, but while he did not admitted to himself at that time, he was extremely envious of him too. Viktor also said that he thought that Andy and I already consummated our relationship, because it was obvious to him and everyone that Andy loved me, and that I loved him too. I told him what Andy always said about waiting with having sex after our wedding. I confirmed to him that I did love Andy very much, but when he betrayed me, I questioned myself if I was just getting used to having him around, being comfortable in his company, and that when I believed that I loved him the way I thought I did, perhaps I did not.

It was all very different with Viktor and not just because we had great physical compatibility. We both liked the same things, reading, music, movies and theater. We liked to go museums, or just walking around the parks. To us a good evening was to be home, have a nice dinner, curl up on the sofa and read the books we were interested in, or simply just cuddle up next to each other and talk about anything and everything. He often told me that when he was with me, he felt like he was with his equal, and that statement meant the world to me. He trusted me one hundred percent without any hesitation or doubts, despite my relatively young age, which we never, ever discussed from our marriage point of view.

My nineteenth birthday came around two months after we got married and he threw a surprise birthday party at our home. Viktor invited all of my colleagues and their families if they had any. After the party, which was on a Saturday night, we drove to my parents and spent Sunday with them.

"I know that the two of you are just newlyweds," my mother said during dinner. "But is there any plan to present me with a grandchild?" She asked. I was taken aback a little bit, not as much because of her question, parents always wondered about having grandchildren, but because I personally never thought about it. The thing was, Viktor already had a child and he never talked about the possibility that perhaps someday we will have children of our own. Viktor and I had not used any protection, I suppose we'll let nature take its course, and besides, I was not familiar, but was aware of various types of protections, such as the existence of condoms, which Viktor never used, nor that I took any birth control pills.

"Irene," Viktor told my mother, he called her by her first name instead of "mama", like son-in-laws traditionally called their wife's mother. "If someday Angie tells me that she is expecting, it would make me very happy. If she never be able to conceive, I would love her just the same." He said kissed my hand. So there we were, my parents wanted to have a grandchild and we certainly did our part to fulfill their dream.

Time was passing real fast and by the fourth month of my leadership, every single folder was correct and every error was corrected. I made a speech during our usual Thursday afternoon meetings that I would personally strangle anyone who makes one more error, or files one document in the wrong folder. Indeed, I was doing spot checks and things were looking good. The military academy expanded their student body with another two hundred cadets because they also added prison management and interrogation method classes. Not just because Colonel Toldai, my brother-in-law, the Commandant of the military academy, promised me during my first general meeting that we could hire four more employees, rather because of the extended cadet numbers, I began to interview potential co-workers.

I ended up with Beáta, Liz, Marga and Rita; all had a lot of experience working in HR offices, or military offices around the country. Two of them were married and their husbands were cadets at the academy, which had zero meaning to me because I went by qualifications and experiences. All of them had good references and they seemed to have nice nature. I hired that four out of some thirty-five applicants, and I sincerely hoped that I made the right decision, as it was my first time hiring anyone.

My six "old timers" got along fine and I designated four of them to cross train the new employees. A couple of weeks later, Marianne asked me if she could talk to me in private. After closing my office door, she hesitantly sat down.

"Angie, you know me by now, I am not the kind of person who would talk about others, but you also know my background, so you are aware of the trauma I have suffered when I was a child," she began.

"Yes, of course. I told all of you before, you can tell me anything," I assured her.

"I think that Rita is being abused by her husband," she said quietly and looked up at me. "She had bruises all over her arms, that is why she is wearing long sleeves when it is so hot in the office. Please don't tell her that I told you, but her husband is a very jealous man and even if she just looks at another man, there would be a beating later on." I suppose she noticed that when she was training her, as I assigned her that task.

I thanked her and I assured her that I would keep the information confidential, and that I would talk to Rita on my own terms and that day forward, I began to keep a close eye on the beautiful young woman. Rita had flowing red hair and her face lacked any makeup, probably because her husband didn't allow her to wear any. I began my *"getting to know"* task by inviting each girl to have lunch with me in the cafeteria on different days. I began with Beáta, few days later I took Liz, and on the following week I treated Marga, I left Rita for last, I didn't want her to become suspicious. It was not the first time I had done that, I treated my old crew for lunches all the time, just to bond with them, nothing else.

Rita and I took the stairs to the second floor but she hesitated to enter the cafeteria. I told her that I was just like that at the beginning, and that I was there to protect her from the "wolves". We got our food on the tray, and as always, it was hard to find an empty table. I noticed one, the one I didn't want to take myself, but we had no choice. There were empty seats here and there, but not two together. Captain Bartha, also known as Attila, the Hunter, was sitting by himself at the table that seated four.

"Captain, are these seats taken?" I asked politely. He pointed at them.

"They are now," he said and we took the seats opposite from him. He already finished his lunch and was just killing time, selfishly occupying a table that four other people could have used. "So, who is this beautiful young lady?" He asked and began eyeing Rita.

"I am Rita," she introduced herself. Attila rose up and shook her extended hand.

"Did anybody tell you just how beautiful you are?" He asked her in total disregard for my presence. That was actually the first time that we were in close vicinity since I got married to Viktor.

"Captain Bartha," I put down my sandwich and focused my eyes on him. He gave me a look that could kill. "Please don't make me nauseated, we are trying to have lunch." He completely ignored me and focused his attention back on Rita, so much so that he switched seats so he would be sitting opposite of her and not me. I could feel the tension in Rita.

"What you usually do after work?" He asked her while playing with a toothpick.

"I go home and make dinner for my husband," Rita replied. I thought, *good girl*.

I did not say a word, I just grinned which irritated Attila to the max. "I don't mind," he said without shame, but I had enough. I put a smile on my face and turned to Rita.

"Rita, never mind Captain Bartha's selfish attitude, he gets a hard-on every time a new female employee starts working here. He made a bet with woman I know that within three weeks he would take my virginity. He lost the bet and it cost him five hundred forint." I told her calmly.

"Shut up," he hissed at me.

"You must stay away from him if you don't want any trouble. He can be very charming and very persuasive," I added to my previous comment. He slammed his fist down which caused people look into our direction. "Oh, and very hot tempered." I added. Attila got up and left.

"Oh, thank you," Rita said and sighed with relief. "As you know, my husband, Zoltán Bujtor, is a cadet here, he is a very jealous man. I am his second wife and apparently his first wife cheated on him all the time in his absence. That is why he moved me here too. He told once me that he ever caught me cheating, he would kill me and the man who I was cheating with." She told me, almost whispering to me.

"Rita," I turned to her. "I am deadly serious about Captain Bartha. He was very nice to me, he acted as he was protecting me, but all along he had alternate motives. I can't tell you what you can and cannot do; all I can do is to warn you about him. Please, be very careful. I know that he is a good-looking man, very handsome, but that is all, nothing else."

"Thank you for telling me," Rita said and we continued our lunch. Not even twenty minutes later a tall, burly looking young man stopped by our table. I wondered how he passed the physical test, but there he was.

"What are you doing here?" He asked.

"Excuse me?" I asked him and at that very moment I began to develop some ill feelings about him. "May I help you?" I inquired again. He gave me nasty look.

"I wasn't talking to you," he hissed at me.

"But I was addressing you," I said and looked at my co-worker. Rita's face was as red as a paprika.

"Honey, Angie invited me for lunch, she invites one girl at a time," Rita tried to explain, evidently to her husband.

"So who is she?" He asked her, still addressing only his wife.

"She is my boss," Rita said. I got up and stretched out my hand for a shake. He looked at it but did not take it. I pulled my hand back and I knew that I was dealing with a very dangerous bully.

"I am Angie Toldai," I introduced myself to him. The name did it; he finally looked at my direction.

"Commandant Toldai is you father?" He asked, obviously he found me young enough to be one.

"No, he is my brother-in-law, but Major General Toldai is my husband," I informed him. I glanced around us and there were a lot of people paying attention to our table and what was going on. "Cadet Bujtor, may I suggest you return to your class and let us finish our lunch?"

He looked at me long and hard and then he turned to Rita. "We will continue this conversation at home." With that threat, he left us. Rita dropped her fork, burst into tears and rushed out of the cafeteria. I picked up our trays and placed them on the tray collection table as I wanted to dash after her, but at the door Major Hetvényi stopped me, he taught logistics at the academy.

"Mrs. Toldai," he stopped me from leaving.

"Hello, Major Hetvényi, how are you?" I asked after shaking hands. He pulled me to the side from the door.

"Mrs. Toldai, what just happened at your table?" He asked. I had no choice but to tell him everything, including the brief, but tense exchange of words with Rita's husband.

"Is there something I should be aware of?" I asked him.

"We are ordering Cadet Bujtor to undergo psychiatric evaluation. He picks fights during physical training (PT), and if anyone says anything, even slightly derogatory; he would threaten that person with physical violence. He failed three consecutive PT tests and this is only his second month here. Those signs are not good, wouldn't you agree?" He asked.

"I completely agree. I am also very concerned about his wife's well being. It was brought into my attention by a co-worker that Mrs. Bujtor is being physically abused at home as well. I personally felt threatened while he was addressing her," I told him. We agreed that we will keep each other informed on any further developments, but deep down inside me an alarm went off very loud and very clear.

I took the stairs to go back to my office on the first floor and as I reached the stairway's door, the sound of whispers caught my ears. There was another set of stairs going all the way down to the basement, which served as a storage area for old furniture and various old office equipment.

Without making a sound, I tiptoed down the stairs and I recognized the woman who was standing with her back to me, it was Rita. "I don't think that it's a good idea," I heard her saying, and all of a sudden, my blood boiled when I heard the man's voice.

"I will protect you, I promise," I heard Captain Bartha's voice. "You can stay at my apartment, he would never find you there." He said while trying to convince her to stay with him.

"But he knows where I work," she objected to his pressure filled suggestion. Attila laughed.

"He won't dare to approach you there," he tried to assure her. "Besides, that tiger woman who is your boss would throw him out in no time." She remained silent for a moment.

"Zoltán is going to hurt me, I just know it," she told him. "He has a gun at the apartment and he threatened me with it more than once."

"I have a gun too, I will protect you," Attila promised her yet again. I pulled back and went up the stairs, into my office. I was greatly troubled by the turn of events. He was actually waiting for her, perhaps even witnessed her husband's behavior in the cafeteria. I only had bad feelings about the whole episode and despite what Attila told her, that the "tiger woman", referring to me, would protect her, how could I? I had no weapons of any kind, and by the time I could call security, it would be too late for all concerned.

A few minutes later Rita also returned to the office and I wrote her a note. When she walked by my office I called out for her and handed her the note. She looked at me and tried to smile. In my note, I warned her about the danger of hooking up with Captain Attila Bartha. He unleashed his charms way too much and way to often. I knew that it was only a matter of time before someone is going to collect on them. She read the note and left without a word.

MY LIFE AS I KNEW IT

"YOU CAN'T LEAVE me here, all by myself," Viktor said and pulled me back on the bed. It was a Saturday and I wanted to do some much-needed laundry. His uniforms were not a problem, the quartermaster's department took care of them, but everything else needed to be washed. Terri, my sister-in-law had a woman come to clean her house once a week and we hired her as well. I seldom had time to clean, although I actually enjoyed housework. Unfortunately I worked longer hours than usual because the end of the school year was upon us and we were getting busier than ever. Cadets in most of the classes were about to depart for their two-month long vacation with the exception of those who enrolled in variety of classes that were only available during the two vacation months, July and August. The specialized classes that Viktor was teaching could be picked up as extra semesters, and there were plenty of students for that too, so he had to work all summer.

"Are you being afraid without me?" I asked and kicked off the comforter to the floor. He pulled me on the top of him and kissed me.

"I would not want to live without you," he said in a tone of voice that I had no doubt that he spoke the truth.

"Good thing that you don't have to worry about that," I said and I slid my hand down to his erection. Oh, yes, he was ready. I did not wait for an invitation I lowered myself on his throbbing manhood. Viktor closed his eyes as he whispered my name, as always.

"Angie, don't move," he said. I stopped. He knew what I liked and what gave me the most pleasure. Feeling him completely inside me was not just a simple act of sex, it was a confirmation that we had become one. I looked down at him with the desire that only matched his, and then I bent over to kiss him. His lips were always soft and his tongue was always ready for venture. He put his hands on my buttocks and sat up, steadying himself with the headboard behind him for support. I moved with him, we did not separate not even for a moment.

It was his favorite position because he had access to my breasts and my lips. It always amazed me how he handled me, as if I was a precious doll. While his tongue moved along my neck, down to my breast, his hands were busy too. Just as I was close to climaxing, he slowed down his movements, as apparently he was not done with me yet. He rolled me over and after putting a pillow under my buttocks; he began to move inside me slowly, managing to give me additional pleasure in other ways too.

Viktor was breathing heavily, yet his kisses never stopped. He whispered things to me that we only spoke in our intimate times. They were all sweet things, like how much he loved to do this or that, but basically we were more physical than conversational. That morning, for some reason was different than many others. Within a short period of time, he pleasured me twice without any break in our lovemaking. We made love slowly and leisurely, because we believed that we had all the time in the world. When he climaxed, somehow it was different too, it felt like desperation, for reasons I didn't know why. I thought, but did not dare to say out loud, that it was such a pleasure filled love making that I would have been surprised if I didn't get pregnant.

Eventually all housework what I intended to do was accomplished by six in the evening, and after taking a quick shower to wash away roaming around the house mostly in the afternoon, we decided to call his brother that we won't be making it for our usual Saturday night dinner. Instead, we went back to the same place where we had our first dinner together. Viktor was talking about the backyard rose bushes that needed pruning, and while I listened to his words, my eyes feasted on his handsome face. I smiled at him and he noticed the change in my mood.

"Did the subject of the rose bushes put a smile on your face, or there is something else on your mind?" He asked jokingly while he caressed my hand above the table.

"I was just thinking," I begun. He smiled.

"Oh, oh," he said playfully.

"I was just thinking how perfectly happy I am," I told him. He lifted my hand to his lips and kissed it. "Just how many nineteen year old girls can say that she has good job, a handsome loving husband and a beautiful home?" I added but did not expect a reply. "I could not imagine how I would go on living without you if you had to go off to fight a war and not come back to me." Just the thought of separation made tears rush into my eyes.

"I am a soldier," he said quietly. "My job is to protect my country by any means necessary, even if it could cost my life. I love my daughter, but the love I feel for you is totally different." His green eyes were expressing the love that I had always craved. "Angie," he said quietly. "You are my guiding light, you are my everything."

I have no idea what the food was that I ate, but I could hardly wait to get out of the restaurant and get home. We barely made it through the door, when we began to peel the clothes off from each other. We had that kind of love, that kind of passion. I praised God for turning my life into the right direction and that I was smart enough to accept the job that was offered, so I could be at the right place and the right time to reconnect with my Viktor.

Summer classes were longer than regular semester hour, but at the same time they also got extra credits as well. Longer hours at the school meant less time spent together, but neither of us complained as at least we had a chance to see each other a couple of times a day between his classes, which time I would also took my breaks. Sometimes we even managed to have lunch together, and of course, we spent all after work hours at home, or visiting my in-laws. In many ways I felt very fortunate because many military wives were unable to live in the same vicinity where they husbands served.

Rita returned to work after a month of unpaid vacation because her husband left for his home village and would not leave her behind, even if it meant that she might lose her job. I was not without compassion and it never crossed my mind to let her go. I knew just how much her income meant to her and her undeserving husband, Zoltán.

Her first day back on the job, Rita would not remove her sunglasses despite the fact that it must have been hard for her to see indoors wearing them. When she finally took off the glasses, she had one eye swollen shut, and the other one, while it was in the process of healing; it still showed signs of beating. Her long sleeve outfits were another indication that her husband's habit of wife beating did not change. She told me confidentially that she was very much afraid for her life, and when I asked her why she didn't leave him, she stared down on the floor in front of her.

"Because he told me that he would find me and kill me along with the person who helped me to get away," she told me. I knew that she believed his threatening words because I surely did.

"The thing is; and I don't want to encourage you one way or another as it has to be your decision alone, but if this beating continues, you will end up dead one day," I said to her. Rita acknowledged that she was aware of that, and that she was on the verge of making a perhaps life altering decision.

"If I can do anything, please let me know," I assured her. Honestly, I did not know what I could truly do for her. In those days I didn't know any city that had shelters for abused women or children, or both, unlike these days when they exist. I could not invite her into our home because it would surely endanger our lives, although after my encounter with her husband in the cafeteria, I had concerns of my own about her husband's mental state.

A week before the regular school year began, and when the cadets, new and returning ones had to go through routine medical and mental evaluation, I received a phone call from Major Hetvényi in regards to the returning of Cadet Zoltán Bujtor, Rita's husband. He failed both evaluations, physical and psychological, and that he was instructed to out-process within four working days.

Hanging up the phone, I immediately contacted the Security Department and talked to Captain Mihalics about the situation. He provided me with a direct emergency line telephone number, and he instructed me how to code that into our telephone system. If there was an emergency and we dialed that number, they would immediately know where the emergency was. Since they were located in Section B, the next section to ours, they were relatively close which gave me a semi-peace of mind.

After I hung up the phone with Captain Mihalics, when the last customer left, I locked the door and called a quick meeting. I told everyone that there was a possibility that we may have an unhappy customer one of the following days, and I instructed them to program their telephones just like I did. I looked at Rita and she nodded, she allowed me to tell her co-workers who the person was, the one we had to especially look out for.

I remember that day very well because the morning before was the first morning when I woke up so nauseated that even just the smell of coffee that I loved made me sick. On the previous night when Viktor woke me to make love, I noticed that when he touched my breasts there was a slight discomfort to his touch, but it did not bother me so much, so I did not say anything. The vomiting was another subject because he heard me through the bathroom door and knocked on it with concern. I told him that I was fine but I would be skipping breakfast. Since I was still nauseated as we drove to work, I took a plastic bag with me, just in case.

The scenario repeated itself on the following morning, not by choice but from necessity, I made an appointment with a gynecologist for that afternoon. Her office was a fifteen-minute walking distance from the academy and without Viktor's knowledge; I took some time off, which I made up later for my appointment. Dr. Fehér was a middle-aged woman with a beautiful, reassuring smile. After the examination she asked me to get dressed and meet her in her office. I was fast becoming concerned that something was wrong with me, but when she sat down and was smiling, I thought, *it could not have been so bad*.

"Well, Angie, congratulations are in order, you are eight weeks pregnant," she informed me. I stared at her and then I finally smiled. *Yes,* I thought. *I knew exactly when that happened*. I vividly recalled that particular morning when instead of doing laundry, we made love over and over again, and how I felt that something very special was happening between us.

Dr. Fehér gave me a booklet and asked me to set up a visit schedule with one of the receptionist, which I did. When I returned to work it was two-thirty in the afternoon. I called Viktor and I was in luck, he was between classes. I told him that there was something very important I needed to tell him, but it was so important that I could not talk about it over the phone. Viktor was puzzled but he was more than willing to stop by after his next class, which was due to end at three forty-five. I agreed that it was fine and went back to work.

He arrived at the time he promised, he taught classes at Section C and he was a fast walker, it did not take him more than a few minutes to get to my place of work. When he arrived, I asked him to close the door to my office. I already lowered the blinds for maximum privacy.

"So what is so important that you had to tell me in person?" He asked and pulled me onto his lap. He was nibbling on my neck and while I wanted nothing more than to make love, being in an office or not, what I needed to tell him was even more important indeed.

"Would you still love me if I gained a lot of weight?" I asked and he had a surprised look on his face.

"I would love you in any shape and form, sick or healthy, skinny or fat," he assured me.

"Well, I suppose that is a good thing because seven months from now I will be real fat with a big stomach," I told him. He shrugged and all of a sudden he looked at me when what I said sunk in.

"Angie," he whispered my name. "Angie, are we having a baby?" He asked and his face radiated nothing less than sheer happiness when I whispered back, a *yes*.

We were kissing when we first heard what sounded like a big popping sound coming from a close distance, and there were two more but much louder. I peeped through the blinds and I saw Zoltán, Rita's husband standing inside the office, he got in using the flap door and he had a revolver in his hand. I motioned to Viktor to remain quiet and I picked up the phone and dialed the code number that went directly to the Security Department's emergency line indicating where the call was coming from.

Viktor also had a gun, but he never had it on him while conducting classes, he kept it in his small office that opened from the teacher's lounge. I wished that we locked the door, but I doubted that it would have helped us; he could have fired through the door as well. Viktor hugged me and I silently prayed that Zoltán would just disappear into thin air when my office door was kicked wide open and he stood there pointing a gun at me.

"You bitch, you encouraged her to leave me, didn't you?" He asked. I did not reply because it was clear to me that even if I had denied his accusation, it perhaps would just pour oil onto the fire.

"Cadet Bujtor," Viktor said in a soothing tone of voice. "Please put down your gun and leave, nobody is going to stop you."

"General, I have no quarrel with you. That bitch you are protecting is the one I have a problem with," he said and motioned with his gun.

"Cadet Bujtor, she is my wife and we are expecting a child, please, exercise compassion," Viktor pleaded with the obviously disturbed man. My eyes fell on the floor just outside my office door and with shock and fear I noticed a trail of blood that was flowing down toward the counter. At that very moment I knew that Rita was shot and I wondered who the first victim was, sadly, I had my suspicion.

"General, I am ordering you to step aside," Zoltán yelled at Viktor and raised his gun. Instead of obeying him, Viktor pushed me behind him and by doing so; he protected me with his own body. When the next shot and then another rang out, I honestly did not understand what just happened until Viktor sprung around and grabbed my hands before collapsing to the floor. I suppose I was in a temporary shock as I tried to scream but no sound would leave my throat. What I was experiencing could not possibly be real, that is what I was keep telling myself. I fell to my knees next to Viktor's bleeding body and it was then when I began to scream for help.

As tears flooded my face, I looked up at Zoltán with all the hate I could muster. He raised his weapon and fired, but nothing happened, apparently the gun either was out of bullets, or jammed, I found out later that it was the latter. He jumped right at me and kicked me on my side and in my stomach, which I tried to protect with my hands, and as he repeatedly kicked me there, he broke two fingers on each of my hand. From the pain I moved my hands and he began to kick me in the stomach over and over again. I could barely move from the pain, but as if I was moving in slow motion I turned my head. It was then that I noticed something shiny under my desk, a simple arm reach away. It was my letter opener that I couldn't find earlier when our mail was dropped of

He was kicking my sides, left and right, but somehow I managed to roll ever so slightly. Frankly, there was so much pain that the new ones did not even register yet. I reached my arm out and grabbed the letter opener and quickly as I could, I pulled my arm back. After Zoltán rolled me on my back and sat down across my stomach, he wrapped his hands around my neck, he was trying to strangle me. With my broken fingers hurting like hell, I wrapped them around the handle of the letter opener and with that little energy that I had left; I jammed the letter opener into the side of his neck. He screamed out of pain and let my neck go, leaving his fingerprints on my skin.

The very same moment when amidst bleeding profusely, he pulled out the letter opener from his neck and tried to stab me with it, I saw two military policeman with weapons drawn in the doorway. They yelled at Zoltán to put the letter opener down, but to everyone's surprise, he laughed and lifted his arm to stab me. Two shots were fired, each of the military policemen used their weapons and Zoltán fell dead on the top of me. I knew that I was seconds away from passing out, so when one of the military policemen bent over me, I looked straight into his eyes and I said as loud as I could. "Save my husband, save the General first." And with that said, I lost consciousness.

THE AFTERMATH

I BLINKED AND I tried to open my eyes that turned out to be a difficult task. I had a horrible headache, my mouth was bone dry and I had difficulty moving any of my body parts. The first image that came into view was the IV stand on my left side; it was blissfully dripping and automatically pumping fluids and painkillers into my left arm. I heard a familiar voice.

"Call the doctor, she is coming through," it was Terri, my sister-in-law's voice telling that to someone. It took me almost forever to turn my head, and then I saw her sitting by the right side of my bed, holding my right hand, very carefully I may add. My second and middle fingers on both of my hands were broken; I already knew that after Zoltán's first kicks.

"Viktor," I called out my husband's name. "Where is he?" I asked but Terri did not reply. I considered that a bad sign.

"Mrs. Toldai," I heard a voice and when I managed to look to my left, I saw a man, possibly in his early sixties in a white coat. His name was stitched onto the left pocket of his coat and it read, Dr. Keleti. He introduced himself, which confirmed his name. "You are in a military hospital in Budapest, you were brought in by an ambulance after an attack on your person."

"Where is my husband?" I asked stopping him from talking about me.

"I am pleased to tell you that General Toldai survived the shooting. Although I am not his primary physician, I did assisted during his surgery. I will talk to you about his condition in a little while. I want to discuss your injuries first," he told me. Since I knew that Viktor was alive, I was a little bit more willing to listen to him about my condition. "You suffered a concussion, a bruised kidney, three broken ribs, bruised spleen and broken fingers on both hands. You are very much visibly bruised from the outside. Everything I mentioned will heal by themselves with time. Other than the bruising, there was no damage done to any of your vital organs, which is a miracle by itself. We taped your fingers together as well, they will heal too, and no surgery is necessary." Terror struck me like a freight train.

"My baby, what happened to my baby?" I asked with panic.

"I am very sorry to tell you, but you lost the baby," he informed me. "We checked you out thoroughly and our OBGYN Specialist confirmed that you won't have any problem conceiving again." My heart sunk and my eyes immediately became clouded with tears when I recalled how happy Viktor was hearing the news that we were expecting.

"Please tell me about my husband," I asked after a moment of silence.

"He was shot twice in the chest, severing one of the arteries that supply blood to the heart. He lost a lot of blood after being shot and we also encountered difficulties while we tried to stop the bleeding. While he was on the operating table, your husband suffered a major stroke," he informed me. *And the bad news just keeps on coming*, I thought.

"He suffered a major stroke, what does that mean?" I inquired.

"His brain did not receive sufficient blood and oxygen because of the severe internal and external bleeding. Time will tell the extent of any damage, given there is any," he told me. "He is presently unconscious, which is fairly common after a major surgery such as your husband endured. Luckily, he is still young and he is in excellent physical shape. We are hoping that the damage was minimal. Naturally we will keep you informed," he promised and then he gave instructions to the nurse before leaving.

Terri and Nicholas, my brother-in-law returned to my bedside after the doctor left. "Was anybody else shot?" I asked, although I suspected that there were other victims as well.

"Captain Bartha was shot in the head as he was getting out of the elevator, he died at the scene. Your subordinate, Rita Bujtor was also shot and killed by her husband," Nicholas told me. My heart sunk even deeper learning that innocent lives were lost in such a senseless way. I wished that I could turn back time to take some sort of preventive measures that I had not, but could have taken.

I have to give credit to Terri; she remained by my side as much as she could. On the third day after the shooting, I was finally able get out of bed but only with help, and even though I was still in a great deal of pain, they tried to reduce my morphine dosage. Terri pushed my wheelchair a few doors down the hall where Viktor was still in intensive care. Despite the fact that no visitors were allowed in there, given the circumstances that I was also a victim and not only the victim's wife, they allowed me to visit Viktor for a half an hour twice a day.

A week later, still moving slowly, I managed to walk but still not without help. I had to lean on Terri, Nicholas or my parents, depending on who was there at those times when I visited Viktor. All of the women whom I worked with, basically who worked for me came to visit, more than once, but Marianne came almost every day. It was a big sacrifice and I tried to discourage her from doing so, but she would not listen to me. The Military Hospital in Budapest was forty-five minutes away with the local train, plus an additional fifteen minutes with a streetcar.

My parents also arrived on the following day of the shooting and I found out from them that Terri and her husband, Nicholas, took turns staying with them, not wanting to leave their children in a twenty-four hour care of their baby sitter, regardless that she was rather reliable and willing. I praised God and the doctors, because two weeks after the shooting, Viktor was moved into my semi-private room from the intensive care. We were treated somewhat differently because only two of us were in the large hospital room that usually held up to four people. There were hospital rooms where they had even more people, sometimes eight or ten to one room. I just assumed that Nicholas pulled some strings, but I have never asked. I simply thanked him for being there for us.

Terri and Nicholas took a great liking to my parents and Nicholas told me that while he stayed with my genuinely caring parents, he realized just how much he missed his own parents. Nicholas and Viktor's parents perished due to carbon monoxide poisoning when Viktor and he barely survived. They used their fireplace in a cold winter night, but they failed to notice that the chimney's smoke exit was blocked, sending the poisonous fumes through the house. They were already teenagers and they were sent to live with their elderly aunt, who passed away since then.

At the beginning of the third week, Viktor, just as his doctors hoped, regained consciousness on his own. Unfortunately, it was then that we learned with great sadness, especially I felt devastated, that Viktor could not talk, and that he could not move his legs. However; I was told by the doctors, they found it interesting that Viktor was able to move his arms and they considered that a good sign. All of the cases that they had before, a major stroke victim, such as Viktor was, normally lost the use of both, legs and arms.

The doctors tried to assure all of us that there were excellent therapists in the hospital; they mentioned that because Viktor was facing some strenuous physical therapy, prescribed to him by his primary surgeon. They were making arrangements to transfer Viktor in a week's time into the rehabilitation department, given that his wounds would continue to heal without any complications. They were able to repair everything that was damaged around his heart and there were no signs of any rejection of the artificial artery, or any signs of infections.

Viktor was aware of his surroundings, which was a good sign, it also meant that he didn't suffer any memory loss, or if he did, it had to be minimal, time would truly tell. They give us a sounding board on which I pointed at a letter or number, and he would confirm the letter with a squeeze of my hand. The first thing I asked him, if he knew who I was. He made me spell out the word "love". I assured him too that I loved him more than ever; he smiled when I told him that. He asked me a question that broke my heart again; he wanted to know about our baby. There was no reason to lie, I replied, may be the next time we will be luckier, instead of telling him straight out that I lost the baby. It was a very difficult time for me too, but I was determined to be strong for the man I loved. Tears rolled down on his face, which hurt me greatly to see him in such a sorrow. It felt as if was being kicked again. I sincerely hoped that it was the first and the last time that I saw him cry.

The days' activities began to slow down and so did the flow of visitors. We still had plenty though; my colleagues visited in intervals and Marianne still came every day, even if only for a few minutes. I appreciated all of their concerns and affords. A couple of days after the shooting, I was visited by the academy's military police as well as two police detectives from Gödöllö's police department. I told them exactly what happened, right from the beginning. They asked me what I thought about Cadet Bujtor's shooting of Captain Bartha.

I was honest when I told them about Attila's woman chasing habits, and I did not feel bad about that, although without a doubt I felt sad about his untimely death. He was very good-looking man, nice when he needed to be and well liked by most, especially by woman. They inquired about my "relationship" with him, to which I replied that there wasn't one. He tried and failed to seduce me, albeit I left out the bet that Klára and Attila made, wanting to leave her out of the whole thing.

Of course, the subject of the letter opener came up and they asked me why I did not try to use it earlier. It was a strange question because it could have been labeled as a deadly weapon. I repeated the details about being on the floor while being assaulted by Zoltán, and how I noticed the mail opener that I must have accidentally dropped earlier because I could not find it when I wanted to open the daily mail. They told me that even if the two military policemen did not shot Zoltán, he would have bleed out because the mail opener severed a major artery in his neck. I asked them if Zoltán would have bled out before or after he stabbed or strangled me?

At first they just stared at me without any acceptable reply, and then they eventually nodded and told me that it was a valid question without having any answer for that. I inquired about what was going to happen, would I be charged with stabbing Zoltán? They actually smiled and informed me that there was no reason to continue their investigation because Major Hetvényi, my colleagues and more importantly, the Security Department that I contacted two days prior to the bloody event, backed up my story. On the following day they returned with my typed confession, which I read thoroughly and after finding it correct, I signed it without any further delay.

A month later I received a letter from the city's court magistrate in which I was told that I was officially exonerated from any wrongdoing, and that they closed all inquiries into the matter. The final conclusion was that a mentally unstable man by the name of Zoltán Bujtor with a long history of domestic and public violence, in a fit of jealous rage killed Captain Attila Bartha, an instructor at the Gödöllö Military Academy, after accusing him of having an affair with his wife, Rita Bujtor. It was never proven that they indeed had an affair, as there were no witnesses. Rita Bujtor died from the bullet wound to the head and one to her heart; both of them were fatal shots. Major General Viktor Toldai, a teacher at the Gödöllö Military Academy was shot twice while protecting his expectant wife, the shots hit him in the chest. MG Toldai survived the attack. Mrs. Angelina Toldai, two months pregnant at the time of the incident, suffered a concussion, broken ribs and fingers on her hands, bruised kidney and spleen. Due to extensive blows and kicks to her body, Mrs. Toldai suffered a miscarriage and also numerous superficial injuries. The court found that Mrs. Toldai acted in self-defense when she stabbed Zoltán Bujtor in the neck during his attack on her person. Since Mr. Bujtor died during the attack, the court concluded with the decision that the case was closed.

Well, it was certainly good to hear that I would not be punished for trying to save my own life (I am being sarcastic here). Nevertheless, it was one less thing to worry about. My main concern was Viktor because his mental state was not the best. He was a very physical man, active in sports; he played tennis and soccer at the academy. Viktor never stopped exercising; he did everything, all the physical training, also known as PT that included a three to five mile run, push-ups and sit-ups every single morning. I have seen him doing sit-ups and push-ups even at home, along with some milder version of weight lifting.

I strongly believed that Viktor was greatly disturbed by the fact that he was unable to attend to himself, and it was also terribly embarrassing for him. He was the type of person who always wanted to help others, and laying there on the hospital bed, unable to do anything on his own, it made him feel like as he was in infant, versus the bright, intelligent and always witty man that he was before the shooting. I hoped that he would again become active after the extensive therapy sessions that were coming up in the near future.

I was released from the hospital three weeks after the shooting and although there were serious reminders on my body of the attack, I knew that with time they would all heal. I tried to put all the sadness that I felt about losing the baby aside as I made it a priority to get Viktor into better shape, to assist with his speech and physical therapies. I stayed with my parents for the first month, but at the beginning of the second month I returned to work. I had a serious discussion with Nicholas, not as an in-law, rather as an employee.

Nicholas suggested that I should take more time off, but I was persistent on returning to work because I toiled too hard to let it out my control again. I did make a promise to him that I would strictly work eight hours, and that I would take at least a half an hour lunch because he didn't go for me working through lunch to have that time off. He also made me promise that I would not work on weekends. It was an easy promise to make as I intended to stay in Budapest during my weekends, to spend both days with Viktor at the Military Hospital Rehabilitation Center. During the week, right after work I headed for the HÉV, which was the local commuter train and from there I took the street car to the hospital to spend a couple of hours or more with my husband.

Viktor lost a lot of weight because he barely ate. I knew what he was thinking; he thought that if he didn't eat, he didn't have to go to the bathroom in a bedpan. It was a ridiculous thought but that was Viktor for you, he was ashamed to ask for it. Time and time again the nurses assured him that it was part of their job and there was nothing to be ashamed about. I begged him to eat more but he refused, despite the doctor's threat that if he is not going to eat more than he will be fed through his nose.

Tears of anger shone in his eyes and with a bleeding heart I acted as if I did not notice. I read newspaper and magazine articles to him, what he selected that is after my pleading. I had the distinct impression that Viktor lost his will to live and it made me depressed a great deal too. I had enough burdens of my own to carry and I prayed real hard that he would snap out of it real soon.

My first day back on the job, as one may expect was very stressful. As soon as I got out of the elevator and walked the few steps toward our office, I stopped at the door and with trembling hands I unlocked the door. I expected blood on the walkway but there was none. When I reached my office, which had its door replaced and left open, I held my breath to look inside. There was no sign of blood as the entire office was cleaned and re-carpeted in my absence.

I made the coffee and looked at the piles of paperwork neatly stacked on both sides of my large desk. The employees began to arrive one by one and I was very touched that they brought me a huge welcome back bouquet of flowers and pastries to go with the coffee, just as I did for them on every Wednesday to break the week in half. I was hugged by every one of them, and they of course inquired about Viktor's condition. I tried to be brave and gave them a weak smile, and then I thanked them for asking. I told them that we are taking baby steps every day, and I prayed that someday he will be back in his normal form, at least I had to have faith in it.

Four months after the shooting, Viktor began to regain his speech and two months later he was almost able to speak just about anything with the exception of pronouncing long and complicated words, those came some time later. That was the good news, the bad news was that his legs were not co-operating or, as the physical therapist told me in private, he didn't thing that Viktor was concentrating enough on trying to improve his condition.

His primary military doctor, Colonel Alföldi and I had our discussions about Viktor's mental condition, and we both agreed that he needed not just physical therapy, but also some sort of consultations with or without me. I completely agreed and we scheduled one for the following week. It was my job to tell him and when I did, his blood pressure shot up. I told him that not only did he need consultations, but I did too. Frankly, although I told him nicely, I did not care if he protested at all, I was determined to bring him out of his depression to a level where he actually wanted to get well.

As we both waited for our psychotherapist to call us in, I held his hand and unlike in the past when he gently caressed my hand with his fingers, he simply let me hold his hand, he did not try to hold mine. The therapist was a very well dressed woman in her mid-fifties and I pushed Viktor's wheelchair next to a chair that was offered to me. The therapist took the other chair opposite from us. She introduced herself as Dr. Sarah Benkö, and she confirmed who we were by repeating personal data, name, age, and our professions.

"I would like General Toldai to tell me briefly what happened that day," she asked him. Viktor looked at me and began to stare at the wall behind the therapist. "Mrs. Toldai, would you like to tell me?" She addressed me with her question realizing that Viktor was not going to reply.

I looked at Viktor and I began to tell Dr. Benkö in a slow monotone voice about what happened, basically the same story that I told the policemen. She asked me if I felt any guilt about stabbing that man in the neck. I laughed.

"Dr. Benkö, have you ever been on the floor, lying next to your bleeding husband while somebody is trying to shoot you? When he failed to do that, he began to kick me on my sides, on my back and in my stomach. All I could think of was to protect the life of my unborn child and to get help for my husband whom I did not know was dead or alive. So your question, forgive me for saying this, sounds a lit bit out of this world to me. That man had his hands around my neck and I had difficulty breathing because he was strangling me when I noticed the letter opener. I was barely half conscious when I stabbed him. So to answer your question, my answer is to you that I just wish that I had found that letter opener sooner and stabbed him when he entered the office."

"Mrs. Toldai, please do not misunderstand my question. I did not ask that question to insult your intelligence. I am simply trying to understand your mental state, if you feel guilty or somewhat responsible for that man's death." She told me.

"No, I don't," I replied. "I am here to help my husband, I am not seeking any assistance," I told her. She made some notes.

"General Toldai, it appears from your doctor's note that your physical therapy is not up to speed. Do you want to talk about why you are not cooperating with your physical therapist?" She asked him.

I sat on the chair and listened to the therapist's voice as she tried to convince Viktor that if he shared his thoughts about what happened, she would be able to help him overcome whatever was troubling him, but Viktor remained silent. The therapist looked at me with questions in her eyes.

"Dr. Benkö, it is only my opinion, and I am no expert by any means, that Viktor is a very physical person, very athletic and very independent. I always categorized people in two groups, givers and takers. We are both givers, so I believe that it troubles Viktor a great deal that he shifted into the takers group. Takers are not necessarily people who just want to get and take as much as they can, they are also people who cannot help themselves and who must accept help from the givers." She nodded in acknowledgement and she took down more notes. All of a sudden I heard Viktor's voice.

"Don't you dare speak for me as I cannot talk for myself," he said it very slowly. "I do not want you here."

"General Toldai," Dr. Benkö addressed him. "Actually what Mrs. Toldai said makes a lot of sense."

Viktor did not look at me at all and he pulled his hand out from mine. "Dr. Benkö," he said her name painstakingly. "My wife is way too young to understand life. She is only nineteen years old and she does not need me in her life any longer. As a matter of fact, I am thinking about filing for divorce. Please take me back to my room," he said. I got up to do that and to talk to him that he doesn't know what he was talking about. He lifted his hand to stop me. "Dr. Benkö, I do not want her around in the hospital anymore, please tell Dr. Alföldi. Thank you." He said slowly.

Devastation is a mild word compering how I felt in that moment. Where was that all coming from? I had no idea. My feelings for Viktor had not changed; I loved him with the same passion as I have always done, if not more. So what if he could not make love to me? He, as a person was more important to me than having sex. Sure, it was important part of a marriage, but not the most important, at least not to me. The thought that he wanted to get rid of me hurt more than being kicked and strangled.

Dr. Benkö called for an orderly to roll Viktor back to his room and when they left her office, she told me what I have already known, that Viktor was severely depressed. She also told me as an afterthought, that Viktor being forty-two years old and myself only nineteen had a scaring effect on him, meaning; he felt that he could no longer provide me with what I was used to, and therefore, because he loved me so much, he would rather not see me and think about what he could not do or provide. Seeing me caused him even more depression. I told her that I had no intention to agree to any kind of divorce for any reasons, and that I was going to fight him in court, if it comes to that. I would fight on the basis of his mental instability, for not being capable to make sound decisions. She smiled for the first time when I said that.

"You are wise beyond your years and it is apparent that you love him very much," she remarked as I walked to the door. I turned around.

"Indeed I do. Please Dr. Benkö, do not give up on him because as I told you, I never will," with that said I walked out the door.

SOMEONE FROM THE PAST

SLEEP BECAME A luxury as I could not think of anything else but Viktor. I went to work every day and I did the best I could, while I tried to make sense of Viktor's behavior towards me. I loved him just the same, yet he treated me with silence and he often called the nurse to tell him or her that he wanted to be alone. I had great many conversations with his treating physician Colonel/ Dr. Alföldi, and he admitted that even the psychotherapist accomplished very little success with Viktor. He agreed with my observation that his refusal to talk to me, and often even as much as look at me steamed from the fact that if we talked in numbers, he went from one hundred percent down to almost zero percent being a senior ranked officer, a teacher, a man, but especially being a husband to a young wife.

My concentration at work lacked motivation but nobody said a word, and often one or more of my subordinates brought me food because I simply would not leave my office, not even to take a few minutes break. As if I was on autopilot, I looked at all the paperwork and signed them, shamed to admit, sometimes even without checking it. I was just not myself. I have to say, that thinking about those days, what I called '*days of darkness*', I received unspoken support from all sides, from my in-laws, my co-workers and of course, my own parents.

Almost eight months passed since the shooting and Viktor's speech greatly improved, sadly I already knew that he would not be returning to active duty that he loved, although he would still be able to teach from a wheelchair, but I had serious doubts that he would be willing to do that. He was still struggling with physical therapy, but he did make small steps with the help of the parallel bars. His stubbornness set back the therapist from making any progress with him.

It was a Friday afternoon and left work early to catch the HÉV, the local train to Budapest. I got to the hospital at two o'clock when Viktor was in the process of physical therapy. I walked in and said hello, as usual he did not respond he was just quietly sitting in the wheelchair. The therapist welcomed me loudly, just to make a point. He was young man and I asked him some questions about how things progressed on the previous afternoon.

"Just ignore me," Viktor said, loud and clear. "Moreover, why don't the two of you just get the hell out of here."

I had a sleepless night, we had unusual problems at work with payroll, two of the women were out with sick children, the train was crowded and so was the streetcar. I was simply exhausted. I promised myself months ago that I would never get mad at Viktor, but hearing him being nasty with me without any reason, I just lost my temper. I walked up his wheelchair. He looked absolutely terrible with dark circles under his eyes and his face needed some serious shaving. I stopped right in front of him. He didn't look up at me at all.

"Viktor, what is this about?" I asked him. "Are you feeling sorry for yourself? May I remind you that you were not the only victim of that horrible crime? Three people were killed and I was injured too. I didn't even have a chance to grieve for our child that was unable to be born to enrich and complete our lives. You, Viktor, all you have to do is to get well by following the instructions of your therapist. For the past eight months everything was about you, always about you Viktor. What about me, Viktor? What about me?" I said and I could feel tears rushing into my eyes but I was determined not to cry. He just sat there with his head hanging as he stared down at the floor in front of him. I took a deep breath. "All of that I can deal with, but I cannot deal with the fact that I no longer know who you are. Because you are not anyone I have known for years. You are not the same person I had dinners with, walked in the parks with and who made love to me. I just don't know you. If that person I still love more than anybody else in the world is still in there, in your heart, I want him back and I want him back soon." I didn't wait for a response; I walked out and went back to Gödöllö.

Arriving back to the city of Gödöllö was refreshing after the hustle and bustle of the big city. The supermarket was about a comfortable ten-minute walk from the train station and because my refrigerator was almost empty, I decided to buy something that did not need much preparation to eat. When I got to the store it began to drizzle, but I figured that by the time I was done shopping perhaps it would stop raining. The store was located another fifteen minute walking distance from our house. Well, it did not work; the rain got heavier and was coming down rather hard.

I was standing outside the store, under the canopy, when I heard my name. "Angie." I looked around but I didn't see anybody I knew, until a car stopped by the sidewalk and the driver rolled the car's window down. It was a man wearing an Army uniform and he was calling out my name. I saw the dark car earlier but I did not pay attention to it. "Angie," he called out to me again and I could not believe my eyes, it was Captain, now Major Mark Hegyes, the very same one who I worked with at the Ministry of Defense, he was the aid to Viktor, then LTG Toldai.

He pushed the passenger door open and I made a run for it. I got in and I looked at him with genuine surprise. "I can't believe that it's you. What are you doing here in Gödöllö?" I asked. He pulled out from the curb and drove to the end of the parking lot and stopped.

He was hesitant to say it but eventually he did. "I am here to teach the second semester that Viktor taught," he finally told me. I smiled; I understood that it had to be done. "How are you doing?" He asked and touched my hand. He did not try to lift it or kiss it; he just touched it like a sympathy touch. I shrugged and sighed.

"I am all right, I guess," I replied because I did not have a better answer.

"Look, I already rented an apartment and it's only five minutes from here. Why don't I cook dinner for you tonight?" He asked. It made me smile; I remember how he used talk about how much he enjoyed cooking.

"Maybe some other time, Mark. I appreciate your offer but I am very tired, very upset and very hungry. I need to get home," I told him.

"Well, in that case my offer makes perfect sense. All you have to do is just relax, you can even take a nice long bath while I cook, and then we eat and talk. I think that it is a relatively good plan, don't you think?" He asked. It felt good just talking normally to someone other than the people at work. I took a deep breath and agreed.

Mark was right; his apartment was only a few minutes away. He parked his car as close to the entrance door as was possible, and then he asked me to wait in the car, he would be right back. Mark disappeared in the doorway and not even two minutes later he returned holding an umbrella. It was truly a gentlemanly gesture; I smiled and thanked him when he opened the car door. I still got wet a little bit, for which he for some reason apologized for.

"It's not your fault that I got wet," I replied as we stepped into the short hallway of his apartment. "Besides, it's only water and will dry in no time."

"That's true," he agreed and helped me out of my light jacket, which he hung on one of the hangers in the hallway closet. "Come on in," he said and motioned toward one of the doors. He took my shopping bags and carried them for me.

"This is your home, so lead the way," I told him.

"Okay, so here on your right is the kitchen, on your left is the bathroom and straight forward is the living room," he said and opened the door ahead. It was a nice size living room and I was pleased to realize that Mark actually had good taste in furniture. I always wanted to live in a place where there was less furniture and more space, that is why I loved the place Viktor bought. Mark had just enough furniture to provide comfort, but not too many that made people feel as if they were in a labyrinth. I looked around and nodded.

"This is very nice," I complimented him. "Where do you sleep?" I asked.

"I was hoping that you would ask that," he said with a sheepish smile. I was not sure if I should have felt embarrassed or intrigued.

"I didn't mean it that way," I mumbled and then I added. "I grew up in one room which was a living room and bedroom combination," I explained.

He laughed. "I was just joking, I know exactly what you meant. I know many people who lived the same way." He opened a door that I had not noticed. "This is the bedroom." He showed me inside. I did not go in just glanced around from the door. It was nicely furnished as well.

I was debating where I should sit because my clothes were wet, and as if he read my mind, he opened one of the shrunk's door and removed a jogging outfit and handed it to me. He disappeared into the bathroom that opened from the hallway and I heard water running in the bathtub. He came out a few minutes later and waived to me to go in there. "Why don't you take a nice long bath and change into the jogging suit. You can hang up your clothes to dry," he suggested. After a moment of thinking I grabbed the dry outfit and stepped inside the bathroom. "There are clean towels in the cabinet," he yelled after me.

"Thanks," I yelled back. I have never seen such a clean bathroom; it looked as if nobody lived there. I sunk into the bubble bath and stretched out as far as I could. It was heavenly. I closed my eyes and said the same thing as I did each time I went to sleep. I prayed that by the time I opened my eyes, what happened, the shooting and the beating appeared to be just a horrible nightmare.

"Angie," I heard Mark's voice and he touched my arm.

"What happened?" I asked and looked around momentarily confused. He took a couple of steps back, he had a huge beach towel in his hand which he was lifting up so he could not see me if I stepped out of the water.

"You fell asleep in the water," he explained as I wrapped the towel that he was holding earlier around me. "I'll be in the kitchen," he said and left, giving me privacy to dry off and get dressed.

There were clotheslines above the bathtub and once I drained and rinsed out the bathtub, I hung up my skirt and blouse to dry. Realizing that my bra was also wet, after a two second debate, I thought, *hell with that too*, the top part of the jogging suit was loose enough not to be noticed that I had no bra on.

I went back to the kitchen and I noticed that he also changed into dry clothes as well. "So, are you ready for some good food?" He asked standing next to the stove.

"Well, actually I am," I replied.

"Have a seat at the table," he told me and just then I noticed that it was already set.

"Your place is spotless," I remarked. "Do you have a housekeeper?" I asked.

"Don't insult me," Mark replied. "I have been looking after myself it seems like forever, and the Army also teaches you discipline too."

"Sorry," I told him, he just waived my apology away.

"So here is the deal," he said. "I baked some chicken breast with potatoes, this is a sauce I made the other day, it is actually called salsa. I have a Mexican cookbook, you see. I also tossed some lettuce and tomatoes together for salad." While he talked he transferred the food into serving dishes and brought them to the table. I followed his every move and he did everything effortlessly.

"My favorite foods," I replied with a smile. "I remember that you said that you like to cook, but how did you get interested in cooking?" I inquired.

I listened to him as I ate enjoying every single bite. I haven't had decent meal in weeks, not because of the lack of not having any at my parents' house, or at my in-laws house, I just simply did not want to eat when I thought about Viktor's refusal to consume more than a few bites at a time. Mark told me about his mother, how she taught him to cook since she didn't have a daughter, only two sons. I felt good being there with him and I also felt incredibly comfortable. I couldn't help but to smile as he talked, occasionally looking up at me as if he wanted to make certain that I was still listening.

As Mark was talking about his family, I watched as his lips moved and out of the blue, I remembered how he looked at me when he woke me up at that army garrison when I was yelling after having a nightmare. How he gently wiped off the perspiration from my forehead with his handkerchief, and then, as if it was only yesterday, although it was over two years earlier, I felt his lips on mine. I clearly recalled how we promised to each other that it would never happen again, just to kiss for the second or and third time with a passion I didn't know he felt about me. And there I was, sitting in his kitchen, having dinner with him and listening to stories about his family. I began to wonder if he ever thought about those moments and those kisses, and I was unable to decide if I wanted him to remember or not.

"Sorry, I forgot the drinks. What would you like to drink?" He asked, but before I could reply, he listed my choices. "Beer, wine, hard liqueur, coffee, tea, lemonade, diet Coke or water." I laughed.

"Wow, you put me on the spot here, so many choices," I said. "Diet Coke would be fine." I made the selection. He sighed.

"That is an excellent choice because from all of those drinks I offered I only had diet Coke and water," he confessed with a grin and went about to pour one for each of us. After dinner he told me to make myself comfortable in the living room, he was going to join me in a few minutes. I offered my help with the dishes but he quickly ushered me out of the kitchen. The sofa was comfortable and I laid down putting a couple of throw pillows under my head.

He joined me ten minutes later and I wanted to get up but he gently pushed me back down. Mark set down by my feet and he lifted them up when he sat down, so my feet were on his lap. I was too tired to object or protest, and he was not doing anything anyway. He asked me if I wanted to listen to some music or have the television on.

"No, thank you," I replied, and then I added. "You are enough entertainment for me." He stared at me for a brief moment and smiled.

"You have changed a lot," he said quietly. "How come you cut off your beautiful hair?" He asked. I sighed. I wasn't really up to telling him stories but he was acting like someone who really cared, he was somebody from the past that I actually cherished.

"Do you remember Andy?" I asked. He rolled his eyes.

"Do I ever," he remarked. I told him everything about what happened. The long engagement, my pleading for a wedding date, I even told him honestly about wanting Andy physically and how he wanted to wait and then, how he betrayed me. Mark shook his head. "You went through a lot." He commented. He could not possibly know half of the emotional turmoil I had lived through. I also told him about how in a fit of anger I cut off my hair and how I offered it to the stunned Andy.

"Well, I would have been shocked too," Mark told me. "Have you seen him privately since then?" He wanted to know.

"Yes," I replied. "He came to show me the documents about the finalization of his divorce. He asked me to marry him."

"What did you say to him?" Mark asked.

"I told him the truth that I did not love him anymore," I told Mark. "The truth is that I thought about him less and less even before I met Viktor again, and almost never after." I pushed myself up on my elbow. "It is so strange that first Viktor came back into my life and now here you are."

"I believe it is called, destiny," he remarked and looked at my hair. "I'll be right back," he said and left for a couple of minutes. When he came back into the living room he was carrying a fresh towel and a comb. "No matter how cute you look with wet hair, I don't want you to catch cold," he said and not waiting for my permission, he began towel dry my hair. Once he thought that it was satisfactory for his liking, he began to comb my hair the way he liked it. I just sat there like a schoolgirl who waited for her mother to braid her hair. It was a kindly gesture and I was genuinely touched.

He stopped next to the couch and as I turned to him, he lowered himself on his knees. Mark did not try to touch me, he just looked at me and after taking a deep breath he finally said something that I very much hoped that he won't say.

"I have hoped and dreamed that someday you will be in my home, just like this," he said quietly.

"Like this, totally wet?" I asked jokingly. He shook his head.

"Please, don't make a joke about this situation," he said and gently touched my face. "I think that I fell in love you when we shared that room at that garrison down south, but I have felt something, something very special about you earlier when I first walked through that office door at the Defense Ministry." I wanted to make a joke about how much we disliked each other, but as if he knew what I was about to say, he put a finger on my lips. "I may never get another opportunity for a time like this, a time when I am finally able to tell you how I feel about you," he continued and as I looked into his eyes, I saw something in them that reminded me of somebody else, namely Andy. He looked at me the same way so many times and left me disappointed that many times as well. "When I wrote that letter to you, I was sure that I would never see you again, and that you would be happily married to Andrew. Several months ago, someone mentioned that Major General Toldai got married to a beautiful young lady by the name of Angelina. I'll admit, it was a big blow at that time."

I turned my head and stared toward the window. It made me wonder for a brief moment, how can such a thing, like mentioning names from the pest could hurt so much. Was I damaged so badly that I will never be able to fully recover and being loved again? I did not know about that, but what I knew was that I was sitting in front of a man who did nothing but loved me hopelessly for over two long years. I could not just ignore his words. Did I love him, no, did I like him, yes. I was sure of that.

I knew that he was waiting for a reply but what could I tell him? I could not tell him that I always had been in love with him, because it would have been a sheer lie. I was ever so desperately in love with my husband that every cell and fiber of my body was missing him, but at the same time; I was hurting by his rejection. It was not a physical rejection, rather, a more serious one, he wanted to reject me from his life for reasons that were not clear to anyone, especially not to me who hadn't done anything wrong to him. Not just yet.

Mark leaned forward and softly kissed me, our lips just barely touched. He got up from his kneeling position and he pulled me up from the sofa. I felt very tired, very weak and I was certain that I could not stand on my own two feet. He scooped me up as if I was weightless and took me into his bedroom. I did not protest because I was too weak, both physically and emotionally.

He stopped by the right side of the king size bed and he just stood there for a brief moment still holding me in his arms. I lifted my arms that felt very heavy as if a couple of bricks were pulling them down. I finally managed to touch both sides of his face and I kissed him. Yes, I kissed him and he kissed me right back. His tongue forced my lips open and entered my mouth, entered to search and dance with mine. Oh, yes, that kiss certainly brought back memories.

He gently put me down on the top of the bed and leaned over me. I pushed him away, breathless, and I just wondered how I could still feel that way towards someone I hadn't seen for so long. His sheer presence and the touch of his lips stirred up desires in me while without a doubt or question, I loved my husband. Mark stared at me for a half of second before he drew me close to his body and kissed me again, with more passion than he had ever done before.

At the end of that kiss I gently pushed him away. "I am sorry, Mark, I just can't. This is all very, very wrong." I told him. "I like you more than I should, but I do love Viktor very much and I would never break my wedding vows. I felt, and now I know that it was a mistake coming here. I am so very sorry, I did not mean to lead you on." I told him. "Perhaps, I should just go home." He shook his head.

"I know that you are tired and I would not be a friend if I let you go like this," he said and pulled the comforter over me. "I am forever hopeful that you come to me someday, but just looking at you, I know that you don't love me. Your thoughts were not with me when we kissed. Tell me, am I right?" He asked.

"You are an incredibly good man, Mark. I am very grateful that you are not trying to take advantage of my weak and tired condition. I'll be fine by tomorrow, I promise that I will get out of your way." I replied.

"You can stay here as long as you like," he said and pulled away. "I'll be sleeping on the sofa, it is comfortable. Do you need the second comforter?" He asked.

"I am fine with one, thanks," I assured him. He bent down and kissed me on the forehead. Before he closed the bedroom door, he turned around.

"You know Angie, you are like a dream to me. A dream that someday I hope will come true." I was touched and saddened by his words, but it was clear to me that it was the right thing to do not to get involved with him. Sure, I went to his apartment voluntarily, but getting intimate with him never crossed my mind. In my mind he was a caring friend, just like he was on that nightmare filled night in that southern border garrison, what seemed like a lifetime ago when in reality it was only two years earlier.

I fell asleep a few minutes after he left the room, but not before I thought about something that would help motivate Viktor with his physical therapy. That idea made me smile and I was looking forward to the following day.

I woke up at four in the morning and I wanted to go home before I went to work. I got dressed and without making any noise, I headed down the hallway that led to the outside. I passed by his sofa and for a brief second I watched him as he slept lying on his back.

Mark was handsome and very peacefully as he laid there. He pushed the comforter off from himself and I was free to the view of his entire body that was perfect. I smiled, picked up my shopping bags that were left in the hallway; they did not have anything perishable in them, and left the apartment.

THE BIRTHDAY SURPRISE

THE EARLY MORNING weather was still a little bit crispy as I walked home from Mark's apartment. I took my time walking and there were hardly any people around with the exception of those who wanted to catch the early train into the city. Because I walked slower than usual, it took me twenty minutes to get home. I actually enjoyed the walk as I had a chance to think things over, not to mention the fact that I almost forgot something very important. It was Viktor's birthday.

I had a semi guilty conscious about kissing Mark but I had to give him credit, he didn't change, he was still the same officer and a gentleman that I have always thought he was. *Why should I feel guilty?* I thought. While I realized that by going over to his apartment it could have easily given him the wrong impression, but on the other hand, he clearly knew that I was the wife of a senior ranked officer, regardless what condition the General was in.

I thought about our kisses and I am not ashamed to admit that they felt good, they felt energizing. If someone had asked me, how could I kiss another man, other than my husband, I would have replied that because I was certain that my honor would not be broken. I trusted Mark and I always thought of him as a very good friend, but nothing more. What other nineteen years old with sexual experience turned down a handsome and willing man from making love to her, with a husband who presumably would never find about the affair. That may be true, but I was not that kind of person. Mark came back into my life at a perfect time when I was down in the gutter both emotionally and physically. With three of Mark's kisses my spirit was lifted because they made me realize just how much I still loved my husband, Major General Viktor Toldai, and how much more I needed to motivate him by any means possible to get well and come home to me.

I took a quick shower and I just barely got dressed when there was a knock on the door. "It's Nicholas," he replied when I ask who it was. I opened the door with great concern, I thought that something might have happened and that I missed the phone call. "Good morning," he said in a tone of voice that relaxed me.

"Good morning," I answered and looked at him questioningly. "Is there something wrong?" I finally blurted out. He shook his head.

"Oh, no, nothing is wrong. I was just driving by and saw your lights on. I thought perhaps I can give you a drive to work," he offered. I smiled and thanked him. We drove the ten-minute distance almost in silence, with occasional questions about work. When we arrived to the academy's building Section A's entrance, where I worked, before I got out of his car, I turned to him.

"Nicholas, are you and Terri planning to visit Viktor today?" I asked.

"Well, we were thinking about it since this is his birthday," he commented. "Why are you asking?" I smiled.

"I have a special birthday surprise for him, a sort of morale booster," I confided in him. He stared at me curiously and being a smart man, just like his brother was, he realized what I was talking about.

"Ah, I see," he grinned. "I don't have any meetings scheduled for this afternoon as I planned to leave early, so we can go before you come by, would that be alright?" He asked.

"That would be perfect," I agreed. "I have to speak with his doctor first anyway." I added.

My co-workers immediately noticed that there was an improvement in my mood and they said so. I suppose they hoped that it would keep up for a longer period of time as I had a dark cloud hanging above my head and around me since the shooting. Every one of them went for counseling at the academy after the shooting, and they were doing much better. They also dropped their request for a metal detector for the door.

I could hardly wait until three o'clock when I left work and dashed home to change and get the birthday present ready for Viktor. I arrived at the hospital a quarter after four and instead of going to visit Viktor right away, I went to look for Colonel/Dr. Alföldi. After I found him I had to wait another twenty minutes until he finished with his rounds. Per my request he also called in the Charge Nurse by the name of Andrea, who bonded with me throughout the months, almost a total of nine months since we first arrived there by ambulances. After she entered and closed the door to Dr. Alföldi's office, I took a deep breath and asked several sensitive questions about Viktor's condition. I was assured that other than Viktor's legs, there were no physical limitations to his activities.

I went on telling them about my my surprise birthday present for which I needed their permission and cooperation, especially Dr. Alföldi's. Initially both of them just stared at me and after exchanging looks, Andrea shrugged. Dr. Alföldi looked at me a while longer without expressing any opinion, but then he put down his glasses and smiled.

He told me that he only needed to think about my suggestion for a brief moment, and then he mentioned that normally these sorts of surprises were not requested. He and Andrea both agreed that my idea had a good potential for changing Viktor's attitude and his outlook on life once he received his birthday gift. The only other thing I requested was privacy as there were no locks on the door. Once Dr. Alföldi agreed to my plan, Andrea said that she would put a "do not disturb" sign on the closed, but not locked door.

I walked into Viktor's room just as Terri and Nicholas were about to leave. Nicholas blinked at me and Terri gave me a big smile and we all hugged. Once they left, I closed the door and pulled the divider curtain all way around the bed, not that he had to share the room; he was all alone in there.

"Hello, darling," I said and bent down to kiss him. I noticed that his face was shaved, perhaps because of his birthday, I didn't know, and it did not matter. "How was your day today?" I asked relatively cheerfully because I knew what he was going to say next and he did not disappoint me, but that day he couldn't hurt me, at least not yet.

"I told you not to come and open that curtain," he told me, although surprisingly he did not sound rude, perhaps a little bit harsh, until he noticed that I was wearing the dress that he liked me to wear.

"I will open the curtain after I present your birthday gift to you," I told him.

"I don't want anything," he said, leaving the hurting part out of that sentence, which was "*from you.*"

"It's too late, I already got it," I told him. "Would you be sweet and close your eyes, please?" I asked him.

"I don't want to play any games," he mumbled but he closed his eyes anyway. When I changed into another dress after getting home from work, I put on what Viktor called the 'zipper dress', which had a zipper from the neckline all the way to the bottom. For the safe side, I always wore a belt with it just in case the zipper pulled apart, but it never did. As I mentioned, it was the dress that Viktor loved when I wore it and it brought me back a number of pleasant memories.

"Sweetheart, I promise you that this is not a game," I assured him and took off my high heel sandals and my belt, unhooked my bra and removed it along with my panties. "Keep your eyes closed," I asked him again, and then I climbed on the bed and laid down next to him. His eyes came wide open and looked at me with surprise when I pulled back the blanket as well.

"What in the world are you doing?" He asked. I leaned above him and kissed him. He turned his head but I reached out and turned his head back towards me. I pushed myself up and gently sat across his hips. I leaned forward and kissed his eyes, his neck, and his chest and regrouped over his lips. "Please, stop." He said but his voice was not convincing. With my hands caressing his chest carefully, especially where the scars were, I kissed his stomach and I looked up at him. "Somebody will come in," he protested but he didn't ask me to stop again.

"It has been arranged that there will be no interruptions," I told him and sat up across his legs.

"What?" He asked and looked toward the door that was not visible from the closed curtains.

"I need you to unzip my dress," I asked and waited. He didn't move he just stared at me. I leaned forward and kissed his lips softly, and then I let my tongue go to work. He stubbornly kept his mouth closed until I reached down and touched his private parts. He opened his mouth and I kissed him deeper and ever so passionately that he gasped for air.

"Oh, God," he murmured. I set back up and I looked at him with challenge in my eyes. It was a sheer joy watching as he slowly lifted his arms and with his right hand, he slowly pulled down the zipper all the way down to the bottom, just as he used to do. The dress fell open and I let it drop from my shoulders down to the ground. His eyes fell on my breasts and I pulled myself up to offer them to him. He touched them softly and then he kissed them. I bent down to kiss him again and then I pulled myself back when I noticed that within seconds he was fully erect.

"Angie," he whispered when my hands touched him and stroked him for a brief second or so, before I carefully lowered myself on his firmness. "Oh, Angie," he murmured my name. I did not move for a minute, I simply just enjoyed feeling his much missed hardness inside of me.

"My love," I told him with a smile. "You may be a General, but today, on your birthday, you are my Chief of Staff." He looked at me with wide eyes and for the first time in almost nine months, Viktor laughed. I began to move and he held my hips with his hand, giving me a notion about the movements and the rhythm that he wanted, what he desired from me. He didn't forget how to please me and when he was about to climax, he touched me in a certain way that was an almost guarantee that we reached our maximum pleasure together.

My breathing was labored but I didn't mind and I just stared down at the man whom I loved with all my heart, my body and my soul. I carefully lifted myself off from him and laid back down by his side, and despite the narrow bed; he managed to put his right arm around me. "I love you, Angie," he told me and kissed my forehead.

"I love you, my husband," I replied. "Get well and come home with me soon." He nodded that he would, but I made him promise out loud.

Sometime later I got up and got dressed in the bathroom, cleaned and covered him back with the blanket. I opened the curtain and the door, and also removed the sign that was taped there by the Charge Nurse Andrea, it read, "Do Not Disturb, Therapy in Session". I showed it to Viktor who shook his head and laughed again. His laughter was like beautiful sound of ringing bells to me.

There was a knock on the door; it was Dr. Alföldi with Andrea tagging behind him. When they walked in, he took one look at Viktor and then at me, as I was sitting on the chair next Viktor's bed. "Well, I'll be darn," he said with a grin. "This is the first time that I have seen you smile, General," he commented. "I trust that you liked your birthday present." I just smiled, did not say anything.

"Indeed, Colonel, very much indeed," Viktor said and squeezed my left hand that he was holding. It was a routine check as the doctor was just finishing his final round for the day along with the Charge Nurse. After finding everything in order, they left the room. It was getting late and I still had a lot of travelling ahead of me, I wanted to get home while it was still daylight outside. He did not complain, he understood.

I leaned over him and kissed him, but he would not let my hand go. "Angie, I have said some nasty things to you, and I acted terribly towards you, are you able to forgive me?" He asked. I kissed him again.

"Darling, there is nothing to forgive. You saved my life and took the bullets for me. How could I ever forget that? I love you for everything that you are."

As I stepped outside the hospital's exit gate to the busy street, there was only one thing on my mind; I got my husband back.

GOOD THINGS COMES TO THOSE WHO WAIT

MY BIRTHDAY GIFT to Viktor had a magic quality, according to the physical therapist. Viktor, like a madman threw himself into therapy and just over two months later he was standing in the doorway of our home. He was still walking with the help of a walking stick, but it was more like a security piece of equipment than anything else. Almost an entire year passed since the shooting and finally our life was getting back on the right track. I had a surprise waiting for him and it was the first thing that he noticed. Across from the entrance, there was a sign hanging that read, "Welcome Home, Viktor Senior."

The expression on his face was priceless and I seriously doubted that he noticed that there were others present, such as his brother and his family, and my parents too. He tossed the walking stick and picked me up and swirled me around, and then he put me down just as quickly. "Are we having a baby?" He asked. I nodded.

It was an all and all celebration and felt like a new beginning for us with Viktor finally being home and with the new life growing inside of me.

There were inevitable changes in our lives. Viktor and I talked it over before he decided to leave active service after twenty-six years of various duties and of course, promotions. His retirement request was approved shortly, but there was a request attached from the Defense Ministry. They suggested that wasting the knowledge that Viktor accumulated would be a big loss to the country, and because he enjoyed wide popularity at the academy, they offered him a permanent teaching position for as long as he wanted it. Viktor had concerns with that, because Major Mark Hegyes, his former aid at the ministry, and his substitute at the academy during the last few months of his absence, was popular and as well respected. Based on Viktor's recommendation, the Commandant granted Mark a teaching job at the academy in a different area which he was also familiar with as well.

Thank God, I had a trouble free pregnancy, and almost exactly nine months to the day when I presented Viktor with his 43rd birthday present in the hospital, our son, Viktor Toldai Junior was born. He was a healthy baby and loved by all of us. We were blessed with good health and life was good once again.

EPILOG

LIFE IS REALLY fascinating and I tried to keep up with all the happenings in our friends' lives. During the party celebrating the birth of our first child, we invited everyone from my office, and Viktor also invited some of his friends, including Major Mark Hegyes, his brother Nicholas and Terri with their children and of course my parents.

Mark sat down next to me as I cuddled Junior on my lap. He began to ask questions about Marianne, my shy colleague from work. I told Mark that she was wonderful and kind, and also very lonely. I briefly told him about her background so he could understand her personality better.

"Would you mind if I ask her out?" He inquired. I looked at him and smiled.

"Mark, as far as I am concerned, you and I were never more than friends. Regards to Marianne, I always liked her, and you have a personality that would be a perfect match for her. You are a kind and gentle man, the kind whom she needs." I told him as an encouragement.

He took my advice and after a couple of unsuccessful attempts, and with my helpful encouragements, they began dating and six months later, they were married. As I congratulated them after the wedding, Mark whispered into my ears. "I will always love you."

I whispered back to him. "And I will do the same my friend, as a friend."

They were seemingly happy and I was pleased for them, unfortunately after three years, they moved to another duty station and with time, we lost contact.

In reference to Joe, after that incident in the grocery store when Captain Attila Bartha came to my aid, I have never seen him again. I heard from someone who lived in the same village as he did, that several years after what happened between us, he got married and had a daughter. I wondered sometimes if the young pregnant woman in the store was his wife, the one whom he publicly degraded.

I know that I have seldom mentioned Viktor's daughter from his first marriage, and there is a good reason behind that. There was not much to write about. They lived in Florida, in the United States and she came to visit us for a couple of weeks every year. It appeared that she was completely brainwashed by her mother, and while she was polite with us, there was always a chill in the air when she was in the company of her father. Although Viktor never talked about her, I was certain that he thought of her because he loved his daughter unconditionally.

Sometimes, despite some sad and dramatic times in our lives, it is good to remember and recall episodes from it. To this day, I still don't know and now I don't even care to figure it out why Andy refused to be with me, yet, drunk or not, he gave in to the charms of Judy, his brother's former mistress. At times, especially at the beginning of our marriage, Viktor, since he knew Andy, asked me about him, and I told him honestly that in those days, what Andy had done to me caused indescribable pain. Of course, I added, we make plans and God decides which one will actually happen.

Obviously Andy had issues about intimacy when it came to me, which worked out for the best when I unknowingly at that time, I had already met the man of my dreams. He was an Army Major who was promoted to Colonel and who selected me to be his secretary and later his office manager straight out of school, and whom I followed when he was promoted to General. We knew each other well, but only as a boss and close employee, and then as friends, love came later but stayed with us for a long time to come.

You may wonder what happened to Andy. He interrogated everyone on a daily bases at my former place of employment about my whereabouts, and he did not believe that nobody knew where I had moved to. They were telling him the truth all along, but he thought that they were protecting me from him. Five years after I left that job, the company was sold to General Motors, in the United States, and because of the great improvements and better changes in television and radio technology, my former department was dissolved and the employees were transferred to other branches within the large factory.

Andy became a weekly visitor at my parents who did not tell him either where I lived and worked. Because his visits were routine, I knew when he was going to be there, so I did not visit my parents on those weekends, especially in the beginning when he visited them the most. We have never bumped into each other, thank God for that. I was not afraid of him, but as we learned from history, a disturbed person cannot be trusted with personal safety. After a few months, he gave up and never visited my parents again.

On a Friday afternoon, about a year after I moved to Gödöllö, outside of Budapest, my parents by sheer accident met with Andy's parents at the market place. It took them almost fifteen minutes before they stopped saying just how bad they felt about what happened, and that how much they loved me like a daughter. I actually believed them because I loved them too. It was not like in the case of Joe, when his mother hated me just because I was born into a different faith, which later, despite being a firm believer in God, never came up in any of my relationships with co-workers and especially not with Viktor, who knew all along that my parents were Jewish.

Andy's parents told my mom and dad, that after my "disappearance", and because he could not find me, he went into a depression and was hospitalized. By the time my parents met Andy's parents, according to them, he was fine again and back to work in another part of the factory. He told them that he was not going date or planned to marry again. My mother assured them that it was only a stage and it will pass too, just like all of us got over sadness and disappointments. They never heard, saw or talked to Andy or his parents again, and neither did I, nor that I wanted too.

Just a week after our little boy's second birthday, I gave birth to our daughter whom we named Ilona. She was an incredibly beautiful baby, as was our son too.

Viktor continued teaching at the military academy, until one day totally unexpectedly; he received a job offer that was way too good to refuse. It was almost like his old job but as a civilian at the Hungarian Embassy in Washington, D.C., in the United States. When he told me about the offer, I was stunned, but he relaxed when I told him that it was one of my childhood dreams to go to America.

A couple of months later after he signed the contract with the Foreign Ministry, we made all the necessary arrangements, locked down our house to where someday we intended to return, and we were ready for what I considered our big adventure.

Never in a million years I would have dared to imagine the events that occurred six months after our arrival to Washington, D.C., events, unimaginable events that effected the rest of my and my children's lives. You may read about it in the novel, titled: *"The Angie Chronicles: The Resurrection"*.

Edwards Brothers Malloy
Thorofare, NJ USA
May 7, 2015